John Francome has been Champion Jockey seven times and is regarded as the greatest National Hunt jockey ever known; he is now a frequent broadcaster on racing for Channel 4.

John Francome (together with co-author James MacGregor) has gained terrific acclaim for his previous bestselling novels.

'A captivating read . . . goes at a cracking pace all the way'   *Woman and Home*

'The racing feel is authentic and it's a pacy, entertaining read'   *The Times*

'A thoroughly convincing and entertaining tale'
                                                                 Daily Mail

Stone Cold

John Francome

HEADLINE

First published in 1990
by HEADLINE BOOK PUBLISHING PLC

First published in paperback in 1991
by HEADLINE BOOK PUBLISHING PLC

10 9 8 7 6 5 4 3

ISBN 0 7472 3483 3

Printed and bound by
Collins Manufacturing, Glasgow

HEADLINE BOOK PUBLISHING PLC
Headline House
79 Great Titchfield Street
London W1P 7FN

ACKNOWLEDGEMENT

The author would particularly like to thank Terence Blacker for his invaluable help in the preparation of his manuscript.

Chapter 1

The air-conditioning in the large blue Mercedes had been pumping out cold air for forty-five minutes, but the sweat was still trickling down the two rolls of fat on the driver's neck. The smell in the car – essence of Harry Short, mingling with stale cigar smoke – was none too sweet but Harry didn't mind. He was a good three stones overweight, it was the hottest summer on record and he was just about to become the most successful racehorse trainer in Britain. If that wasn't an excuse for generating a bit of your own heat, what was?

Harry shifted his bulk in the seat of the car and smiled, an unnerving sight. Just over six foot tall with straight brown hair cut brutally short at the sides, he looked like a bouncer who somewhere along the line had got lucky, which is what he was. There was a high colour to his cheeks, suggesting a man with a temper straining at the leash like an angry Rottweiler. Sometimes the leash snapped. Right now the thought of his

1

horse Pendero getting beaten this afternoon made him grip the large steering wheel so tightly he could feel the moisture squeezing from his palms. It had been a year, a year of planning. If it all went wrong, he really didn't know what he would do. Some act of mindless violence probably.

He loosened the collar of his shirt where a waterline of sweat was visible.

'Can't happen,' he muttered. 'Cannot happen.'

He pressed a fat finger at the car radio and the sound of strings filled the car. Mantovani, he loved it. Sweet, soft and easy – everything Harry Short was not.

There were two ways to win the flat trainers championship, Harry reflected. One was to be born into a rich racing family, like the two chinless wallies above him in the current winners table, Edward Denton and Ian Gardem. Harry winced at the mere thought of them. Without inherited wealth, those two couldn't have held down a job mucking out, let alone training expensive horses. Their success had been assured the moment their mothers had lain back and thought of England. No way was Harry Short hung up on class – he just hated any bastard that went to public school.

Then there was the other way to the top, Harry's way. He had been born into a poor family in Doncaster. Everything he knew about horses he had learnt from the gypsies who camped south of the racecourse. He understood horses – or, rather, they understood him and his none too subtle methods. Briefly he had wanted to be a jockey but, as little

Harry became big Harry, the dream receded.

He worked the clubs for a while, on the security side, but racing was what mattered to him. Thanks to a spot of friendly pressure – Harry didn't like to think of it as blackmail – he landed a job as assistant to a trainer with an unfortunate fondness for curb-crawling on Saturday nights and, within a couple of years, he had seen more of the underbelly of racing than the Dentons and Gardems would see in a life-time. When his boss was obliged to retire after some-one thoughtlessly exposed him to the press, Harry Short took over the yard.

Today, ten years later, Harry was a name to be reckoned with. He wasn't liked by those who ran racing, or by other trainers. He wasn't much liked by his owners either; he treated them with careless con-tempt. But he did get winners when it mattered.

Like at 3.30 this afternoon at Ascot with a four-year-old called Pendero.

Harry smiled. It was the sweetest deal you could imagine. Pendero had run four times this season and his form, which read 4-3-5-2, was enough for the handicapper to give him nine stone for the race at Ascot. But then, on this occasion, the handicapper was himself working under a handicap. He didn't know, for example, that Pendero's best distance was a mile and a half. All he knew was that the horse was better than average over a mile. He didn't know either that last time out, his jockey had been warned that if he was seen doing anything more strenuous than breath-ing during the race he would get a good hiding. He didn't know that, just to make sure, his trainer had

3

put an extra stone of lead in his weight cloth to anchor him.

The Kings' Food Handicap, Ascot, was hardly the richest race in the calendar, being worth a mere £20,000 to the winner, but for Harry Short it mattered more than a classic. It would give him what he needed to crack the magic circle of fashionable trainers: a blue-chip owner rather than the fly-by-night builders, nightclub owners and footballers that he mostly dealt with at present. A moneyed lord would do it but an Arab was even better. It gave you credibility, class – suddenly everybody would want to know him.

Harry had set his sights on Ibn Fayoud al Hassan, which translated as Son of Fayoud of the House of Hassan. His English friends called him Ibn or Ib for short. The house in question happened to be royal. In Arab terms that meant rich, too, which was more than could be said for most of the British variety.

It was rumoured in the business that young Ibn Fayoud was in a spot of financial bother. He was something of a playboy, very different from his famous wealthy father. According to Harry Short's sources, he owed a cool £600,000 to Reg Butler Ltd, a chain of bookmakers much respected by gamblers on account of the risk of quite serious injury to the person if you didn't respect them.

Jack Butler now ran the firm. He was thirty-six and not an unreasonable man; he knew you didn't go around breaking the legs of rich Arabs who owed you a bit of cash – at least not if the Arab in question had a daddy for whom the honour of the family was more important than a mere six-figure gambling debt. On the other hand, the Butler family honour mattered too. Once the word spread that Jack was owed six hundred big ones by someone who was still walking around in perfectly good health, his reputation would take no end of a hammering. So one of Jack's men had a quiet word with Ibn Fayoud to the effect that, if he didn't see his way to clearing the debt plus interest by the end of the season, Mr Butler would have no alternative but to take his problem to the Sheikh.

It was at the Newmarket Craven meeting that Ibn Fayoud, now desperate, was approached by an unlikely benefactor in the form of Harry Short. He had heard of Ibn Fayoud's little problem and he had a solution. In three months' time he would give the young Arab a stone cold certainty to clear his debts in one. All he would expect in return was that Ibn Fayoud should move his nine horses, currently being trained by Ian Denton, to Harry's yard. Ibn Fayoud had agreed.

Harry had booked a good apprentice to ease Pendero's task. With the seven-pound claim reducing his weight, the horse couldn't lose. The apprentice could even make a cockup and still win. Harry chuckled. Cockup? It was hardly the right phrase when his apprentice was one Kelly Connor.

The day started badly for Kelly. She'd had to ride out three lots before setting off for Ascot in her rusty Saab. Then she had a puncture on the way to the races. By the time she reached the weighing room, Harry Short was steaming like a pressure cooker.

'Walked the course yet?' he snapped by way of

introduction. This was their first meeting.

Heads turned in the weighing room. Harry Short's rages were legendary and this one was warming up nicely.

'My car—'

'I'm not interested in your fucking car.'

Kelly sighed. 'I'm here,' she said, her smile sweet, her tone razor-sharp and so quiet that only Harry could hear. 'I know the course. If the horse is good enough, I'll win. Nothing else matters. All right . . . sir?'

Harry was taken aback. He wasn't used to back-chat, not from female apprentices anyway. He flushed a deeper red. 'Get yourself ready then,' he growled and strode out of the weighing room.

It had taken five years for Kelly Connor to reach this moment, five years of hardship and dedication, five years of trying to make the world ignore the fact that she was bright, intelligent, goodlooking and female. Racing, she discovered, had no time for looks in a jockey; it distrusted brains. Her appearance – dark, slim, pale-skinned – which, in any other profession, would have been an advantage, was for her a liability.

Ever since she left school, she had worked for Bill Templeman, who kept a small string of horses but had a big reputation as a trainer. Bill and his wife Annie had been impressed by the way Kelly rode from the day she'd arrived on their doorstep. They had expected competence – after all, she was Frank Connor's daughter – but Kelly had something more: judgement yoked with an iron determination to win at all costs. There was a touch of class to her.

Bill had given her as many rides as he could but, with only twenty horses in his yard, the chances were limited. It had been Kelly who had pushed her career forward by ringing other trainers, riding work for as many people as she could, picking up whatever spare rides were going. Soon she had established a reputation as one of the most professional apprentices riding, and great value for her seven pounds. All she needed now was the opportunity to do well for one of the big stables. Then she would be on her way. The call from Harry Short asking her to ride Pendero at Ascot was what she'd been waiting for.

She had hesitated briefly. Short had a reputation as a ruthless womanizer – there had been talk of stable girls in his yard being the subject of his hefty, unpleasant attentions – and she was not naive enough to think that she was the only good apprentice available. So why her?

'Just get to the course in time for us to walk it,' he had ordered.

Kelly dismissed Short from her mind as she pulled on her silk breeches and changed into the orange and black colours of Pendero's owner Colonel Twyford. She had more important matters to think about.

In a small, tidy flat in Newmarket, Frank Connor sat in front of his television, occasionally glancing at his watch. Kelly's race was in forty-five minutes' time. It was unlike her not to ring him from the racecourse as soon as she arrived. Both of them had become used to this ritual, which had nothing to do with advice – Kelly was beyond needing help of that kind from her father – but was simply a ritual. 'Good luck, girl.' 'Thanks, Da.' It set them both up for the afternoon.

Normally Frank would have dismissed any worries about Kelly from his mind. An important spare ride, a notoriously difficult trainer for whom she had never ridden before: it was hardly surprising that she had forgotten to phone. After all, nobody knew the pressures of racing better than Frank Connor: Irish champion jockey at nineteen, winner in one season of both the George VI, the Gold Cup and the Irish National at twenty-three, and then at twenty-nine washed-up, just another has-been with a dodgy past. He knew all about the ups and downs, the winners and the losers. Most of all, the losers.

Frank Connor hated memories – there were no trophies in his flat, the only framed racing photographs were of Kelly – but recently the past had been stalking him like a hungry wolf. Not the winners, the laughs in the weighing room, the champagne, the congratulations, but the other side: clipped instructions over the phone, secret meetings, the look of bewilderment on trainers' and owners' faces, the jeers of the punters who knew, almost by instinct, that Frank boy, yesterday's folk hero, was now Connor, just another bent jock on the skids.

Once they got their claws into you, there was no escape. Frank had started drinking – not champagne in the Members' Bar now, but whisky on the morning of the race. The whirlpool of corruption and failure dragged him down faster with every season. There were scandals, rumours: he lost the best job in Irish racing, that of stable jockey to Tim Collins. Soon the only spare rides he was offered were dodgy jumpers, non-triers; the only trainers who used him were those who hadn't heard that Frank Connor was finished.

'Stop it,' Connor whispered to himself, trying to concentrate on the television, which was showing the race before Kelly's. That was the thing about the past. It wouldn't let you go. Even when you thought you'd shaken it – a new chapter, a new generation, a new future – it played itself again and again.

He opened a can of alcohol-free lager and thought of the day when he'd lost it all. Driving to Naas with his wife Mary to ride a novice that would surely bury him, the past caught up with him on a bend in the road outside Cork. Maybe it was the booze racing through his veins, or the worry, or simply fear. Whatever the cause, the result was the same. Connor's car had left the road at seventy miles an hour; he had hardly hit the brakes before it piled into a tree. He had regained consciousness twenty-four hours later and, when they had told him, he wished that he hadn't. Mary, one of the few people in Ireland who had trusted him, was dead. Killed, and by what? Racing? Corruption? No. Frank knew there was only one answer: Mary had been killed by her own husband.

His life had changed that day. He had quit racing and had never touched another drop of alcohol. In an attempt to escape the past, he had brought his daughter Kelly to England and settled in Newmarket where he worked part time in a garage. He had never spoken of the past to Kelly and had never encouraged her passion for horses. He had done everything in his power to stop her working in a yard after she had left school but racing was the only thing that interested her.

In spite of himself, Frank had willed her to succeed. He gave her advice on race-riding and, more importantly, warned her of the pitfalls and temptations ahead of her. But not only was Kelly a good little rider, she was wise, cooler by far than he had been at her age. It began to look as if she might just make it as long she, too, could escape the past.

The telephone rang and Frank leapt across the room.

'Kelly,' he said happily. 'I was worried that—'

'Have you spoken to her?'

It was the voice that, over the past week, he had come to dread.

Frank hesitated. 'You'll be finding out soon, sure enough.'

'Connor, we mean business. We've asked you for one little favour. One little item of parental influence.'

'You've . . . you've got nothing to worry about.'

'Good. Because all you had to do was explain very gently to your little girl not to try too hard this afternoon. We really hope you've done what you were told.'

'Have you finished?' Connor gripped the receiver with anger. 'I have a race to watch.'

'Oh, we're watching too, don't worry. It's going to be just like the old days. Watching a Connor pulling the back teeth out of a good thing.'

Frank Connor slammed down the receiver. In the background, the television commentator was reading out the runners and riders for the 3.30 at Ascot.

Just like the old days. The past was back. The past was now. But this time he was ready for it.

Kelly Connor had weighed out and was trying not to think of her father as she stood, waiting for Harry Short to collect the saddle. Although winning on Pendero was all that mattered now, it bothered her that she had been unable to ring Newmarket. Her father had been quiet and preoccupied over the last few days; Kelly had sensed that he had something to tell her but for some reason was holding back. Perhaps if Pendero won it would cheer him up.

The assistant to the Clerk of the Scales approached her. 'Call for you, Connor,' he said, nodding in the direction of a telephone in the corner. Kelly smiled with relief.

'I'll keep an eye on your saddle.' Damien Gould, one of the older jockeys Kelly seemed to meet every time she went racing, stood beside her. 'If Fat Harry turns up I'll give you a shout.'

'Thanks, Damien,' said Kelly. 'I won't be a minute.' She gave him the saddle and hurried across to the telephone.

'Hi,' she said eagerly.

'Hello.' The cool, laconic voice was not that of her father. 'This is Giles Williams, Associated Press. Do you have a moment?'

'A moment?' Kelly tried to conceal her impatience. 'I'm about to ride in a race.'

11

'Sorry,' said Williams dismissively. 'I'm not much of a racing man myself. I work on the magazine. Now,' the man ignored Kelly's attempt to interrupt him, 'I don't want to do the interview right this minute but I was hoping to set up a meeting when I could come down and see you at work for a sort of "Day in the Life of a Leading Woman Apprentice" piece.'

'I can't think of that—'

'Hopes, ambitions, boy friends, what you have for breakfast – human interest stuff. Anyway, I'll call you at your Mr Templeman's tomorrow morning, if I may. I think it could do you a bit of good, don't you?'

'All right. Tomorrow morning. Listen, I must go now. I—'

'Are you going to win?' Williams' voice was deceptively casual.

'Hope so.' Kelly hung up. Quickly she tried to phone her father but his line was engaged. She returned to where Damien was standing.

'Would you believe it? Some bloody journalist wanting an interview.'

Damien smiled with a hint of envy. It had been years since he was asked for a press interview. 'Lucky old you,' he said.

At that moment, Harry Short bustled into the weighing room to collect the saddle. Kelly was grateful that he hadn't seen her talking on the telephone. No doubt that would have been a cue for another public exhibition of bad temper.

'Thanks, Damien,' she said quietly.

Gould watched her as she listened to Harry Short's instructions. Pretty little thing, she was. Too pretty for this game. For a moment, he felt bad about the task in hand, but then he thought of the money. Five grand to make sure a girl apprentice didn't win. It was going to be so easy, it was almost criminal.

Would she win? Kelly pondered the journalist's question as she walked out to the paddock. The previous night, she had looked at the form and concluded that, even with her seven-pound claim, Pendero would be lucky to run into a place. Yet Harry, for all his bluster, was a shrewd trainer and his confidence was infectious. You're only as good as your last race, they said, but Kelly knew that this particular race mattered more than most. If she won a good, televised handicap at Ascot, the offers would start coming in. On the other hand, ride a bad race and nobody would want to know.

As if reading her thoughts, Damien Gould winked at her as they made their way through the crowd around the paddock. 'Good luck, sexy,' he muttered. Kelly smiled.

Pendero looked magnificent. A strongly built grey, he was bred to be a sprinter but by some genetic queue-jumping had inherited his great-grandfather's stamina. He had been weak as a two-year-old but last season had won a couple of good races over a mile. Yet this year, nothing.

Harry introduced her to the horse's owner Colonel Twyford, a red-faced old enthusiast who looked as if his heart would give out with too much excitement.

'He's straightforward,' said Harry, speaking to her with a quiet authority which Kelly found strange after his behaviour in the weighing room. 'Just settle him halfway down the field and aim to hit the front at the furlong marker. He stays well and he's got plenty of speed, so make sure you don't get into trouble.'

The sun was warm on Kelly's back and her confidence was growing with every stride as she cantered down to the start. Pendero was class; he didn't pull but took a nice hold of the bridle and had a long, easy stride that seemed to eat up the ground. For the first time, she understood what it was like to ride a real racehorse. Used to pushing tired, scraggy second-raters round the likes of Wolverhampton and Leicester, she now knew what she had been missing. It was like a pub pianist being let loose on a Steinway grand.

When she reached the start, Kelly let Pendero stop blowing before getting the girths checked and then made her way behind the stalls as the starter called out the jockeys' names and the handlers began to load them up. Pendero was drawn between Damien's horse Come Tomorrow and a big black horse ridden by Paul Clark which was known to be difficult to load up and normally entered the stalls last.

'Where you going?' Damien called across as they waited in the stalls.

Kelly pulled down her goggles. 'Halfway,' she shouted, and at that moment Clark's horse barged into the stalls and head-butted the front gate. Clark whipped the hood off its head and, within two seconds, the starter had pulled the lever and they were off.

Kelly caught hold of Pendero's mane as he sprang

forward and was immediately into his stride. Once her body had adjusted to the new pace, she let go and settled him into the middle of the field as planned.

The ground was riding on the fast side and, as the field raced down the hill and picked up speed, Kelly found that she was only just able to hold her position. Even in this company, the race would not be run at such speed to the finish, so Kelly settled Pendero and waited for the pace to slow down. They had taken the bend at the bottom of the hill and were facing the uphill run to the finish that would sort the field out when Kelly felt Pendero hit his stride and begin to feel comfortable. He seemed to prefer galloping uphill and as they reached the final bend, she moved easily up into fifth place.

She took a quick look round. Nothing was going as well as Pendero. All she had to do was steer him and they'd be certain to win. She was imagining the post-race TV interview when the horse directly in front of her began to tire. There was room enough to move up on his inside but she was going so well that cheekiness of that sort was a needless risk. It was as she pulled to go round on the outside that it happened. Suddenly a horse appeared from nowhere and knocked her off balance towards the rails. Pendero briefly lost momentum but, in the time it took him to find his feet, the gap on the rails had disappeared. Kelly suddenly found herself tightly boxed in behind a horse going backwards.

She looked across at the jockey who stayed tight on her outside. It was Damien.

'You're going nowhere, sexy,' he said, almost

conversationally. 'You're staying with me.'

In the stands, Harry Short gripped his binoculars with rage. 'She's losing her place,' he hissed through his teeth. 'The bitch has got herself boxed in.' Nearby, a pale, good-looking young Arab looked away from the race as if his last best hope had just died. On the rails, a bookmaker smiled.

One hundred miles away, Frank Connor groaned as he sat in front of the television. 'Oh, jeez, Kelly,' he said. 'They've done you now.'

The horse in front of Pendero was losing ground so quickly that, short of standing up in the irons and pulling Come Tomorrow's back teeth out, Damien Gould had no alternative but to go on, leaving Kelly behind him but now lengths off the leader. Those few immobilizing seconds would be enough to earn him his money. He kicked on. Maybe his horse would run into a place.

Behind Damien, Kelly Connor despairingly pulled Pendero from the rails and into Come Tomorrow's slipstream. The horse had lost his stride and, with less than a furlong and a half to go, the two leaders were battling it out some six lengths adrift of her. Briefly, like a distant echo, Kelly heard the voices which had haunted her ever since she had started riding in races. No strength, these women jockeys, no battle in them, no bottle. She changed her grip on the reins and, once again, Pendero was running. As Kelly passed Come Tomorrow, she knew she was riding for nothing now but her own pride.

Pendero felt as if he was giving his all but, a furlong from home, Kelly picked up her whip and gave him

one good crack behind the saddle to make certain.
The response was immediate. The early pace began to
tell on the leading horses and, as Pendero lengthened
his stride, they lost their rhythm, began to come back
to him. There was just a slight chance. No strength,
no battle, no bottle. With a hundred yards to run
Kelly gave him one more crack, and then rode him out
with hands and heels as the final uphill run took its
toll on the leaders. Fifty yards from the post she
passed them and won going away by a length and a
half.

'She did it!' Frank Connor danced around the flat in
Newmarket, laughing, tears in his eyes. The television
was showing replays of the race's final stages: each
time it looked as if Pendero could not possibly win
and each time, in relentless slow-motion, she did. The
commentator's words, 'Superbly ridden race . . .
look at the way she kept him balanced . . . a tremen-
dously promising apprentice', filtered through to
Frank. Today it was all worth it, the pain of the past,
the hardships; he only wished Mary were alive to see
this moment. It was the best day of his life, better than
any of his own big winners.

There was a ring at the door. With a joyful whoop,
Frank bounded across the room. Maybe it was a
neighbour, come to congratulate him. Or the milk-
man collecting payment. Or Jehovah's Witnesses. He
didn't care, he'd tell them all about his brilliant
daughter. Beaming with pride, he opened the door.

Two men stood before him, their hands hanging
loose at their side. They wore heavy combat jackets

and dark glasses. One of them placed a large booted foot in the door before Frank could slam it. They pushed their way in, bolting the door behind them.

'So,' said the larger of the two men. 'We hear congratulations are in order. Mind you, we're not surprised. That's why we stayed close at hand to help you celebrate.'

Frank backed towards the wall, his eyes darting from one to the other. He knew why they were here and he knew he had no chance of escape, but he didn't intend to go down without a fight.

The smaller of the two men yanked the telephone lead from the wall and with a weary sigh pulled a baseball bat from inside his combat jacket.

'You're a loser, Connor.' The man looked down at the weapon in his hand almost regretfully. 'You were a loser as a jockey. Then you lost your wife. Now you've landed your daughter right in it.'

As the man spoke, Frank lashed out at him with his right fist but missed as his target moved sharply to the side. The weight of his body kept Frank moving forward as another baseball bat crashed into his skull.

Pendero's lad could hardly speak for excitement as he led Kelly and his charge through the crowd at Ascot on their way to the winners' enclosure. He'd quite forgotten that he had been among those who had assumed his guv'nor had taken leave of his senses when he booked a girl apprentice for the ride. 'Brilliant,' he gasped, looking back at her as he scurried along with one hand on the reins.

'I couldn't have done it without him,' Kelly

beamed. She was thinking of her father and the call that she would shortly be making to him.

Ahead, she saw Damien Gould glance round at her as Come Tomorrow was led away to be unsaddled. For a moment, Kelly held his stare with undisguised hostility.

'You ain't won nothing yet, sweetheart,' he said quietly.

Kelly looked away. There was something in the confidence of that leathery, taciturn face which, even in her moment of triumph, nagged at her like a distant alarm bell.

Chapter 2

'You nearly cocked that one up, didn't you?' Harry Short stood with his binoculars hanging round his neck in front of him as he reached out to pat Pendero. Apart from a dangerously high flush on his face and beads of perspiration on his brow, Harry showed little emotion as, amidst cheers from the crowd and shouted questions from a gaggle of pressmen, Kelly dismounted in the winners' enclosure.

'Someone didn't want us to win, that was all,' she said bending down to undo the circingle. It had been too much to expect gratitude or congratulations from him. Her father had often told her never to expect anything from a pig but a grunt, and she smiled to herself as she thought of it.

'In this game, darling,' said Harry with the first hint of a smile, 'no one wants you to win anything. Ever. Don't forget to weigh in.'

Kelly took off the saddle, gave Pendero a final pat

and, half answering requests for her first reactions from the press, skipped down the steps into the weighing room. In spite of her apparent coolness, her mind raced with thoughts of the future. She knew that one race would hardly change her career overnight but it had been a spectacular win and it had been on TV. It was a breakthrough, the first significant rung on the ladder to the top.

She stepped on to the scales and called out her number to the Clerk at the desk, who looked up to check her weight. He was in his fifties, a typical racing functionary with horn-rimmed glasses and black hair slicked down with a military parting. There was something absurdly fussy about the way he looked at the scales, then down at the book in front of him, and then back at the scales. Kelly smiled.

'You're five pounds light,' he said.

At first Kelly thought he was joking, but Clerks of the Scales were not known for their sense of humour. She turned quickly round to look at the face of the huge black scales. She had weighed out at eight stone seven; now she was a shade under eight stone two. As the nightmare engulfed her, she felt sick to her stomach.

'It's not possible,' she said quietly. 'I put the lead in myself.'

'Stay on the scales, please,' said the Clerk. 'Mr Morley.' He called over a steward who was standing nearby. 'The winner's five pounds light.'

Nick Morley, one of the new generation of stewards, walked quickly over to the scales, his

22

expression intent, to confirm what the Clerk had just said. Then he walked off to get a message announced over the tannoy system.

Word of what had happened spread from the weighing room well before the announcement was made. Kelly stood, pale and drawn, as Morley returned to her. 'The stewards will see you in five minutes,' he told her. 'You'd better give me your saddle and weight cloth.'

'*Objection to the winner by the Clerk of the Scales*,' droned the public address system as if announcing the late arrival of a train.

'Bitch!' Harry Short burst into the weighing room like a tidal wave. Nick Morley quickly moved between him and Kelly. 'Who was the bastard who paid you to do that?' screamed the Yorkshireman.

In a low, shaky voice, Kelly said, 'It wasn't me. I don't know how it happened.'

And then she remembered who'd looked after her saddle and the look on Damien's face as they walked in.

'You're bent,' Short was yelling, his eyes bulging in their sockets. 'I'll see you never get another ride.'

Morley pushed him back, more firmly this time. 'Any more of that, Short, and you'll be in front of the stewards too.'

Outside the weighing room, journalists were straining to hear what was being said. 'D'you have any comment, Harry?' one called out.

Short looked at Kelly with hatred in his eyes.

'You bet I do,' he said.

* * *

Jack Butler was chatting to a fellow bookmaker when the announcement came through. *Objection to the winner of* – coolly he held up a finger like a man trying to catch the weather forecast on a distant radio – *Please hold your tickets*. And then someone rushed up to the two men with the full story.

'Oh dear,' said Jack. 'I'd better check where that leaves us.' There could only be one result from this inquiry. He cuffed his friend on the shoulder. 'See you later,' he said.

As he pushed his way through the crowd, race-goers nudged one another and nodded in his direction. One or two of the more daring said, 'Wotcher, Jack!' or 'Got any tips, Jack?' as he brushed past them. But he ignored them. Pillocks. These were the sort of people who stood behind him making idiot faces and waving as he talked to camera. Just because he appeared in their living room, the familiar TV bookie, they seemed to think they owned a part of him. Nobody owned Jack Butler.

On the other hand, Jack Butler owned a few nobodies – indeed a few somebodies, now that he had Ibn Fayoud in his pocket.

He looked at his watch. If he skipped off before the next race, he'd have a couple of hours with an ex-girl friend who lived nearby before driving back home. Time for a spot of the auld lang syne. He had earned it this afternoon.

As he made his way back to his pitch on the rails Jack felt good, but not as good as he had antici-pated. The look on that girl's face as she was pulling up after the post was troubling him. Ecstatic, over the bloody moon, and, to be fair, she deserved to be pleased with herself – she had ridden a blinder. Five pounds would have made no difference to the result. He just wished he hadn't seen her face. It was like offering a child the biggest and best ice cream in the world and then knocking it out of her hand as she was about to taste it.

An odd, unfamiliar feeling nagged at him. What the hell was it? Guilt? Conscience? Jack shook his head as if insulted by the very thought. She was young, good-looking, talented; Kelly Connor would survive this. He thought of the stewards' inquiry, the scandal, the avenging fury of Harry Short. Maybe she wouldn't survive it. It wasn't his problem, was it? Suddenly he wanted to be away from the racecourse. Upstairs with Linzi, that would fix it.

Twenty minutes later, after Pendero had been officially placed last, Jack gave an older man who worked for him a large manila envelope filled with £20 notes. 'Jim, get this to Gould. I have some urgent business to see to.'

Kelly had never attended a stewards' inquiry, but she had heard all about them from her father. The stories he told made them seem absurd occasions, a line-up of bowler-hatted old buffers most of whom knew more about pig-sticking in the Punjab than riding a finish on a tired three-year-old. As she walked into the stewards' room at Ascot, she saw that, in this at least, racing had changed little since her father's day. The atmosphere was as tense as that of a courtroom. Only Kelly had no one defending her.

Colonel John Beamish, the senior steward, looked at Kelly with some distaste before turning to Nick Morley, the acting steward.

'Mr Morley, perhaps you'd get proceedings under way.'

'Yes, sir.' Nick Morley took a step forward. 'The facts are straightforward.' He spoke with a clipped formality but Kelly sensed a note of regret in his voice. 'The horse Pendero was given nine stone by the handicapper and its jockey Kelly Connor claims seven pounds. She weighed out correctly at eight stone seven. On weighing in, having won the race, however, she was found to be eight stone two pounds.'

Kelly looked at Colonel Beamish. 'The reason—'

'You'll get your chance in a moment,' the colonel said briskly. 'Please be quiet.'

'Listen to your elders and betters' was the implication. It was like being back at school.

'I looked at the weight cloth, of course.' Nick Morley reached down behind his chair and produced Kelly's saddle and weight cloth. 'There's nothing wrong with it. None of the lead could possibly have fallen out on its own and as both the Clerk of the Scales and Miss Connor are certain that she went out at the correct weight, I can only conclude that lead was removed expressly and on purpose.'

The steward on Beamish's left roused himself. 'Of course jockeys do lose weight during a race.'

The colonel allowed the full fatuousness of this

remark to sink in before chuckling humourlessly. 'If Billy Bunter was riding round the Grand National,' he said, 'the loss of five pounds might be understandable. But Connor,' he glanced at Kelly's trim form as if assessing a yearling, 'is hardly likely to lose that much over a mile and a half, I would think.'

There was another silence before Beamish said testily, 'Well, Connor? What do you have to say for yourself?'

Kelly was grateful that a full five minutes had elapsed since the moment when she looked at the scales and realized that she had been cheated out of the race. Sitting alone, she had been assailed by feelings of bewilderment and disappointment. As she thought of her father's reaction, her eyes briefly filled with tears. But now she felt only a cold, implacable anger towards Damien Gould and who-ever else had destroyed her ambitions and possibly the one career that she cared about.

'I have only this to say.' Kelly spoke with quiet dignity. 'I wanted to win this race more than any other I've ridden in. Nothing would persuade me to lose a race. I'm innocent.'

'None of which explains why you were five pounds light.'

'I believe I have an explanation for that.' The three stewards looked at her intently. In the silence, the sound of the stenographer's pencil could be heard. 'After I weighed out, I was waiting for Mr Short to collect the saddle and I was called to the phone. I gave the saddle to another jockey for what must have been a minute or so. I can only think—'

'A phone call?' Beamish interrupted. 'You're just about to ride in a race at Ascot and you're wandering off to chat on the phone?'

'I thought it was my father. He likes to wish me luck. But—' Kelly faltered, sensing that her story was beginning to sound absurd '– it was only a journalist wanting an interview.'

'A journalist.' Colonel Beamish made a note on the pad in front of him. 'I see.'

'So what you're saying,' – Nick Morley took up the questioning – 'is that you were called deliberately to the telephone and, while you were away, the lead was removed from your weight cloth.'

'Yes, sir.'

'And who was this journalist? Someone we can talk to?'

'Someone called Giles Williams. Associated Press. I hadn't heard of him.'

'Williams?' Colonel Beamish looked at his fellow stewards. 'Nor have we,' he said.

'And the jockey?' Of those questioning her, only Nick Morley seemed interested in her version of events.

'That,' said Kelly quietly, 'was Damien Gould.' And then, as it suddenly came to her, she added, 'If it wasn't him, it was the trainer.'

Harry Short rarely gave interviews to press or television. Even in moments of triumph, after one of his horses had won a race, he gave the wrong impression. Red-faced, inarticulate, arrogant, he couldn't even be described as a rough diamond. Harry Short was merely rough.

But today, for the first time in his life, he needed the press. He wanted all the publicity he could get. Nobody did that to him and got away with it.

'So, Harry,' the smooth-faced television interviewer looked warily at the angry trainer, 'it would be fair to say you're a disappointed man at this moment.'

'Bloody right,' said Short. 'Wouldn't you be if you'd just been cheated?'

'There's an inquiry going on as we speak so perhaps we should be careful—'

'Careful?' Short's eyes flashed with anger. 'I'll be as careful as she was to make certain she lost me that race.'

'You're referring to—'

'I'll say it now, I don't care who knows it.' Harry Short turned to the camera, ignoring the interviewer's attempts to interrupt him. 'I gave Kelly Connor her big chance today and she's fitted me up. I don't know why or who's paid her but only one person could remove five pounds from that weight cloth. It was her.'

'Turning to the race itself—'

'I curse myself for putting her on Pendero. Never trust a Connor, that's what they used to say when her father was riding. And she's a definite chip off the old crooked block. She's finished in this game.' Harry Short stabbed the air with an angry forefinger, spitting as he spoke. 'Finished, got that?'

'And now,' the interviewer said hastily, 'while

we're waiting for the outcome of the stewards' inquiry, let's catch up on the results from elsewhere.'

Still scowling, Short stormed off.

The interviewer listened to his producer on the headphones. 'Yes, of course it was slanderous, but don't worry, we're not talking about Jeffrey Archer. She's only a bloody apprentice, for God's sake.'

'It's a lie, sir.'

Damien Gould knew all about stewards' inquiries, he'd been up before them more times than he could remember, and he knew Colonel Beamish. Stand to attention, stare ahead like a private on parade, throw in a few 'sirs' and you were halfway there. 'I don't know why she would want to say that about me.'

He sounded so plausible and looked so innocent that for a moment Kelly felt that maybe she'd been wrong about him.

'But did you look after her saddle?' The colonel allowed his impatience with this inquiry to show.

'Of course, sir. She got a telephone call and she asked me to look after her saddle.' As soon as the words were out, Kelly knew she'd been right.

'I never—' she interjected.

'You've said your bit, Connor,' Colonel Beamish snapped without looking at her. 'Go on, Gould.'

'Anyway, as we're not allowed to leave our saddles unattended, I agreed to keep an eye on it for her. And that's all I did.'

Nick Morley leant over to Colonel Beamish and whispered something in his ear.

'Yes, all right,' the colonel nodded. 'Step forward,

Connor. You've heard Gould's testimony. Have you anything to add to it?'

Kelly said, 'If Damien Gould was so keen to help me, I'd like to know why he boxed me in two furlongs from home and tried to stop me making my challenge. Why wasn't he trying to win the race himself?'

'Gould?'

'I don't know what she's talking about, sir.'

'And then after the race,' Kelly continued, 'why did he say "You ain't won nothing yet, sweetheart".'

'Gould?'

'That's not true, sir.'

Colonel Beamish made another note on the pad in front of him. 'It all sounds rather flimsy to me, Connor,' he said wearily. He turned to Gould once more. 'Do you have any further comments on what Connor has had to say for herself?'

'I do, sir, but I shall keep them to myself if I may. After all,' he looked at Kelly and smiled coldly, 'there are ladies present.'

'Thank you, Gould, you may go.'

After Gould had left the inquiry, Harry Short was called in to give his own abusive detail of events. Kelly stood beside the stipendiary steward trying to hold back her tears. When Harry had finished, Colonel Beamish asked the other stewards if they had further questions. They shook their heads. Harry was dismissed but Kelly was told to wait outside while they made their decision.

Barely one minute later she was called back in, and

while she was being given the inevitable news that Pendero had been disqualified and placed last, Nick Morley was relaying the same information to the public.

'We will of course be referring the matter to the Jockey Club.'

Colonel Beamish's last words to Kelly were too much and as she turned and opened the door to leave, she quietly began to cry.

Another day's racing at Ascot was over, but the Members' Bar was still noisy and crowded. Winning owners, surrounded by friends, family and hangers-on, relived their moment of victory over bottles of champagne, forgetting the countless times when they had driven home in silence after another expensive and disappointing day. This moment was what they owned racehorses for: they drank to the jockey, the trainer, the lad, all of whom were making their way home at the end of another working day.

Racing journalists who had filed their copy hung around the bar, moving from group to group, accepting free drinks, picking up gossip. The talk was of a highly promising two-year-old owned by a shipping magnate that had trotted up on its first public appearance and was now ante-post favourite for next season's Two Thousand Guineas, of the breathtakingly close finish to the big race of the day, and, of course, the astonishing business of Harry Short's girl apprentice who had lost her race in the weighing room. Poor old Harry. You'd think he'd know better than to trust a Connor. Just like her father, that girl. Brilliant, but bent.

Yet the noisiest party in the Members' Bar was not being held by a winner and was avoided by journalists. For Ibn Fayoud, to go racing without treating a few friends to champagne at the end of the day was unthinkable. Here the conversation rarely touched on racing (although Serena, who said she had once been girl friend to a member of the royal family, claimed to have had a seriously successful gamble on the colt), it was about London, parties, who had spent the night with whom.

Ibn Fayoud, who took his pleasure quietly, observed his friends with a smile on his face. He liked to take them to the racecourse because they protected him from the tiresome racing people – trainers, bloodstock agents, advisers to his father – who would try to impress him with their knowledge of and interest in his horses. Since the age of thirteen, Ibn Fayoud had taken what he wanted from life. His teens and early twenties were a riot of sexual and narcotic excess. Now he was like a little rich boy in a toy shop. He went out, he partied, he took his friends racing, but he was bored. Nothing mattered to him. Or almost nothing.

'Ib, God you're so silent down there.' The blonde publicist for a high-profile London nightclub leant towards him, flashing an expanse of tanned cleavage. 'What evil plans are you hatching now?'

Ibn Fayoud fixed her with his dark eyes and smiled. 'I'll show you later.'

The fact was that, although Ibn Fayoud had stopped feeling anything in about 1983, he was now assailed by something approaching concern. That bloody horse, that bloody fat trainer, that bloody little girl. Between them they had ensured that his debt to Reg Butler, Turf Accountants, topped the million mark. Pounds. (Fayoud was almost certain it was pounds.) If Butler jerked his lead, there was no way he could pay it off without speaking to his father.

Now that *was* a problem. Sheikh al Hassan did not share his son's view of Western life as a fun-palace built for his own diversion. The Sheikh believed that, if you had money, you should behave responsibly; he actually had religious objections to some of his son's wilder stunts. His threat to send Ibn Fayoud back to Qatar where he would have to work as Minister of something or other, was not an empty one. Jack Butler had the power to have everything he enjoyed – women, parties, horses, Ascot – taken away from him if he so wished.

Ibn Fayoud shuddered. Then he stopped thinking about it. He was good at not thinking about unpleasant things.

Outside, in the deserted members' enclosure, a tall man in a suit and a bowler hat walked with a young girl, deep in conversation.

'Hope you don't mind talking out here,' Nick Morley was saying to Kelly Connor as they wandered slowly down towards the racetrack. 'The weighing room lacks privacy.'

'No, that's fine,' Kelly said. 'I prefer to be outside. I was beginning to feel like a prisoner in there.'

Nick Morley smiled. 'I'm sorry about the inquiry. The colonel is not the gentlest of inquisitors.'

'Particularly with women apprentices.'

'He belongs to the old school. I spoke to him later about it.'

Kelly glanced at the steward in some surprise. After the formality of the inquiry, his friendliness was welcome.

'You know that Gould was lying in there, don't you?' she said.

'Among the stewards, Damien is hardly renowned as a reliable witness. I don't think he's told the unvarnished truth to an inquiry in his life.' Nick leant on the rails and looked across the course. 'That's off the record, by the way.'

For the first time, Kelly looked at him as a man rather than as a Jockey Club steward. He wasn't unattractive. He was in his thirties, tall, strongly built, with straight, sandy hair and a squarish chin. Although it occurred to her that he might be using the sympathetic approach to break her down, he seemed uneasy with the role that had been thrust upon him.

'Hadn't you better tell me what happens now?' she asked.

'I've been instructed to take more statements, make a report of what happened and then file it to Portman Square advising as to whether you should appear before a formal hearing of the Jockey Club. In the meantime, you're not suspended.'

Kelly sighed. 'I suppose I should be pleased.'

'It could be worse. Oh, and you're not to talk to the press.'

'Unlike Harry Short?' There had been much talk in the weighing room of Short's comments to the press.

'Short's a bad man to cross,' said Nick. 'Try to ignore his remarks.'

'Even when he insults my father?' For the first time, the anger and hurt Kelly was feeling flashed in her eyes. 'I want to find out who was behind all this.' She started walking back to the weighing room.

'Kelly.' She turned, surprised that a steward should use her first name. Nick was still standing by the rails. He looked serious. 'Keep yourself to yourself for a while. Don't play the detective. Let us do the investigating, OK? I'll be in touch.'

It was only when she had returned to the weighing room and was dialling her father's number that the significance of Morley's remark filtered through. *Don't play the detective.* That could only mean that he believed her story.

There was a continuous low tone at the end of the line. Kelly tried again without success.

'Bloody phones.' She slammed down the receiver, collected her racing gear and headed home. It really wasn't her day.

Frank Connor's flat looked like a hurricane had swept through it. Tables had been overturned, the contents of drawers strewn about. The screen of the television had been shattered and there were gaps on the mantelpiece where he'd kept his few items of value: a silve cigarette case, a silver frame round the photograph of his wife, a set of antique china plates.

None of this Kelly saw when, with a growing sense of dread, she pushed open the unlocked front door and stepped into the flat. For a moment she was transfixed by the full horror of her father's body lying on the carpet, his head covered in blood and bone splinters showing through his temple.

'Dad!' she cried, stumbling across the room. She crouched beside the still figure, afraid even to touch it. Frank Connor's eyes stared unseeing out of a face contorted with pain. 'Oh my God, Dad.'

Chapter 3

In racing, as in life, rumour breeds on rumour. Within days of Frank Connor's death, the word on racetracks and in stable yards throughout the country, repeated and embroidered upon in the bars of Newmarket and Lambourn, was that the ex-jockey had paid the price for falling into crooked company. Nobody knew the details – maybe it was a gambling ring, or doping, or drugs – but everybody knew the truth about Connor. As a jockey, he had sold his soul to the devil; as a civvy, he had continued to work in some capacity for his corrupt paymasters. Somewhere along the line he had crossed, maybe double-crossed, them. He had been on the run, hiding out in Newmarket, but they had found him out, warned him off, stopped him once and for all.

Frank Connor, small-time failed hood, deceased. Frank Connor, victim of just another gangland killing. The winners, the glory days, were all but forgotten.

Almost lost in this swelling symphony of gossip and hearsay, a sad minor theme in counterpoint, was the story of his only daughter Kelly. Tragic, really. A talented enough rider, strong, balanced, with the knack of getting the best out of a horse, but caught in the same gin-trap of corruption as her father. Harry Short was no angel but when Harry pointed the finger, you had to take note. If he said he'd been stitched up by an apprentice with dodgy connections, then that was the way it was. All right, so she hadn't actually been suspended, so Morley of the Jockey Club had gone on record as saying no specific guilt in the matter had been proven but, in this game, there was no smoke without fire. It all added up; sad, but true.

Initial police investigation did nothing to still the rumours. The Newmarket constabulary reported that there was no evidence that the killing involved anything as melodramatic as gang revenge. It was the considered opinion of their officers that the deceased was the unfortunate victim of a break-in which had gone wrong. There had been several robberies in the Newmarket area, thieves working on the sound assumption that racing people liked to keep a spot of ready cash under the floorboards and out of the grasp of Her Majesty's Inspector of Taxes. How were the thieves to know that Frank Connor didn't have two pennies to rub together? This incident had all the hallmarks of a robbery – the flat had been torn apart, several items were missing and it had taken place on a Saturday afternoon when many people in the industry were at the racecourse. It was unfortunate for Mr Connor that he had been at home when the break-in occurred. Police issued descriptions of three men, already suspected of robbery with violence in the East Anglia district and now wanted for questioning in connection with the murder of Frank Connor.

Racing's rumour-mongers knew better. Yet again, the police had got it wrong.

Kelly Connor was in too great a state of shock to listen to the grapevine. All that she knew was that the most important person in her life, the man who had brought her up since she was eight, a gentle, wounded, wise man, was now gone. There was no hate in her heart, not yet, only pain and bewilderment.

During the time that Kelly had been working for Bill Templeman she'd become firm friends with his wife Annie. Just as Annie had confided in her when her marriage to Bill had been going through a shaky time, so Kelly had revealed her anxieties and ambitions. It was to Annie that Kelly turned for help now.

'Christ, whatever's the matter with you?' had been her first words when Kelly appeared through the back door. Before she had a chance to say any more, Kelly burst into tears and flung her arms round her, sobbing uncontrollably.

While Annie hugged her tightly, Kelly blurted out an account of what had happened. When the worst was over, Annie made her drink a large mug of sweet tea. She stayed up with her talking about anything and everything until they were both exhausted, and then she took Kelly upstairs and put her to bed.

For the first few difficult days Kelly stayed with the Templemans. Annie fielded the inevitable calls from

the more ghoulish members of the press who smelt a
story and were prepared to lie, cheat and bribe to get
at it. She protected her from the news that several of
her husband's owners had rung him to request that,
whatever happened, he did not put the apprentice
Connor on their horses in future. Smoke, fire,
rumour – Bill Templeman's oft-repeated support for
his protégée could do nothing against them.

For the two days before her father's body was
released for burial, Kelly spoke little, spending many
hours in her room, thinking of the past. The race at
Ascot was all but forgotten and, in her grief, she gave
little thought to her career beyond the conviction that,
at this moment, any plan to live by riding seemed an
absurdity. If a life with horses had led her father to his
death, she would earn her money elsewhere. Perhaps
her schoolfriends had been right – being a jockey was
no job for an intelligent, good-looking girl.

After Frank Connor's body was released by the
police, the autopsy having confirmed that he had been
killed by three blows to the cranium with a blunt
instrument or instruments, Kelly found the old
determination and resolve slowly returning to her.
She politely rejected Annie's suggestion that her
father should be buried near Newmarket, insisting
that she would fly home with the body and see it
interred in Adare, County Limerick, where he had
been raised and lived during the years before it all
went wrong. Annie offered to come along.

'No,' said Kelly. 'I want to do this by myself.'

'I just wish I could help.'

Kelly looked at Annie's lightly freckled face and

smiled for the first time in days. 'You can,' she said, giving Annie her keys. 'You can keep the cat fed.'

Annie returned Kelly's smile and the two women hugged each other. 'I hope it goes all right,' she said.

It was a wise decision. A funeral in England would have attracted gossips, journalists and rubber-necking members of the public. The ceremony in Adare was simple and affecting. The small village church was packed with people, many of whom had known Frank since he rode his first winners at local point-to-points. To his friends in this neighbourhood, rumour meant nothing, particularly if it originated from across the Irish Sea. All they knew was that Frank Connor was a fine, kind man who rode horses like a young god and who had been unlucky.

'Ashes to ashes.' The ringing tones of Father O'Brien could be heard in the town square as Frank Connor's body was laid to rest. 'Dust to dust.' Kelly stood alone at the foot of the grave, slightly apart from the rest of the congregation. 'Dust to dust.' These last few days had been as near to a living hell as she hoped she would ever suffer. She had gone to sleep crying and had awoken with tears in her eyes. Part of her had died with him.

She looked up from the coffin, across the wild green fields of County Limerick. Her father had not died in vain. She had come through.

'The Sheikh is waiting for you upstairs.' A tall black American held open the door of Sheikh al Hassan's London house in Eaton Square, scanning the street with apparent casualness.

'Thanks, Tom.' Nick Morley stepped into the house, noting with approval that Sheikh al Hassan's security arrangements were as subtly impregnable as ever. An ex-SAS man himself, Nick could appreciate the lengths to which the Arab potentate went to avoid kidnappers, assassins and political enemies. A few yards down the street, a man was washing a Daimler, eyeing anyone who approached the front door. Upstairs, he happened to know, another member of the Sheikh's entourage would be seated before a bank of television monitors covering all approaches to the house. Tom, whose euphemistic title was 'butler', was a fully trained security guard, as were most of the staff of twenty who ran the household. Here, even the pantry maid included marksmanship and kung-fu among her job qualifications.

'Mr Brompton-Smiley is with him, sir.'

Nick nodded. Of course, he would be. Simon Brompton-Smiley, international racing manager to the Al Hassan family, one of the most assiduously courted men in British racing and, in Nick's private view, a slimy, worthless creep. Admittedly Nick was biased, having known him since they were both at Harrow. Then little Simey was a pitiful creature – pale, ingratiating, the school sneak. These days, Nick tried to treat him with respect; after all, as the Sheikh's bloodstock adviser, he had to work with Brompton-Smiley, but it was not easy. Where the world saw a self-assured, pin-striped little man with greased hair Nick saw a jumped-up schoolboy, a sneak made good.

'Simon, how are you?'

'Nick.' Brompton-Smiley greeted him at the top of the stairs. 'Good of you to be so prompt. The Sheikh has a dinner, so perhaps we could sort this out within the half-hour.'

Nick smiled coldly. 'Suits me.'

The two men made their way into a large drawing room hung in perfect taste with eighteenth-century sporting pictures. With its Chippendale furniture, and a well-known Stubbs over a blazing log fire, the room suggested the lifestyle of one of the great landowners of the past, a Lord Derby or a Duke of Norfolk. Nick knew several Arab owners, but only Sheikh al Hassan seemed so effortlessly at home with Western culture.

The Sheikh sat on a sofa by the fire, a small, neat man in a dark suit, sipping iced mineral water and reading *The Times*. He welcomed Nick with a natural, gracious authority. Brompton-Smiley poured them both a mineral water as the Sheikh discussed the plans for a yearling Nick had bought for him the previous week at the Kentucky sales. No one listening to their casual conversation would have guessed that the colt in question had cost the Sheikh just short of three and a half million dollars.

'The problem we need to talk about,' Sheikh al Hassan said, as the two men settled into their chairs, 'is unfortunately a human rather than an equestrian one, namely—' he frowned at the thought '—my son. You probably know that he's in something of a mess.'

'Mess, sir?' It was unwise, Nick knew, to give the impression that everyone in racing knew about Ibn Fayoud's debts which, naturally enough, they did. 'I hadn't heard.'

The Sheikh smiled. 'Of course not,' he said. 'Simon can probably fill you in on the details later but the fact of the matter is that my son's well-developed appreciation for the good life has recently got rather out of hand.' He sipped thoughtfully at his mineral water. 'Now, much as I believe that the young should be allowed to make their own mistakes – and after all my son is, on paper at least, an adult – his financial situation is such that I can no longer stand aside. Like any family, we have our name to consider.'

Nick nodded. It was one of the Sheikh's favourite tricks to talk as if the Hassan dynasty, which was worth several billion dollars, was not that different from any other family – his, for example, or even Tom's downstairs. It was only the scale of their opportunities and difficulties which set them apart.

'A month ago,' the Sheikh continued, 'I was obliged to tell him that, unless he made a fresh start, there would be the most serious consequences – for him, of course, but also for me. Since then, I have been informed by an impeccable source' – Brompton-Smiley pursed his lips self-importantly – 'that my son's gambling debts have, if anything, increased. More seriously, he appears to be obligated to a particular bookmaker, Mr . . . ?'

'Butler,' said Brompton-Smiley.

'Jack Butler?' Nick winced. 'That's not good. He's tough.'

'Tougher than my son, I fear. Very reluctantly, I have to consider sending him back to Qatar for a course in home economics.' The Sheikh smiled wanly. 'An open-ended course.'

'What about his horses, sir?' So far, nothing Nick had heard surprised him. Ibn Fayoud was a nuisance, an embarrassment. British racing could do without him.

'His horses I shall sell unless Simon advises me to hold on to any of them. On the whole, they seem to have as disastrous a track record as their owner.' The two Englishmen laughed dutifully. 'Of course, none of that concerns you.'

'I'm sorry to hear about all this, sir.' Nick glanced over to Brompton-Smiley, whose expression suggested that worse was yet to come.

The Sheikh shrugged. 'Family life,' he said wearily. 'I can see no way to avoid stories in the press. Already the gossip columns are talking of a rift between my son and myself. When he is sent back to Qatar, there will doubtless be something of a fuss, particularly in the racing press. And that's why I've asked you here.' He glanced at his watch. 'I'll make this brief. Because of the probable scandal, I feel inclined to move my principal racing interests from the United Kingdom to France.'

'France, sir?' Nick tried to sound as calm as he could while his mind was racing at the implications of the Sheikh's remark. 'I would have thought that any family problem would be well known there.'

'The prize money is better and they don't have bookmakers,' said Sheikh al Hassan more firmly. 'I find I have something of an aversion to bookmakers.'

'The Sheikh and I have been looking into the economics,' Simon Brompton-Smiley added. 'It makes sense both on the training and—' at this point he was

47

unable to keep the smile off his face '—the bloodstock side.'

'That,' Nick said weakly, 'would be a major decision.'

'Not that major.' In Sheikh al Hassan's world, steps were taken in a brisk, businesslike way. It wasn't that he lacked sympathy for the hundreds of people whose livelihoods were affected by the change, simply that he didn't think of them. Life was too full of first-hand problems to worry about side effects.

'On the bloodstock side alone, we have some hundred or so animals,' Nick said quietly.

'We'd move them,' said Brompton-Smiley with the smugness of a man who, as international racing manager, would be unaffected by such a radical move. At a stroke, a handful of large trainers with whom the Sheikh kept his horses would find their yards devastated. He owned up to forty per cent of the horses with some of them and replacement owners of his calibre didn't just fall off trees. The face of British breeding and racing would be changed, and Nick would lose his principal source of income.

'Naturally,' the Sheikh said, 'we hope that you will continue to buy and sell on our behalf, but from France.'

'I'm very grateful, sir,' Nick smiled palely, 'but, as a member of the Jockey Club, I have my duties here.'

'You'll just have to make a choice.' Brompton-Smiley made no effort to hide his pleasure.

The Sheikh stared at him with piercing eyes and the international racing manager shrunk back into his chair. He had gone too far.

'Any choice that Nick may or may not have to make,' said the Sheikh, 'will be in a month's time and not before. He should think it over, the decision need not be hurried. And, of course, my son may find a way out of his difficulties so that the move will be unnecessary, although personally I doubt it.' The Sheikh got to his feet, the cue for Nick to leave. 'Let's all think about this, shall we? We'll talk soon.'

Simon Brompton-Smiley showed Nick out. 'Don't fall for the old options open line,' he said on the doorstep. 'The Sheikh has made up his mind, I'm afraid.'

'We'll see,' said Nick, turning on his heel and marching briskly down Eaton Place, past a man washing his car.

It was good to be riding again. An early morning mist shrouded Newmarket Heath as the first lot from Bill Templeman's yard made its way to the gallops. It was cold, with the first hint of autumn in the air, and a sullen silence hung over the string. Later, after breakfast, when a watery sun showed through the mist and the larks chattered high in the sky, the lads riding out would talk and laugh, but for now they sat hunched and silent, sleeping in. If one of the horses jigged about or bucked, it could expect a sharp dig in the ribs and a curse from its bleary-eyed jockey.

Kelly was gradually getting back to normal. Yes, it was good to be riding out again.

She had flown in from Dublin the previous evening and, despite Bill's offer of a few days' compassionate leave, she had insisted on working. The following

Saturday, a promising two-year-old called Diamond Dealer was due to make his first appearance on a racecourse at Kempton. Kelly had ridden him in most of his work and, since she would be riding him on Saturday, it was important to see how he went today. Bill, a man of few words at the best of times, had agreed, but only with considerable reluctance. Kelly had put it down to embarrassment over her father's death.

There had been a time when Kelly had dreaded riding out. The life of a stable lad was harsh and full of frustrations and, even in small yards, newcomers were treated with leery suspicion until they proved themselves. For a teenage lad, this was a relatively simple process; during his first week, he would be dumped in the yard's water trough after second lot. If he reacted to this initiation ceremony with loud good humour, he was in, one of the lads. If he cried or complained to the head lad, he could expect no mercy.

For girls, it was different. You didn't chuck girls in water troughs. Their initiation ceremony was more subtle.

Before Kelly had arrived, there had been only one girl working in the yard, a wiry, ginger-haired teenager called Bonny, who was tougher, louder and could pack a harder punch than most of the lads. For this reason, she fitted in easily and was treated with a certain wary respect. The fact that she was known to be meeting the much-feared head lad in the horsebox after evening feeds may have helped her position too.

Kelly was different. She was well spoken, quiet and her good looks noticeably raised the sexual tension in the Templeman yard. Worse than all this, she rode neatly and well, and was riding work for the boss within a couple of weeks of arriving. All this hadn't done much for her popularity.

One by one, the older lads tried it on. Bullying, nagging, threatening. Come to the pictures, Kelly. Come and watch a video round at my place. You need a friend in this yard, Kelly, a protector. One by one, Kelly turned them down. She was there to ride horses, not extend her sexual experience. She wasn't interested.

At first it was just names. Fridge. Prick-teaser. Dyke. Kelly ignored them. Then they would tell her insultingly filthy jokes. She laughed at them. Even when one of the lads marched around the yard holding a pair of black knickers, claiming that he had broken into the Fridge, Kelly smiled and went about her work.

At one point, she considered giving up racing altogether. The persecution, the loneliness in the yard were getting worse by the day. She had decided not to speak to Bill or Annie about it – that would only make her position worse. After the knickers incident, she had confided in her father and he had simply smiled and said, 'Sure, you'll just have to show them what you're made of. They'll respect you if you fight back.'

So she had. Dennis was the worst of them. Now in his late thirties, he had all the anger and resentment of a man who has been offered the chance of success and has failed to take it. Dennis rode light, was strong and looked good. A few seasons ago, Bill had started giving him the odd ride in apprentice races. But for some reason, the poise and balance that he showed riding work at home deserted him on the racecourse. He rode two winners and that was it. These days, he was given the occasional no-hope spare ride by the guv'nor but, by now, even Dennis understood. He was just another might-have-been on the way to being a has-been.

Dennis resented promise, particularly in the younger lads. He teased them, tried to show them up on the gallops. Behind his cheery, grinning façade, he hated Kelly with a passion.

She had been at the yard two months when Bill had asked her to ride work with Dennis on a couple of four-year-olds. At one point, the gallop went out of Bill's sight before coming round a hill and back into view. Kelly was a neck up on Dennis when she heard a clicking noise from him. Quite coolly, he took his right hand off his reins and held it firmly between her legs. Kelly cursed him and tried to wriggle away but they were riding at racing speed and it was impossible to escape without the risk of damaging her horse. For what seemed an eternity, Dennis held her in a humiliatingly intimate grip. 'Nice,' she heard him say. 'You like it too, don't you?' Sick with anger, Kelly remembered her father's advice. Fight back. She steadied her horse slightly, cupped her left hand under Dennis's foot and, with a swift, businesslike movement, tipped him out of the saddle.

Bill was furious when Kelly pulled up alone and rushed off to catch the loose horse. Shortly afterwards, Dennis came into view, limping, followed by Bill leading the horse.

'What happened to you?' he stormed. Dennis glanced up at Kelly, hate in his eyes. Her look told him all he needed to know: shop me, buster, and I'll shop you. 'He stumbled, guv'nor,' he muttered. 'One moment he was going fine, the next I was on the floor.'

Word of the incident spread through the stable. The new girl had dropped Dennis. He'd tried it on and ended up on his backside. It was the joke of the week. Nobody really liked Dennis, although some of the younger lads were afraid of him. To Kelly's relief and surprise, she was accepted at last. Her initiation ceremony had been completed with honours.

'He'll go close on Saturday.' Kelly patted Diamond Dealer, after pulling up. 'With my claim.' The horse had worked well, getting a previous winner well off the bridle over the last furlong.

Bill nodded. 'We'll talk about that over breakfast,' he said, turning to walk back to his car.

It was not unusual for Bill to ask Kelly to take breakfast between first and second lots, and normally it was an occasion she enjoyed. Conversation with Bill was limited as he stayed absorbed in the morning's racing papers, but Annie more than compensated with a never-ending supply of local gossip. She was also a great cook.

On this occasion, though, something was wrong. The two of them talked to Kelly about the funeral in Ireland, but when she switched the conversation to racing matters they became evasive and Kelly noticed odd glances passing between them.

'So,' she said brightly at one point. 'How do you

think Diamond Dealer will run on Saturday? He went well this morning.'

There was silence. Annie looked significantly at her husband, urging him to speak.

'Was it something I said?' Kelly smiled.

Bill frowned. 'The horse runs,' he said quietly. 'But I'm afraid you're not riding.'

It was as if Kelly had been slapped in the face. Diamond Dealer was her ride. He went better for her than anyone else. It was unthinkable that Bill, her greatest supporter in the past, should book someone else to ride him.

'May I know why?'

'Lady Dereham has insisted.'

The owner had jocked her off? It made no sense to Kelly. 'But I've ridden winners for her. It's crazy.'

'She's not alone, I'm afraid, Kelly,' said Annie gently. 'We've been getting calls all week. It's a serious problem.'

'Not because of Ascot, surely?'

Bill nodded. 'Harry Short is a very powerful man. He's been running something of a character assassination campaign on you. Apparently an extremely large bet on Pendero came unstuck. You were too busy dealing with your father's funeral to notice, but the racing papers gave you a real hammering.'

Kelly looked at Bill in amazement 'But you don't believe I'd do that, do you?'

'Of course not,' said Bill impatiently. 'But I'm not an owner. I'm sure it will blow over in time.' He sounded unconvinced. 'Until then you'll have to sit tight. Can you ride out second lot?'

'Of course I can.' Kelly felt a knot of anger in her stomach. 'I'm not finished yet. Who am I on?'

'Shine On.'

Kelly smiled. It was lucky for her that the yard's star three-year-old was owned by Bill himself, who had bred him. There was one ride she could still depend on.

After she had left to tack up, Annie looked across the table at her husband.

'You should have told her,' she said.

Bill rubbed his eyes. 'I will.' Unusually for a trainer, he hated confrontations, awkward scenes. 'One thing at a time.'

'Forget it.' Annie folded her *Racing Post* briskly. 'I'll talk to her after second lot.'

Later that morning, as she returned her saddle and bridle to the tack room, Kelly found herself reflecting on what had been said over breakfast. The Templemans were honest people, rarely influenced by the racecourse gossip which dictated who was in and who was out at any particular time. There were certain yards where a stable jockey going through a difficult patch could expect no mercy, the best rides would suddenly start going outside, but the Templemans were not like that. Never having been fashionable themselves, they didn't give a damn for the ebb and flow of public opinion. Loyalty, judgement was what mattered to them.

And yet, there was something about Bill's manner this morning which had alarmed Kelly. She was used to his silent moods, which she put down to the pressures of his job, but she had never known him so evasive and ill at ease. In fact, the yard itself was not the same since her return from Ireland. It was as if the lads were party to an embarrassing secret, a conspiracy of silence which excluded her. Maybe it was the Ascot race, or the death of her father, but that would be surprising. Apart from Dennis, whose loathing she now took for granted, they liked her here and, even if they thought she had ridden a bad race the previous day, they would express their views with open good humour.

As Kelly made her way to her car, Annie emerged from the house and walked towards her. 'How about a coffee and a sticky bun in the town?' Annie was ten years older than Kelly and a couple of inches taller. She was also quite a bit fatter due to a passion for anything with sugar in it.

'Let's make it three sticky buns,' Kelly said gloomily. 'After all, I don't have to watch my weight any more now I'm being jocked off.'

'Don't be like that,' said Annie, climbing into Kelly's Saab.

On their way into Newmarket, the two women talked about the horses in the yard. Shine On had been impressive in his work and Bill planned to run him at York and then maybe a big race abroad.

'Sounds like bad news for me,' said Kelly. On the international circuit, she would be unable to claim her seven pounds and most trainers would opt for the experience of one of the top jockeys.

'Depends how you ride him at York.'

Annie suggested a tea-house frequented by shoppers and visitors rather than racing people and, as if to confirm Kelly's suspicion that this was to be more than a casual chat, picked a corner table away from the other customers.

'So,' she said, stirring her coffee. 'Ireland was all right, the funeral?'

Kelly nodded. 'It was as Dad would have wished. I'm glad I took him home.'

'And now?' Annie asked casually.

'Now I pick up the pieces. Ride out. Resume my career. Back to normal except I'm going to look for another flat. I can't bear to be in the old one any more. I keep seeing Dad's body lying on the floor.' There was something about Kelly's tone of voice that betrayed her.

'That's not all, is it?' asked Annie.

Kelly shook her head. 'I can't let it go,' she said with quiet determination. 'Someone murdered Dad. That wasn't a botched break-in. I've got to find out who killed him.' Raking over painful memories, she frowned. 'There was something on his mind the day before he died. I'm sure it was something to do with my race at Ascot. He was so desperate that I should win it.'

'Your dad wanted you to win everything.'

'I know.' Kelly smiled, thinking of her father's enthusiasm.

'Kelly.' There was a new seriousness to Annie. 'You were right. Something is going on. We've been getting calls – not just from owners worried about your riding their horses but anonymous calls.

Threats. They want us to throw you out, sack you.'

Kelly sat bolt upright. 'I don't believe it!' she said. 'Why should anyone want to do that?'

'I think you're right. I think there is a connection between Pendero's race at Ascot and your father's death. Someone somewhere has been playing for very high stakes and they don't want you spoiling the game.'

Kelly could feel her temper begin to rise. 'I told the police it was no ordinary break-in,' she said angrily. 'I'm not going to be scared off by—'

'Look, you'll get going again. The rides will come. But you'll just have to take things quietly. Forget these people.'

'And if not?'

Annie sighed. 'If not, I've overestimated your good sense.'

Kelly agreed, not wanting to prolong the argument, and changed the subject.

After the two women had parted, Kelly drove back to her flat. The events of the morning had made her weary. On her return from Ireland, it had seemed so simple: resume riding and make a few calls to people who could help her. Now she was faced by a choice: on the one hand, her future career; on the other, the memory of her father. She wanted to be a jockey more than anything else, but she knew which she'd choose.

She cursed as she entered the flat. It was warm as if she had left the central heating on by mistake. There were two messages on her answering machine. Kelly picked up a pen in the hope that she would be taking down details of spare rides.

'This is Giles Williams.' Kelly recognized the voice of the journalist who had spoken to her before the fateful race at Ascot. The man sounded drunk. 'I'd quite like to talk to you. Soon. Don't call me. I'll be in touch.' There was a click, followed by a tone.

She didn't recognize the voice of the second caller. 'Hello, Connor. There's a message in the oven to tell you to mind your own business.'

Kelly walked quickly to the kitchen. Nothing appeared to have been moved but the oven was turned full on. That was why the flat was warm. She could hear the sound of her heart beating as, like someone in a dream, she opened the oven door – and then reeled back, gagging, her legs weak beneath her. Looking out of the oven with white unseeing eyes was the corpse of her cat.

Chapter 4

They might have been lovers. In a small French restaurant off Sloane Square, the couple sat at a corner table, their faces lit by candlelight. They talked in low voices, pausing when the waiter put food before them, as if whatever they had to say could not be shared, even by a discreet French boy with an imperfect grasp of English. The understated beauty of her face was framed by the dark curls of her shoulder-length hair – looks which attracted covert glances from other men in the restaurant. But there was something tense about the girl, almost haunted. She smiled little and listened intently whenever the man, sober-suited and authoritative, spoke. He seemed to be a reassuring, comforting presence. An observer would guess that their conversation was troubled, intimate. Maybe he was married. Maybe she was pregnant. Maybe they were just lovers.

But the conversation between Kelly Connor and

Nick Morley was not of matters of the heart, but of life, death and horses.

The call from Nick that afternoon had been well timed. Kelly was still upset and dazed by the events of her first day back at work. He had news of the investigation, he said. They needed to talk. Portman Square? she had asked, and he had laughed almost boyishly. He thought she deserved better than that after all her troubles. How about Au Père de Nico at eight thirty? 'Where on earth is that?' she inquired. He gave her directions and she agreed to meet him there. Maybe it would do her good.

All her troubles. What did Nick Morley know of her troubles? A race lost, a father murdered, a career on the skids – they were no more than the opening scenes of a nightmare which was engulfing her. Alone in the flat, she had shuddered with something approaching fear. What would her father have done under these circumstances? With heaving stomach, Kelly had gone to the kitchen, tipped the burnt remains of her cat into a plastic bag and took it downstairs to bury it in the garden. She was a Connor. They – whoever they were – had underestimated her if they thought she could be cowed into submission by threats and violence. It was at that moment that she had resolved to tell Nick Morley everything that had happened to her.

'Who knows about this?' he asked when Kelly haltingly told him of the latest threat to her.

'I've taken the tape to the police, of course, and told them about my cat, but that's all. I just thought that the Jockey Club should know too. The Templemans have had a few anonymous calls as well.'

'Will you tell them?'

Kelly shook her head. 'No, I've got hardly anything to ride as it is. If they knew I was under that sort of pressure, they'd stop giving me rides altogether. I have to sort it out myself.'

'You're tougher than you look.' Nick smiled. 'I can see why you were less overjoyed by my news than I had anticipated.'

'Of course I'm glad that the investigation has come up with nothing incriminating against me, but it's no surprise. In a way I wish you had pursued it.'

'What?' Nick was used to the tunnel-visioned stubbornness of jockeys but it was difficult to square this cast-iron inner confidence with the slight features of the young girl sitting across the table from him. 'You actually wanted to be hauled up in front of the stewards in Portman Square?'

'Yes, I did,' said Kelly, surprised that he hadn't grasped what she'd been saying. She spoke with a new intensity. 'Someone needed to stop Pendero winning at all costs. Gould tried it on during the race. Then there was the lead missing from a perfectly sound weight cloth. Then my father was killed, there were threats against me, the Templemans. The last thing I want is for the case to be closed. An accident. A misunderstanding. What's that going to do to my reputation if Harry Short's accusing me of everything short of genocide?'

'Everyone knows that Short's a loud mouth. Ride a couple of winners.' Nick sipped at his glass of white wine. 'Ascot will soon be forgotten, believe me.'

'Either that or I'll be dead.'

Nick shook his head and tried to lighten the conversation. 'You're only in danger if you go around screaming "Murder!" every time your father's name is mentioned.'

Kelly looked away. Don't show it, she was thinking. Don't show the pain, the loss, the anger. Why was it everyone seemed to go for the easy way out? If there was a boat to rock, she'd bloody well rock it. In spite of herself, tears welled in her eyes.

'I'm sorry,' Nick muttered. 'That was insensitive. I just . . .' He hesitated. 'I suppose I just don't want to see you hurt.'

Kelly looked at him. 'You're very kind,' she said, and then added, 'for a steward.'

'I wasn't talking as a steward,' he said softly.

There was silence at the table. Not for the first time, Kelly felt an unmistakable tug of attraction towards him. She had always sworn that her private life would take second place to her career until she had established herself, that she would never become involved with anyone remotely connected with racing, and fortunately temptation had rarely come her way. But despite her preoccuption with everything else, something about the man sitting opposite made her resolutions waver.

'Isn't this a touch irregular?' she said. 'Steward enjoying candlelit dinner with apprentice? What would Harry Short say?'

'Somehow,' Nick smiled, 'I can't see Harry spending a night out at Au Père de Nico. Maybe it is a little unusual.' He paused. 'But then so are you.'

Kelly looked away quickly. The thing she needed

least in the world at this moment was to fall in love with a steward. In a deliberately uncouth way, she drank back the rest of her wine. 'I bet you say that to all the jockeys.'

The next morning, Kelly heard from her father. There, among the junk mail and bills delivered while she had been riding out first lot, was an envelope written in a careful, neat hand. It contained a note from Dermot Kinane, an ex-jockey who had been a close friend of the family in Ireland. Puzzled, for Dermot had never been a great correspondent, Kelly read:

Dear Kelly,

I hope you are well, and that you had a good journey home.

There was something I didn't tell you at your father's funeral because it seemed the wrong time, but two days after he died, I received a letter from him. It said that he had a big problem he didn't want to bother me with, but that if anything happened to him, I was to pass on this envelope to you. He said it was very important.

My thoughts are with you at this painful time, Kelly. Please remember that, if you ever need any help, your old friend Dermot is always here.

The Lord be with you.

Your loving Dermot

Attached to the letter was a small blue envelope, marked 'KELLY CONNOR'. In the corner, as if added as an afterthought, were the words 'Very

Confidential'. Sitting alone at her kitchen table, Kelly read the last words ever written by her father.

My Darling Girl,

I only hope that you will never have to read this letter – not because my life is worth anything to me but because it breaks my heart to think of you alone in a world which I have found to be so harsh and unforgiving.

I'm writing this on the morning of your ride at Ascot on Pendero. I hope and pray that you will win – God willing, you will because you have all the ability in the world – but I have discovered over the past few days that there are people prepared to go to great lengths to stop you. I'm told it's nothing personal (it's never anything personal in racing – a fellow who had just put me through the wing at Naas visited me in hospital to tell me it was nothing personal), but the end result is the same. A horse which should win, doesn't.

During the week there had been a number of calls to the flat. If it was you who answered the telephone, they hung up but when you were away riding they spoke to me. They told me that, if Pendero won at Ascot, you were finished as a jockey. Come second, third, last and things would go your way from then on. We have friends in high places, they said. There were also threats to me personally – which didn't worry me. I've been threatened before and doubtless will be again!

Kelly felt the tears fill her eyes as she heard her father's voice speaking through the words on the page.

So why didn't I tell you? God forgive me, I nearly did. The first time's always easy. It's just a race, after all – if you're any good, you can wave your arms about while pulling a horse's back teeth out and keep yourself out of the stewards' room. Why not keep in with the people who really run racing, the villains? I know the argument well because I was once convinced by it. But then they come back. It's another race, the stakes are higher and this time you're being watched more closely by the authorities. Too late you realize that there's no going back. They've got you. In this war, there's no neutral territory. You're either with the enemy or you're not. I went over to the enemy and destroyed my life and that of your dear mother, God rest her soul. On the day she died, I vowed that whatever happened, I would keep you away from them. I hoped you would stay away from racing but it was in your blood. As soon as I saw you riding, I knew you'd make it – so long as they didn't get to you.

So I lied to them. I told them I'd squared it with you. They wanted to talk to you direct, but I said that would frighten you off. Trust me, I said and they did.

This morning I heard from them again. They were double-checking everything was still in order. They threatened me once more, only this time they sounded much more serious. It occurred to me that this was not some two-bit gambling ring. This was big. They have powerful contacts, I know. I feared for you, my darling girl. I began to have doubts as to whether I had been right not to tell you what was going on.

The coward in me hopes that Pendero gets beaten in an honest race this afternoon. But if he wins, it's possible that something may happen to me. If it does, I hope and pray that they will stop there and leave you alone, at least for the time being.

The purpose of this letter is to explain what happened. I did what I thought was right for the most precious thing in the world to me. Remember, always do your best, don't let them hook you, however tempting the bait. Remember what happened to me because I was weak. Do it for your future, for the Connor name, for me.

I love you,

Dad

When Kelly had finished reading, she just sat and cried, a horrible empty feeling inside her. She didn't know if the tears were for herself or her father. After a while she got up and walked slowly from the kitchen into the bedroom. She pulled from under the bed a box containing photographs and cuttings from happier days. Frank Connor jumping the last on his way to a win in the Gold Cup. Frank Connor grinning, mudspattered, in the winners' enclosure. Frank Connor, profiled in the *Irish Times*, relaxing at home with his wife Mary and his five-year-old daughter Kelly.

The Connor name. There was a new coldness in Kelly's heart. Deep in thought, she put her father's letter at the bottom of the box and pushed it back under the bed. It was time for second lot.

'Change of plan,' Peter, the head lad, shouted out to Kelly as she crossed the yard with her tack. 'You're to ride Shine On for a spot of work.'

'Work?' Kelly expressed surprise. 'I thought he was having an easy day, today.'

Peter nodded in the direction of the Templemans' house, where a silver Lamborghini was parked. 'Apparently we have someone to impress.'

Kelly shrugged. It was unlike Bill to change his training plans for anyone.

Ten minutes later, the question in her mind was answered. As she brought Shine On out of his box, Bill and Annie approached from across the yard. With them was a tall, dark-skinned man in an expensive suit that looked oddly out of place among the wheelbarrows and pitchforks of a small stable.

'Hold him there for a second, Kelly,' said Bill. Kelly noticed that, while the trainer and his wife were looking proudly at their horse, the stranger appeared to be more interested in her.

'Please introduce me,' he said quietly.

'Of course.' Bill concealed his disappointment that the man had failed to comment on the appearance of the pride of the yard. 'Kelly Connor. This is Fayoud al Hassan.'

The man walked forward and fixed Kelly with his dark eyes. His handshake was like a caress.

Kelly nodded with a brisk, businesslike 'How do you do, sir.'

'Mr Hassan is Shine On's new owner,' said Bill.

Kelly's eyes widened. She felt like swearing but instead said, 'You're a very lucky man, Mr Hassan, he's a lovely horse.' He was also the one good horse Kelly had been certain to ride – while Bill owned him.

But not even the news that the most promising horse in the yard had been sold to Ibn Fayoud, nor the rumour that the rest of the young Arab's horses would also be coming to the yard, could distract Kelly from thoughts of her father's letter. In the string, taking Shine On for a showpiece half-speed over five furlongs, riding home, her mind was on the implications of his message.

Racecourse rumour, as reported by Annie, had it that there had been a big gamble on Pendero, that a professional gambler stood to gain a fortune if he won. It was now obvious that the horse was a stayer and yet Harry Short's stable jockey had recently ridden him as if his best distance was six furlongs, holding him up for a late run. Although Pendero had finished strongly at Ascot, that was because it had been a truly run race and the leaders had finished tired. Over a mile, the only sensible way to ride Pendero was to use his stamina, not hold him up. Short had been saving him for the Ascot race. Kelly was sure of it.

Then why did he put her up at Ascot rather than one of the top jockeys? Her seven-pound claim was one possible reason; another was that, with an apprentice riding him, Pendero's odds in the market would lengthen. Then Kelly remembered Short's behaviour after the race. He had fastened on to the fact that she was a Connor, played on memories of her father's reputation for throwing races. It was a cheap shot but an effective one. Racing people believed in blood-lines. Even if she were finally cleared by Nick Morley's investigation, she would remain guilty by association in the eyes of many racecourse insiders. In other words, when the race was lost in the weighing room, she was an obvious scapegoat. Was it possible that Short was part of the conspiracy, that he stood to gain from his own horse being beaten?

It seemed unlikely. Before the race he had been tense, after it his fury had seemed spontaneous and genuine. A crook and a bastard Short might be, but it would be surprising if he were that good an actor. His deviousness and dishonesty were in the front window for all to see. Yet whatever went on in that race, Kelly was certain that Short was a part of it. She would have to speak to him. She didn't relish the prospect.

Assuming that Short had been playing it straight, then there remained the question of who stood to lose if Pendero won. That there was a conspiracy Kelly had no doubt. Unfortunately she only knew two bit-part players in the plot. The chance of Damien Gould helping her seemed unlikely in the extreme, unless she could apply pressure on him. Someone somewhere must know what skeletons he had hidden in his

locker. The idea of employing a spot of judicious
blackmail did not appeal to her but what was the alternative? There was little point in appealing to his better
nature when he clearly didn't have one.

A more likely lead was Giles Williams, the journalist. It had been no coincidence that she had been called
to the phone in the weighing room. She doubted if
Williams were a major player – even on the telephone,
he sounded a loser – but at least he might tell her who
had put him up to it. That would be a start.

Trust no one, her father had said. But there was little
chance of discovering who had killed him without
help. Kelly decided that she had to talk to Annie, even if
there was a risk that she would tell her husband. Bill
would have a fit if he knew his apprentice was turning
supersleuth. She also had to tell Nick. He had made her
promise to keep him in touch with developments.
Being part of the racing establishment, he could be
helpful to her, and he had seemed to understand why
she needed to pursue this, and it wouldn't be that painful to see him again. Far from it. Kelly smiled.

'Thinking of your next winner?' one of the lads
interrupted her reverie as the string turned back to the
stable.

'Something like that,' said Kelly, and then returned
to her thoughts. Her first job would be to show the
letter to the police.

Success as a jockey is not just a question of riding
winners. Sometimes you have to be able to handle the
phone as well as you handle horses. No one in racing is
above ringing round for spare rides; one great jump

jockey was nicknamed 'Ting-a-Ling' because of his speed and skill in contacting trainers whose jockeys were injured or couldn't do the weight or were simply out of favour. Kelly understood this and played the game as well as anyone. When it really mattered, Kelly could give great phone.

But this afternoon she wasn't looking for spare rides. She had been to see the inspector in charge of her father's murder case. He hadn't held out much hope, although he had agreed that the letter seemed to disprove the theory about a break-in that had gone wrong.

Kelly had driven straight home and embarked on her own investigation. First of all, she rang round her contacts in journalism. Unsurprisingly, none of them had heard of Giles Williams, which was clearly a false name, and Kelly's description of his telephone manner – a slurred, gin-sodden voice with a wheedling insincere tone to it – covered half of what used to be known as Fleet Street.

It was finally Bob Morrow, one of the older racing correspondents on the *Daily Telegraph*, who came up with a lead.

'That's not his name,' he said. 'And he's not really a journo, more a jumped-up PR man. Now—' There was a noisy inhalation of smoke, followed by a hacking cough '—what the hell was his name?'

'How d'you know it's "Giles Williams"?'

'There used to be a Giles Williams column in the *Life* many years ago. Gossip, jokes, social titbits. This man goes racing every day. He gambles, swears a lot, drinks too much, falls over.'

'So he *is* a journalist.'

Morrow laughed, bringing on another attack of smoker's cough. 'Now, now,' he said, when he had recovered. 'We're not all like that. No, the man gave up writing years ago. There was some sort of scandal.'

'What does he do now?'

'Professional hanger-on. Part-time stringer. Full-time piss-artist. He sells the odd bonk 'n' tell story to the tabloids – Page Three Girl in Raunchy Romps with Royal Romeo, that sort of thing. He's just your basic, traditional smut-peddler really. Tell you what, I'll ask around and ring you back.'

Kelly thanked him.

'Any tips?'

'Yes, Bob,' she said. 'Cut down to twenty a day.'

'Where's that running then?' With a wheezy laugh, the journalist hung up.

Harry Short, Damien Gould. Kelly was tapping the pad in front of her, considering which of these unlikely leads to follow up, when the phone rang. It was Bill.

'Tomorrow evening, at Kempton. Boardwalk runs in the seller. All right?'

'You mean I'm riding him?' Kelly was unable to conceal her surprise. Ascot was barely a week past and all the indications had been that her rehabilitation as a jockey would be a matter of weeks not days.

'Why, did you have other plans?' Bill snapped. 'You'll just have to cancel him, won't you?'

'No, it's just, after last week, I thought that—'

'Don't be bloody stupid. I do have one or two owners who do what they're told. You've got eight stone three with the claim. I think he'll win. I'll see you in the morning.' He hung up.

It hadn't been difficult for Bill to accede to his wife's nagging to give the girl a break. Maybe he was biased, but as far as he was concerned, she was the best claimer in the country.

Kelly put the phone down and skipped around the room. It was the best she'd felt since Ascot. Bill had come up trumps. Abrupt, unsmiling, laconic, he'd kept faith. She grabbed the copy of *Racing Post* that was on the table. Boardwalk was no flying machine, a big clumsy four-year-old who had yet to win a race, but none of the opposition had any form. Best of all, one of them – a horse with a line of duck's eggs beside its inappropriate name of Dead Lucky – was being ridden by Damien Gould. She'd get a chance to talk to him about Ascot.

The sound of the telephone crashed into her thoughts. A wheezing cough at the other end of the line told Kelly that it was Bob Morrow.

'Quentin St John Broom-Parker. A man as phony as his name. That's your Giles Williams.'

'Have you got a number?'

'No, but you'll find him in the bar at the nearest race meeting to London. Big fellow with a Jimmy Edwards tash and a red face, swaying slightly as he bores all around him with a pack of lies about his past. When there's no racing nearby, you'll find him in the Garrick Club.'

Kelly glanced at the racing paper she was holding. 'It's only Pontefract today,' she said. 'If I come down to London now, do you reckon he'll be at the Garrick?'

'He'll have been there since lunchtime like as not. Phone and see. If he is there, by the time you arrive he'll be nice and mellow.'

'Bob, you're a brick,' said Kelly. 'I owe you one.'

Another attack of coughing forced Kelly to hold the receiver away from her ear.

'I'm too old for it now, but thanks for the thought,' Morrow eventually managed. 'By the way, you have to be a member to get in the Garrick.

Kelly grinned to herself. 'Crap,' she said.

The gentleman who answered the phone at the Garrick confirmed that Broom-Parker was indeed there. So Kelly changed to go, but before leaving for London, she wrote a brief letter to Dermot Kinane.

My dear Dermot,

I've just got your letter and Dad's note to me. It meant a lot and I'm very grateful you sent it on to me.

Thanks for your kind offer of help. I'm beginning to put my life together again now and I'm concentrating on my riding to help me get through.

I hope to come to Ireland at the end of the season and I will, of course, come and see you. I miss you and all my friends there.

All my love,
Kelly

Dear Dermot. Always the thoughtful, worried one. There was no need to get him involved in this.

With her thoughts on another, simpler life back in

the old country, Kelly put the letter in an envelope, picked up her coat and left for London.

Bennett had been doorman at the Garrick Club for twenty-three years and had developed a way with unpleasantness. Sometimes tourists wandered in off Longacre and looked about the hall of this famous British institution before he ushered them out. Or members imbibed a little too enthusiastically and had to be helped into a taxi. More often, they simply died; the after-dinner heart attack while slumbering in one of the club's deep leather chairs was a popular way of moving on to the great gentleman's club in the sky. There were low points, of course. First they let journalists in, then literary agents; it would be women members next. Bennett was thankful that retirement was only two years away. These days, everything was changing, even the Garrick Club.

Then a young woman – dark, quite a looker if you liked that sort of thing but a bit too full of herself for Bennett's liking – walked into the club and announced that she was the dinner guest of Sir Robin Day, he could only treat her to his coldly disapproving smile and direct her to the ladies' bar. It was the sort of thing that happened these days. How was he to know that she was up to some sort of mischief?

Kelly walked up the steps into the hall of the Garrick towards the wide staircase which led up to the bar, then hesitated. In front of an open fireplace in the hall, a couple of large leather armchairs were occupied by two men in dark suits. One was reading a newspaper, the other was fast asleep, a rumbling snore like a low-flying aircraft emanating from him. He had a prominent handlebar moustache and a high colour to his cheeks. Choosing a chair with its back to the front door and Bennett's look-out post, Kelly sat herself down.

It took a moment for the full enormity of what was happening to filter through to the brandy-drenched consciousness of the member reading *The Times*. Then he lowered his paper with the look of man whose most precious shrine is being desecrated before his eyes. 'This part of the club is for members only, he said in a voice of strangulated distaste. 'It's not open to—'

'Women?' Kelly smiled. 'Don't worry, I won't be here long.'

At the sound of a female voice, the eyes of the other man snapped open. 'Good God,' he said.

'No, Kelly Connor. Giles Williams, I believe. Or do you prefer the name Quentin St John Broom-Parker?'

Kelly stood up, walked slowly towards Broom-Parker and knelt before his chair like a child about to be told a fireside story. As Broom-Parker attempted to struggle to his feet, she leant forward and tweaked both ends of his moustache.

'I *say*,' the *Times* reader stood up and dithered while Kelly took a firmer hold of Broom-Parker's bristling moustache.

'Be quiet,' she said over her shoulder.

Muttering, 'Where's Bennett, for God's sake?' the man hurried off.

Kelly pulled Broom-Parker's face towards hers and

looked deeply into his loser's eyes. His breath stank of drink. 'Listen,' she said. 'We've spoken on the telephone, remember?'

The colour had now left Quentin Broom-Parker's face. To nod would have been too painful, but he closed his eyes in confirmation.

'I lost the race because of you.' Kelly tugged at the moustache. 'That doesn't matter now. But someone was murdered the same day and that does matter. I think the same people were involved. Follow me?'

A knot of dark-suited Garrick members had gathered in the hall and were muttering anxiously. Who was this madwoman? Broom-Parker's mistress? He always was a game old dog. Doesn't look so clever now, though.

Broom-Parker's eyes swivelled beseechingly towards his friends. Kelly tugged again.

'Follow me?'

A blink of the eyes.

'Now I need to know who paid you or blackmailed you to call me in the weighing room.'

'Right, young lady.' Bennett stood behind her. 'Leave go of this gentleman or I will have no alternative but to use force on you.'

'Throw me out,' said Kelly without taking her eyes off Broom-Parker, 'and the whiskers come too. This won't take more than a moment.' Bennett hesitated. Nothing in his many years' service had prepared him for this sort of situation.

'I need to know,' repeated Kelly.

'I can't tell you,' squirmed Broom-Parker painfully. 'It's more than my life's worth.'

Kelly stared at the pathetic figure for a moment and then let him go. 'OK, I'm going straight to the police.'

With that, Kelly got up, brushed past Bennett and walked calmly out. The fact that she'd already told the police didn't matter. She'd just have to think of something else.

Margaret Stanhope worshipped her employer, Jack Butler. She knew that there were murky corners to his business affairs, that for a suave good-looking man, he had one or two unfortunate characteristics, like a ferocious temper. And, of course, she knew that Jack's private life was something of a carnival. She knew all that because, as Jack's private assistant, she organized him: his TV appearances, his meetings with London's shadier characters, his payments for some mucky chore or other, his alibis to the wife (who could blame him, married to that bimbo?), his hotel rooms.

Not that she minded Jack playing around because she knew that one day he would be hers. She may have been three years older than he was, pushing forty and not quite as pert as the sort of girl he favoured at this precise moment, but one day Jack would grow up, look for a real woman to take care of him, and there she'd be, waiting and ready.

Telephone cupped under his left ear, Jack leant back in his chair, put his feet on the desk, almost kicking his assistant as he did it, and said, 'Well, that's *very* inconvenient.' He winked at Margaret as the person at the other end of the line spluttered some apology or other.

Yes, she was ready. Sometimes a wink kept her in

fantasies for weeks. Once or twice, Jack had casually goosed her as she reached for a file. She had nearly melted away on the spot.

He hung up and stared out of the window, over the roofs of Victoria.

'Right,' he said finally. 'I need to see Ibn Fayoud again. Tell Johnny and Den I have another job for them. And it looks like I'm going to have to attend to that jockey girl.'

'Attend, Jack?' Margaret Stanhope smiled. 'D'you mean—'

'I mean attend,' Jack snapped. 'I want you to do some research on her. Maybe she's not so perfect. Talk to the usual contacts. Find out if she's ever thrown a race. Past boy friends who could use a bit of spare cash. Any relevant details from her private life. You know the sort of thing.'

'Filth.'

'Too right, darling.' Jack was dialling another number. He glanced up, as if surprised she was still there. 'Well, get on with it then.'

Margaret stood up, blushing.

'Yes, Jack,' she said.

Chapter 5

An evening meeting on a Tuesday at Kempton is not one of racing's most glamorous occasions. There are horses, trainers, lads, jockeys, bookmakers and gamblers but the good-hearted enthusiast, the average racegoer, is hardly in evidence. Sometimes it's like a West End performance with all the regulars in place, but no audience.

Kelly Connor didn't care. She was back in the weighing room again after the nightmare of Ascot. She had much on her mind. To her surprise Broom-Parker had phoned shortly after she'd returned home, pleading with her not to mention his name to the police. He had arranged to meet her after racing in the White Lion at Feltham. But her first, most immediate priority was to win again, to show racing's sceptics that she was not a loser, nor bent, but simply a good, strong apprentice on her way to the top. A week had passed without the offer of one single outside ride; she badly needed a winner.

The one and a half mile John Sturgeon Selling
Plate, the second to last race of the evening, was
hardly the stuff of headlines. Between them the eight
runners had won three races; they were racing's
cannon fodder. Some of them would be put over
hurdles next season, perhaps one might be sold to
Barbados or Abu Dhabi in the forlorn hope that they
could win something there, but most of them were
racing in the shadow of the knacker's yard.

Boardwalk was not a joy to ride, Kelly reflected as
the horse made its lumbering way down to the start.
Genuine enough, he pulled your arms out for half the
race until you asked him to quicken, when you found
there was nothing in the tank. It was only because he
belonged to a good-hearted owner, Mrs Prentice, the
wife of a local solicitor, that Bill had persevered with
him. Maybe one day, Boardwalk would pick up a bad
race – like the John Sturgeon Selling Plate at
Kempton. Even if he did win, the owner would buy
him in after the race, so that Boardwalk would have
paid back a small fraction of his training costs. And
Mrs Prentice's idea of a gamble was £10 each way.
Tonight was not about money, but about winning,
fun, maybe a passing mention in the morning's racing
press.

The market, if the desultory interest shown in the
Silver Ring could be described as such, had made
Boardwalk second favourite to a horse called Bite the
Bullet. Also in the betting was Dead Lucky, whose
jockey was Damien Gould.

'All right, sexy?' Kelly had shouted out to Gould as
she cantered past him, almost brushing his boot, on

the way to post. Gould, his face expressionless as a mask, had pretended not to hear. He hadn't expected to see the girl on a racecourse so soon after Ascot. She was riding with a score to settle. That was good.

Bill's instructions to her had been simple. Keep in touch with the leaders, aim to hit the front a furlong out, stay out of trouble. It was that last remark that echoed in Kelly's mind as Boardwalk was loaded into the stalls. The last thing she needed was to be up in front of the stewards again. Forget Ascot, she told herself, ride your race, but stay out of trouble.

Although Boardwalk was drawn on the inside, Kelly hoped to get a good enough break to be able to settle third or fourth. Within seconds of the stalls going up, she realized that this would be a problem. Boardwalk bounded along with more enthusiasm than grace at the head of the second group while two horses, including the favourite, made the running some three lengths clear of her.

Two and a half furlongs from home, Kelly couldn't believe it, she was still riding with a double handful. But she knew Boardwalk well enough not to be fooled. He was one-paced and, even at this lowly level, there were likely to be one or two horses behind her with a touch of finishing speed. Ahead of her, Bite the Bullet's jockey was hard at work while the horse on his outside was clearly beaten. Someone was half a length behind her on her outside but Kelly sensed that she had more in hand than he did. She glanced back to see Damien Gould. This time he wasn't smiling.

In any other race, at any other time, Kelly would have acted instinctively and eased Boardwalk away from the rails so as to take the leader in the final furlong. But seeing Damien made her lose concentration and before she knew what was happening she found herself boxed in yet again. Dead Lucky was struggling to stay in touch, but he was still there nonetheless, and if she just pushed her way out, Damien could easily make a show of snatching up.

For vital seconds, Kelly hesitated. Then she saw that Bite the Bullet, now under heavy pressure, was drifting away from the rails. The gap had barely begun to appear before Kelly was driving Boardwalk through, but he seemed to take for ever to pick up speed. Bite the Bullet continued to drift left-handed as the winning post raced towards them. Kelly was pushing and kicking for all she was worth, with her stick working in her left hand. She'd already hit Boardwalk twice and in desperation gave him a couple more, but it was like living one of those nightmares where you can never quite reach what you're trying to catch.

The two of them flashed by the post. There would be a photograph, but she knew that she had failed to get up.

With despair in her heart, she pulled up, cursing herself. She knew that she should have won and so would everyone else. She glanced across at Damien who shook his head with eloquent disgust, as if to say, 'Women jockeys!'

Of course, they all knew. The lad who led her in, the irate punter who looked up at her with contempt and muttered, 'You're useless', Bill, who made little effort to conceal his anger as she unsaddled Boardwalk. Only the owner was excluded from the common knowledge at Kempton that day: that her horse had been wrestled into second place by an apprentice who couldn't anticipate the obvious. Mrs Prentice fussed about Boardwalk and congratulated its jockey. Kelly smiled politely and went to weigh in.

The last hour of the meeting passed in a haze of disappointment. Kelly had no more rides on whom she could expunge the memory of that first race. She hated losing at the best of times but this was the worst. A misjudged race, a wrong decision, a bad run – they happened to everyone. Kelly tried to put the self-doubt from her mind. There was nobody more certain to lose a race than a jockey with no self-confidence. Gloomily, she remembered the smirk on Gould's face, the surprise and disappointment on Annie's. It was almost more painful than being labelled a cheat. She could imagine the gossip in the bar. Sad about that Kelly Connor. Nice little rider, but no good when the chips are down.

'Hey, come on, it's only a seller at Kempton.'

Cy McCray was a tough little American jockey who had settled in Britain and was now retained by the Ian Gardem stable. Unlike many of the top jockeys, he found time to talk to Kelly without giving her the immediate impression that he wanted to sleep with her, although if his reputation was only half true then he did. As Kelly walked thoughtfully towards the car park after the last race, Cy joined her.

'A race is a race, Cy,' she said. 'I blew it.'

'Hey, bollocks, y'hear?' There was something endearing about the way McCray adapted English slang into his American accent. 'Happens to us all. You'll show 'em on your next ride.'

'Yes, I suppose so,' Kelly muttered, wondering when that next ride would be. Bill's loyalty to his apprentice had been ill rewarded this evening and no trainer could afford to be sentimental. She glanced up to see a familiar trim figure strolling languidly out of the entrance to the Members' Enclosure. It was Ibn Fayoud. With a shudder, Kelly remembered their last meeting, his handshake.

'Cy, do me favour,' she said quietly. 'Keep walking with me to my car. I have an owner to avoid.'

'I know the feeling.' McCray smiled, looking in Ibn Fayoud's direction. 'Old Ib, eh? You don't fancy joining his harem.'

'Nope.'

'It's the first time I've seen him without all his hangers-on,' Cy commented. 'I guess he must be here just to see his favourite apprentice.'

Ibn Fayoud had stopped by a Jaguar XJS. The window on the driver's side was lowered to reveal the unmistakable face of Jack Butler.

'On the other hand, maybe not,' said Kelly, watching as the two men conversed. She had never met Jack Butler but she had seen him racing, and on television of course. In spite of herself, she had to admit that he had a sort of rough charm.

'Talk about the odd couple,' Cy McCray was saying. 'I thought those two were enemies.'

'Really?' Kelly half listened as Ibn Fayoud climbed into the passenger seat. The Jaguar pulled out towards where she was standing with Cy McCray.

'Someone was saying Ib owes Butler a million-odd quid. I wouldn't fancy owing him two bob.'

The car approached them and Kelly could see the two men talking animatedly.

'They seem quite friendly now,' she said.

At that moment, Ibn Fayoud looked across at her. As she nodded politely, he looked away. It was as if she didn't exist.

'Looks like you're off the hook there,' said Cy McCray.

Kelly got in her car and headed east towards Feltham. She'd arranged to meet Broom-Parker at nine thirty. As she reached the outskirts of the town she stopped to ask the way, and then discovered that the traffic on the road past the White Lion was being diverted because of an accident. Kelly parked in a side street and walked.

It must have been quite a crash. As she approached, she could see three blue lights flashing in the gathering gloom. A group of spectators had gathered like vultures on the pavement. Kelly made her way through the crowd, vaguely aware of the chatter of people whose dull lives had briefly been made more exciting by another's misfortune. It was when she heard the phrase 'hit-and-run job' that she glanced into the road.

Behind a police car, which was parked across the road to stop the traffic, an ambulance man was crouching over a body. There was something familiar about the checked suit, lit up by the flashing blue light. She walked into the road.

'Back, please.' A policeman held out his arms as if heading off a loose horse. 'There's nothing you can do for him, dear. He's had it.'

For a moment, she caught a glimpse of the victim's face. It had been bloodied and battered by the impact of the car but, curiously, its handlebar moustache looked as trim and correct in death as it had in life. Turning away, Kelly saw some loose change in the gutter where the car had made contact with its target. There was also a piece of paper.

Kelly picked it up. It was a betting-slip, marked 'REG BUTLER, Turf Accountants'.

Her instinct was to drive – to get in the car, go home, and be safe – resume the life of an apprentice who wanted to be champion jockey. But, with a growing sense of foreboding, she knew she couldn't do that. Broom-Parker had played no more than a small part in the plot to make sure Pendero was beaten, she was certain of that. He was too much of a loser to have been anything more than a hired hand. For reasons of guilt, greed or fear, he had agreed to talk to her. And now he was dead. Pawn, stool pigeon, nobody – it made no difference to these people. To be worth two murders in eight days, Ascot had to be more than a mere gambling scam. Turning away would be playing the game their way. She remembered the words in her father's letter: *Don't let them hook you, however tempting the bait*. Right now the bait was not money or easy winners, just the chance to earn a living by riding horses in races without fearing for her life. But the information she already had marked her out as a target. The men who had killed her father and now Broom-Parker could presumably have something similar planned for her. She'd better tell the police in

Newmarket and also Nick Morley and his Jockey
Club security people.

Kelly asked the policeman what had happened.
Apparently the man, whose body was now on its way
to the city mortuary, was drunk. According to the
barman in the White Lion, he had been putting away
double scotches when he received a telephone call at
the bar. Unsteadily, he had made his way out of the
door, on to the street – and under the speeding wheels
of a hit-and-run driver. The sports car had hardly
braked. It had seemed to slow down briefly after the
impact, as if the driver was considering whether to
stop or not, and then had accelerated off into the
night. Kids, probably – joy-riding was a popular
pastime among the city's bored teenagers. Our red-
faced friend, said the policeman, chose the wrong
time in the wrong town to go for a drunken walkabout
in the road.

Wearily, Kelly made her way back to her car, drove
to the nearest hotel and booked a room. She would
not be going home tonight.

She rang the Templemans' number. They would
still be driving home, so she could leave a message on
the answering machine. That would make it easier.

'This is Kelly here,' she said, trying to make her
voice sound as calm and normal as possible. 'I'm still
in London. I have to go up north tomorrow on a
family matter. It's a bit too complicated to explain
right now but it's really unavoidable so I won't be able
to ride out tomorrow. I'll be back for Thursday,
though. Hope that's all right. 'Bye.'

She hung up. If there was one person she hated

lying to, it was Bill. He was one of the few genuinely honest men in racing. He would curse when he heard the message, even though tomorrow the string would be doing road work and she was not needed. Annie would be suspicious about that 'family matter'. She would worry that Kelly was becoming involved in the sleazy aftermath of her father's death.

Kelly switched on the television and stared blankly at the screen as some mindless cops and robbers show unfolded. At the back of her mind, it occurred to her how different real crime was from the glamorous violence portrayed on the screen. Reality wasn't the wailing siren, the squealing tyres of the cop car, the cry of 'Police, freeze!' in the night; reality was the quiet desperation and nauseous fear of ordinary lives caught up, often unwillingly, in a web of deception, greed and violence. Pointless and destructive.

She sighed and turned the television off. Going up north tomorrow. At least that part was true.

Visitors to Harry Short's yard in Blaworth, which was situated some five miles from the maisonette in Doncaster where he was born, were often taken aback, shocked even, by what they found. Despite the size of the stables and the fact that he belonged to the world of flat-racing where appearances count for something, Short had made no compromises. The yard was squalid and run down, the lads slouched about the place resentfully, the tack was old and dirty with repair patches showing on almost every item of leather. The only things that looked good were the horses, whose coats shone under their shabby exercise sheets. At the end of the day, Kelly thought to herself, I suppose it's them that matter.

It was said that Harry Short's great strength was that he had never tried to imitate smarter trainers, that he played by his rules, was his own man, but even this was flattering him. The idea of smartening up had simply never occurred to him; the appearance of his training establishment was how all yards should look. In fact, for all he knew – which wasn't much, since he never visited other trainers – this was how they did look. The only difference was that he trained more winners than most of them did.

First lot was making its way lazily along a path some fifty yards from the road where Kelly had parked her car. She was not the first person to wonder about the secret of Harry Short's success. If anyone else ran a yard of sixty flat-race horses like he did, they would have been out of business years ago. Yet he just went from strength to strength.

It was true that his horses tended to have brief careers. The idea of giving a backward horse time, of not over-racing his less tough charges, of giving the vet the benefit of the doubt when he said a leg was liable to break down on hard ground – these were alien concepts to Harry Short. Horses were there to earn their living, or rather his living. If they didn't run fast enough, or weren't tough enough, then there were always others. They were the means of producing cash, no more and no less.

As Kelly stood watching the string, her hands sunk deep into her windcheater pockets, Harry Short's Mercedes made its way along the gallops between the

path and the road. He glanced towards Kelly and
slowed down for a moment before speeding onwards.
He didn't like people watching his horses work from
the road but this was only a woman, probably some
jumped-up point-to-point type looking for training
tips. Kelly glanced at her car clock. It was time to make
her entrance.

'That's very strange.' A woman in her fifties, with a
scarf holding a shock of grey hair, stood on the doorstep
of Harry Short's house. 'He never mentioned visitors.'

'Well, isn't that odd?' Kelly shook her head. 'It was
definitely today. Come up to ride Pendero second lot,
he said. I hope he hasn't forgotten – I've driven all the
way from Newmarket. Never mind, I'll wait for him in
the car.'

'By, you will not,' said the woman, opening the front
door. 'You'll come in here and have a cup of tea till his
lordship gets back. It's typical of him to forget to tell me
he's entertaining. Follow me, love, don't mind the mess
in the hall.'

Kelly picked her way through saddles, blankets, old
copies of *Sporting Life*, reflecting that Short's domestic arrangements made his yard looked positively
pristine.

She was on her second cup of tea when Harry blun-
dered into the house like some evil giant out of a fairy
story. He had actually slumped down at the breakfast
table before he became aware of Kelly's presence.
When he did, his eyes narrowed and for a moment Kelly
thought he was going to bound across the room and hit
her.

'What the bloody hell are you doing here?' he said in a dangerous, quiet voice. No one entered Harry Short's house without an invitation and to find Kelly Connor of all people sitting across the breakfast table was like a practical joke in very poor taste. Kelly sat in silence and smiled. An odd rumbling sound emanated from Short before, looking towards the door, he snapped, 'Betty!'

'It's not your wife's fault,' said Kelly quickly. 'I lied to her to get in because I needed to talk to you about your big gamble at Ascot.' Harry got up as if to throw her out. Kelly went on, 'I've discovered some things which might interest you.'

In spite of himself, Harry was curious and he sat down again. It must be important for her to have driven all the way up north and bluff her way into his house. He glanced up at her almost respectfully as he poured himself some tea. If she had the nerve, the sheer bloody brass neck, to do that, then maybe he'd give her a few minutes.

Betty put a plate of fried eggs and bacon in front of the trainer. 'Was there something else?'

'Yes.' He shot a warning glance at Kelly, but then said mildly, 'Any chance of another pot of tea, love?'

After the woman had left, he muttered, 'She isn't my wife. She just comes mornings.' Angrily, as if he blamed them for his loneliness, he set about his fried eggs and bacon. Then he looked up sharply and, revealing more of the contents of his mouth than Kelly wished to see, said, 'Well, get on with it then.'

'Here's what we both know.' Kelly sipped at her tea. She had been right about Short; the way to get him to listen was to treat him as if he were a human being, which he clearly wasn't. But she had to be careful. With this man, an earthquake was never far away. 'Pendero was a stone-cold certainty for the race at Ascot,' she said. 'You had run him over races short of his best distance. Maybe you hadn't tried too hard in them.'

'Say that to anyone else,' Short muttered without looking up from his fried egg, 'and I'll see you in court.'

'What you did with him before Ascot is your business. Pendero was off the day I was riding him, that's what matters. Why did you book me, by the way?'

'Fuck knows.'

Kelly waited.

'I'd seen you ride. We needed the seven-pound claim.' Short looked up angrily as he remembered the events of that day. 'We all make mistakes,' he snapped, 'What's done's done. If you're here because I said certain things about you after the race, you can sod off back south right now.'

'I'm not here for an apology,' Kelly said quietly. Ignoring a dismissive grunt from Short, she continued, 'Since that race, two people have died violent, nasty deaths. I believe those murders had something to do with the race I rode for you.'

Harry Short shrugged. Life, death, it happened, even in racing.

'One of them was my father.'

'Aye, well.' Short was about to say something about Frank Connor, but thought better of it. 'Aye, well, sorry,' he said. 'The reason I put you up was I heard you were good and . . . straight.'

'I am,' said Kelly. 'I didn't lose you that race.'

'So what happened to the weight?'

'You tell me.'

There was a clatter of cutlery as Short reacted. 'What the fuck are you talking about?' he exploded, spraying small bits of bacon across the table.

'You took the saddle. It would have been easy for you to lose five pounds' worth of lead as you saddled up. Then blame me after the race.' Kelly was unable to keep the bitterness out of her voice. 'After all, I'm just another crooked Connor.'

'You're mad. That's not my way. I wanted to win that race. I was done.'

'There's another possibility.' Kelly told him about the call to the weighing room, her father's letter, the death of Broom-Parker. By the time she had finished, Short was sitting back, the greasy remains of his breakfast in front of him. He lit up a cigarette and looked at Kelly thoughtfully. 'If it wasn't me who wanted Pendero to lose that race,' she concluded, 'and it wasn't you, who was it?'

Short shrugged. 'There was a bet. Quite a big bet.'

'Yours?'

'Look, Connor.' The trainer sat up in his chair and looked about the table as if searching for something to throw at her. 'I'm not used to some bloody apprentice waltzing into my house and asking me about my private affairs—'

'So who else was involved?'

'You should know.' A sulky bitterness had entered Short's voice. 'He's just moved all his horses to Bill

Templeman, hasn't he? Bloody Arab bastard.' Short stabbed out his cigarette in the bacon fat on his plate.

'Ibn Fayoud?' Kelly was unable to conceal her surprise. 'What does—'

'Work it out for yourself.' Harry Short stood up. 'I've told you too much already.' He looked at her appraisingly as if, for the first time, it had occurred to him that Kelly Connor was not just another apprentice, but a woman. 'Can't think why,' he added with a telltale catch in his voice.

'I'd better be going,' said Kelly warily, standing up herself and backing away from the trainer.

'Maybe I can tell you more a bit later. Second lot won't take long.'

'Got to get back, Mr Short.'

'Perhaps you'd like to ride a bit of work for me.' The leer was now unmistakable.

'I thought you were never going to let me near any of your horses again.' Kelly made her way through the hall towards the front door.

Short chuckled randily. 'Who's talking about horses?' he called out as she walked quickly towards her car. Kelly waved as she pulled away in her car, and gave a little sigh of relief. Harry Short moving into seductive mode was not an attractive sight.

'Nothing, Jack.'

Margaret Stanhope hated to disappoint her boss. It almost broke her heart when she saw that darting look of irritation cross his face as she brought him bad news. It didn't happen often – when it came to personally assisting, she had few equals – but, when it did, she felt ridiculously guilty. Her point in life was to solve Jack Butler's problems; when they persisted, she felt worse than he did about it.

'What d'you mean *nothing*?'

Margaret shrugged miserably.

'What is she, some kind of nun or something?' Jack Butler was almost ugly when he was angry; it was a side of him that the many thousands of women who watched racing only to catch a glimpse of him never saw. 'She's Irish, isn't she? She's a jockey, she's a looker. There must be something from her past.'

'I've asked around. She had a relationship with a local solicitor a couple of years ago. He's straight as a die. Since then, she's kept herself to herself.'

Jack thought back to Ascot. 'Seems a bit of a waste,' he said. 'What about on the racetrack? Anything there?'

'Just Pendero, nothing else.'

The bookmaker looked at her pityingly. 'I know about that,' he said.

'Maybe,' Margaret faltered. 'Maybe we could . . . fix something up.'

Jack laughed and shook his head. 'You're a wicked old cow sometimes, you really are.'

Uncertain whether to be flattered or insulted, Margaret smiled primly. 'Let me know what you want me to do,' she said.

Bill Templeman was a man of few words. He could talk horses, he could give instructions to a jockey but the confidential fireside chat was not his style. Kelly liked the man but dreaded those rare occasions when their conversations lasted for more than a couple of sentences. When he asked to see her in his study, a few days after her return from Blaworth, she feared the worst.

'Family all right?' he asked, riffling through the papers on his desk.

Kelly remembered the lie that she had had to tell to take a day off work. 'Not too bad,' she said. 'Under the circumstances.'

'Nothing new on your father's death?'

'No, not yet. But I think that—'

'It's not your job to think.' Bill's voice betrayed genuine anger. 'We're still getting calls here about you, anonymous calls. Whoever it is says you're still nosing about in business which doesn't concern you.'

'My father's death concerns—'

'Listen, Kelly, I know you're still upset about your father's death, but if you want to play detective, you'd better give up riding and join the police. You've already lost me one race because you're still hung up on that business at Ascot. If it were up to me, I'd jock you off for the rest of the season. Maybe next year, you'll be a jockey again.'

'I'm sorry.' Kelly hung her head at this unusually long speech. He was right. None of this had anything to do with the Templeman yard. It was run on a shoe-string at the best of times and Kelly was merely adding to his problems. But something nagged at her about what he had just said. 'How do you mean "if it were up to me"?'

'You seem to have an admirer in Ibn Fayoud al Hassan. He's instructed me to give you the ride on

Shine On at York next week. In fact, he wants you to ride all his horses.'

Kelly smiled and sighed with relief. 'Thank you,' she said.

'Don't thank me, thank him. He likes the way you ride them. Bloody fool.'

Kelly knew Bill well enough to be certain that no one, least of all a new owner, would dictate to him which jockey to put up. In spite of this show of gruff disapproval, he was giving her one last chance.

'Don't screw it up this time,' he said, turning back to his correspondence and entry forms. 'Remember you're a jockey.'

Kelly was down to ride a two-year-old called Billy Liar for second lot. He was one of Ibn Fayoud's colts and apparently bone idle. This morning was the first time he was to be given a serious piece of work before running later in the week.

Within moments of climbing on board, Kelly could see why Billy Liar had won few friends at the yard. He was oddly sluggish and lazy, more like a leery veteran than a horse that had never seen a racecourse. Dennis, who was down to ride work with her on another two-year-old smiled with open hostility as they made their way up to the gallops.

'You've met your match there, darling,' he said as Kelly pushed and shoved the colt along, tying to keep him from stopping altogether.

'Really?' Kelly was used to Dennis's sarcasm and had come to pity his jealousy of her. 'What makes you think that?'

'He's a lazy bastard, that's why. He needs a strong pair of legs on him.' He winked across at her. 'Not that I've personally got anything against your legs.'

Kelly laughed and muttered an expletive which Dennis pretended not to hear. She'd show him.

And she'd show Bill. To people in racing, there was nothing more suspect than a professional who allowed outside concerns to impinge on the real world – the world of racing. Outside was dangerous, complicated; outside contaminated the already difficult business of getting horses to win races. To be a true professional, you had to live in a closed world. It's not your job to think. Remember you're a jockey.

From the moment the two horses jumped off to work, Kelly knew she was in trouble. While Dennis was well on the bridle, she was having to work hard to keep Billy Liar up to the pace. After a couple of furlongs, Dennis let out a notch on his reins and moved half a length up on her. Kelly gave her horse a slap down the shoulder; it grunted but failed to quicken.

'This horse is wrong,' she called out. 'I'm going to pull up.'

Dennis turned round and shook his head. 'Legs,' he shouted. 'Told you.'

For a moment, Kelly felt a flare of anger within her. They were out of sight of the guv'nor, so she yelled at Billy Liar and cracked him one behind the saddle. The horse made another noise, more a groan than a grunt this time, and, as his stride faltered, Kelly knew that she had made a serious mistake.

A split second later, the earth was hurtling towards her.

Chapter 6

Sheikh al Hassan had a lot on his mind. The price of oil was tumbling again, one of his most reliable brokers on Wall Street had just been arrested for insider dealing, the acquisition of a highly prestigious London hotel had been held up by a query as to who actually owned it and, back home, one of his sisters had just committed suicide, causing a tremor of scandal throughout the country. The death under somewhat dubious circumstances of a racehorse belonging to his son was frankly the least of his problems.

He looked through the smoked window of his Rolls-Royce and sighed. The traffic on Piccadilly was a great leveller. Salesman making deliveries, out-of-towners visiting a show, executives on their way to a board meeting which would decide the fate of thousands of employees: they all moved at West End speed – that is, not at all. Sheikh al Hassan smiled wearily. In this benighted country, simple solutions – banning traffic, arresting illegal parkers, giving the wealthy and powerful a police escort through the streets – were apparently too complex for its befuddled government.

'There is, I believe, a serious risk of a scandal, sir.'

The Sheikh turned back to Simon Brompton-Smiley. It was bad enough sitting in the London traffic without having to listen to the mumblings of his international racing manager. Mistakenly, he had agreed to let Brompton-Smiley travel with him in the Rolls and discuss the matter of some urgency he had been whining about for the last two days. Now the meeting, which should have taken ten minutes, was being dragged out to three-quarters of an hour. The temptation to open the door and to apply a dark shiny shoe to the seat of the man's pinstriped suit was almost irresistible. If he had been born in Australia or Lithuania or even Manchester, Sheikh al Hassan could have ejected his minion on to the street in the sure knowledge that it would be put down to robust good humour. As it was, he was obliged to behave with decorum.

'I'm so sorry, Simon,' he said, smiling. 'I think I lost the drift of what you were saying.'

'It's your son, sir,' said Brompton-Smiley. 'He has now moved his horses to a small yard in Newmarket run by Bill Templeman. As you know, they were with Ian Gardem.'

'I fail to see a problem there. Maybe he was trying to save some money at last.'

'He then invested in another horse.'

'Ah.' The Sheikh rubbed his eyes. The last thing he needed right now was more bad news about his son.

'A rather expensive horse called Shine On.'

'How much?' Sheikh al Hassan asked the unfamiliar question with some distaste.

'I don't know,' said Brompton-Smiley. 'It was a private sale from Templeman himself but it's got to be six figures.'

'I thought he was broke.'

'Precisely, sir. Then, two days ago, one of his two-year-olds collapsed during a gallop. I've heard, unofficially,' Brompton-Smiley was proud of his network of contacts and could never resist reminding his employer of them, 'very unofficially, that the post-mortem shows that he was got at.'

'Was anyone hurt?'

'Not really. The girl who lost that race at Ascot was riding him. Broken collarbone, that's all.'

At last, the Rolls had broken free of Piccadilly's log-jam and was making its way at something approaching normal speed towards Knightsbridge.

'What exactly are you saying?' Sheikh al Hassan's mind had returned to the important meeting before him.

'Something's going on, sir, and I'm very much afraid that your son is involved. The sooner you make the announcement that you're moving your horses away from Britain the better.'

'I'll need to speak to Morley.'

'I'll arrange that, sir,' said Brompton-Smiley.

The Sheikh's car pulled up outside the hotel where his meeting was to take place. For a moment, he considered letting Brompton-Smiley use the Rolls to get home, but then he thought better of it. There were taxis.

A deputation of dark-suited, middle-aged men appeared at the hotel entrance, smiling like grannies at a railway station. The Sheikh spoke quietly to his chauffeur, then stepped forward to acknowledge them with a courteous inclination of the head.

Standing by the Rolls, Simon Brompton-Smiley turned towards the chauffeur and said something clipped and military. When the man shook his head, he looked at his watch as if yet another important appointment awaited him, and strutted off. There were taxis.

It took a fall at thirty-five miles an hour, a night in Addenbrooke's Hospital in Cambridge, and a broken collarbone to remind Kelly of the life she was missing as a professional jockey. The doctors had told her to take it easy. According to their records, she had not lost consciousness, but she had been badly shaken up. She wouldn't be fit enough to ride for at least a week, but she was able to organize the move to a new flat which Annie had found for her, situated just behind the saddler's shop. It wasn't as nice as the one she'd shared with her father but at least it was cheap. Annie and one of the lads in the yard helped to move what furniture she had. After that she settled down to rest properly. Three days after the accident she agreed to let Nick take her out to dinner.

'Ouch.' Morley winced as Kelly appeared at her front door, her shoulder strapped up, a graze down the side of her face and two blackened eyes. She still managed to look wonderful.

Kelly smiled. 'You should see the other feller,' she

said, easing herself gently into the passenger seat of his Aston Martin.

'And you're telling me you weren't concussed?' Morley looked at her with genuine concern.

'No, I'm telling the doctor I wasn't concussed. I have an important ride next Saturday.'

Nick nodded. Under safety regulations, no jockey was allowed to ride in a race within one week of being concussed. If Kelly's fall had happened on a race-course, she would have been sidelined as a matter of course. It had been fortunate that, by the time a doctor saw her, she showed no signs of having lost consciousness.

'I suppose I'm meant to turn a deaf ear to that.' He grinned and looked across to her as he changed gear.

'It was only a small knock. I'll be fine.' Nick was frowning. 'All right?'

He shrugged. 'Just don't go about saying you had a bang on the head. You're not short of enemies already. You want to be careful what you say.'

Kelly half laughed. 'Funny, that,' she said. 'How I seem to trust you.'

Nick smiled grimly. 'I mean it about the enemies. You'll have heard from your boss that the two-year-old you were riding had been got at.'

'No.' Kelly couldn't help sounding shocked. She stared straight ahead. 'No, he didn't tell me that.'

'A post-mortem showed that the horse had traces of Imobolin in its blood. It's what they call Elephant Juice. It's basically a very powerful anaesthetic. The tiniest amount will knock out an elephant. Hence the name. There was a case some time ago where a vet

107

accidentally injected himself with some. He was dead before he could get back to his car for the antidote.'

'How do you know all this?' Kelly's mind was racing. If the horse had been doped, it could only mean that someone in Bill's yard had been involved. If that was the case, who was the target, the horse or her?

'I heard from the equine laboratory in Newmarket. Officially Templeman should tell me himself, but he hasn't. At least, not yet.' They took a left turn and picked up speed. 'Imobolin doesn't even need to be injected,' Nick went on. 'If you mix the stuff with an absorption agent like DMSO and rub it into the skin it would get into the system within half an hour. Wetting the underneath of the saddle with it would have been more than enough to kill the horse. It was due to run in a couple of days, wasn't it?'

Kelly nodded. 'Nottingham.'

'Were you going to ride him?'

'I'm meant to be riding all Ibn Fayoud's horses.'

'Well, it's a good thing it happened at home and not at the racecourse. Otherwise you might have been much more badly hurt.'

'Tell you what.' Kelly made an unconvincing attempt at cheerfulness. 'Why don't we talk about something other than racing?'

It was an uneasy evening. Nick took her to a small restaurant a few miles outside Cambridge, where they both tried to behave as if nothing untoward had happened. He joked that the other diners were looking at him like a wife-batterer. She found herself talking about her father – the way he had brought her up alone, how he had tried to dissuade her from a racing

career. And, of course, he had been right. If she had
done as he had suggested, become a doctor maybe, or
a teacher, he would be alive today and she would be
living a normal life.

Nick listened intently. Kelly no longer thought of
him as a steward, a central player in the racing
game, but as someone who seemed to understand her
better than anyone ever had, apart from her father.
It was good to talk to a man with whom she felt
comfortable.

Nick looked surprised when she told him this. 'So
there's no . . .' For a moment he looked embarrassed.
'You haven't got a boyfriend, then?'

'No, thank goodness. Life's tricky enough without
that. And you?'

Nick looked away, trying to attract the waiter's
attention. 'I married young,' he said. 'It was a mistake. She was a lovely girl and we're still good friends,
but we just couldn't live together. These days I value
my freelance status. The eligible bachelor.' Kelly
thought she detected a trace of bitterness in his voice.

'Playing the field?'

'Hardly. Concentrating on my career. Looking
after Sheikh al Hassan's bloodstock interests. The
Jockey Club. It keeps me busy.'

'D'you know his son?' Kelly asked suddenly.

'I've met him. He's not exactly on my circuit.'

'Is he bent?'

'What, gay, you mean?' Nick raised his eyebrows.

'No, not that way. I mean corrupt.'

'No. I'd say he was weak rather than corrupt.'

'I believe he was involved in the Pendero business,'

Kelly told him and then went on to fill in the details – Broom-Parker, seeing Ibn Fayoud with Jack Butler in the car park at Kempton racecourse, her conversation with Harry Short. She told him exactly what she had told the police.

'Ibn Fayoud and Butler,' he said eventually. 'They're an unlikely pair.'

There was something subdued about the evening after that, as if the full significance of the events of the past few days was oppressing both of them.

They drove back to Newmarket in virtual silence. Nick spoke quietly as he pulled up outside her flat. 'Call me if you hear anything else.' Troubled, distracted, he looked into Kelly's eyes. Her bruised face gave her a new look of vulnerability. In an almost fatherly way, he placed a hand on her good shoulder and kissed her gently on the lips, like a promise. 'And, for God's sake, take care.' For a moment, he held her more closely.

'Ouch,' said Kelly.

Nick quickly apologized. 'Look, I know that one shouldn't mix business with pleasure, but if I asked you again, would you come out with me?'

Kelly returned his kiss and held it for a fraction longer than she should have. 'Of course.'

The next morning the post brought a letter that was as brief and to the point as it was surprising.

Dear Miss Connor,

I was most distressed to hear of your fall. I hope that you are now well enough to accept the attached invitation to a charity ball on the first evening of the York meeting. I am taking a party of racing people, some of whom you will surely know.

Please confirm that you are able to make it to my personal assistant.

Yours,

Ibn Fayoud

Attached to the note was an ornate invitation to the Marquess of Flaxton's Charity Black and White Ball and a ticket of entry. Kelly shook her head incredulously; Ibn Fayoud had taken her acceptance for granted. Presumably few people said 'No' to him, Well, Kelly reflected as she dialled the Templemans' number angrily, there was a first time for everything.

'You're going to *what*?' Annie's voice all but went off the chromatic scale when Kelly told her that she was turning down Ibn Fayoud's invitation.

'I'm not at my best at parties. My mind will be on the big race. Anyway, I'm not certain that I like him. He's far too smooth for me.'

'Kelly, you don't seem to understand. One of the reasons Shine On is running at York is to give Ibn Fayoud the chance to take a table at the ball. He wants to show you off. He wants to show *us* off, for Christ sake.'

'You mean you're in his party too?'

'Of course. Although I must admit we were obliged to fork out for the tickets – a mere hundred quid each. What we do for our owners.'

'I don't know.' Suddenly Kelly's objections seemed

priggish and defensive. 'I look a sight at the moment, what with my eyes.'

'It's a black and white party. You'll be a wow. Anyway you needn't stay long. Treat it as an education. How often d'you get the chance to watch the mindlessly rich eat and drink themselves into a stupor on behalf of Ethiopia?'

Kelly laughed.

'This is your boss's wife speaking,' Annie continued. 'Accept Ibn Fayoud's invitation. That's an order.'

Margaret Stanhope put down the telephone, stood up, smoothed her tight skirt down and knocked on the door next to her desk. A voice from within muttered, 'Yeah'.

'Newsflash, Jack,' she said, putting her head round the door. 'Our little fish has nibbled the bait.'

Jack Butler puffed on his cigar. 'Brilliant,' he said. 'Maybe she'll get a nibble herself – from the big fish.'

'Maybe.' Margaret smiled at her boss. 'If she's lucky.'

Henry, the Marquess of Flaxton had known hard times. At Eton, he had been fag to a charmless older boy who had wasted no time in introducing Henry to the joys of homosexuality. Today his seducer was a respected Tory backbencher while Henry – in this as in all other matters of pleasure, a broad-minded man – had retained a part-time interest in members of his own sex. But Eton, in those first terms, was tough, frightening. Maybe Henry would have ended up warped and perverse but his unofficial education among the elite certainly helped him along the way.

Then there was the Isle of Wight. For an ordinary Joe, two years spent in the open prison at Parkhurst was no big deal but for Henry, to be starved of decent food, a regular intake of recreational drugs and all but the most basic of sexual activity was deprivation on a grand scale. He was not often given to anger, which required more energy than he had to spare, but two years without life's bounty, all for a small matter of dealing drugs to his friends, seemed little short of scandalous. Of course, since his release, he had made up for lost time, becoming quite a wheel in the charity game, but those two years had stayed with him. The people, the routine, the boredom: frankly, he had been to hell and back.

Balls. That was how he became rehabilitated. Charity parties. Society auctions. It seemed that these days his friends needed an excuse to blow the family money on their own pleasure; it had to be in a good cause. Thanks to his efforts – or rather the efforts of a couple of socially mobile former PR girls who worked for him – several fortunes were directed, with maximum publicity, into the coffers of the needy.

It was brilliant. World starvation was halted in its tracks, Henry became a hero of the gossip columns, and everybody had one hell of a good time. These days, nobody cared what high-grade powder he put up his nose, whom he spent the night with. Henry was all right, a good sort. His heart was in the right place.

The Black and White Ball was going to be a winner. There would be a thousand people there, dressed with varying degrees of elegance in black and white. Some would come in racing silks, or T-shirts with amusing messages, or in clown outfits. Henry had decided on the black-and-white minstrel look – rather apt, he thought, since most of the money would be going to Africa. He had heard that Camilla Welmsley would be all in white, something fluffy and revealing, but with black lipstick. Never was there a less likely vestal virgin. Henry thought that he would probably have Camilla tonight, or maybe Tavic, the black society sculptor everyone was talking about or, hey, maybe both. It was going to be that sort of party.

Ibn Fayoud entered the great black and white marquee. It was decorated with thousands of black balloons, white roses, black bottles of champagne on white tablecloths. He accepted a glass from a black waiter and a kiss from a white puff-ball who turned out to be Camilla Welmsley. A glance at the assembled guests told him what he already knew – that no one looked quite as good as he did. In the dark mourning robes left to him by his grandfather, he was as exotic as Valentino, as dangerous as a black prince of the desert.

One of Henry's PR girls, almost wearing a cutaway schoolgirl outfit, showed him his table. Ibn Fayoud looked at the place settings, noting that the few racing contacts he had been obliged to invite had sensibly been distributed among the more amusing people who had come up from London. God knows what Tavic would find to say to dear, homely Annie Templeman, or what his favourite ex-girl friend, Mina Beresford, had done to deserve the lugubrious Bill Templeman as a neighbour. Ibn Fayoud sipped his champagne thoughtfully. Doubtless Jack Butler and Kelly Connor would discover subjects of common interest.

Annie Templeman had been at the black and white ball for five minutes, and it was five minutes too long. Although she caught sight of a few racing friends, she felt ill at ease among the social butterflies that trilled and chattered all around her. Above all, she felt guilty that she had persuaded Bill, who looked as happy as a man with a toothache, to make an appearance. He had never been a party-goer and it had been against his better judgement that they agreed to join Ibn Fayoud's party. Good owner relations, Annie had argued. The party had seemed like fun to her then. Bill now shot a baleful glance in her direction. 'Two hundred sodding pounds,' he mouthed.

Kelly was late. She'd managed to flood the carburettor on her car. For a moment she stood uncertainly at the entrance to the marquee, the simplicity of her dark long dress in elegant contrast to the exotic fancy-dress all around her. She smiled at the black and white minstrel who approached her.

'Well,' said the Marquess of Flaxton with an appreciative leer made grotesque by his make-up. 'Who's the lucky man you're with?'

Kelly decided to ignore the implication that she could only be someone's girl friend. 'I'm here by myself,' she said. 'I'm with the Ibn Fayoud party.'

'Ah yes.' Henry looked at her more closely, mistaking the dark rings round her eyes for signs of late nights and fast living. 'You would be.'

He took Kelly by the arm to where a man in dark

robes was in earnest conversation with a girl in a skimpy black T-shirt with 'BIMBO POWER' scrawled in white across her chest.

'Kelly!' Ibn Fayoud turned away from the girl, smiled warmly and held out his arms as if greeting an old friend. Kelly managed to turn her head in time for his kiss to miss its target on her lips. 'I'm so happy you could make it, my *favourite* jockey.'

Leaning away slightly as Ibn Fayoud enveloped her in his gowns and aftershave, Kelly found herself looking at a smiling Annie. She crossed her eyes and made a face.

There was something different about Kelly that night. She could see it in the covert glances of the London girls, some of whom had been planning how to look at the Belvoir dance for the past month. She could sense it in the way men talked to her, the sideways glances of strangers. As if, by wearing the simplest of dresses, pale make-up and no jewellery, she had trumped them all.

It was a pity, she thought, that her mind was on Shine On's big test tomorrow afternoon. It was a shame, too, that, because she had unstrapped it for the evening, her shoulder was already aching. Then she looked around at the men on offer, braying nightclub fools mostly, and decided that, even without racing commitments and pain, she would be planning to leave early. This was not her sort of party.

She was nodding politely on the fringes of a group listening to their host talking about himself when she heard a familiar voice behind her.

'So it's true what they say about you and Ibn Fayoud.'

Cy McCray pecked her on the cheek. 'Don't worry,' he said. 'Your secret's safe with me.'

'Duty,' she said with a smile, and lowered her voice. 'Personally, I'd be happier watching television back in the hotel.'

'Hey, tell me about it. Can I give you a lift back there?'

'Cy, you're a gentleman,' said Kelly. 'But I'll be going back with the Templemans. Just as soon as I can.'

'Not before I have a slow dance with you, I hope.'

'Do you think you're tall enough for that?'

'No, but your cleavage looks a great place to rest my head,' he grinned. 'Then you can tell me the truth about Ibn and Butler.'

'I plan to avoid them tonight.'

Cy looked surprised. 'You haven't seen the seating plan then? You've been drawn next to Jack Butler.'

Kelly winced. 'Oh great. That's all I need. Dinner with a bookmaker.'

She should never have come. She would be stuck with a man who, she was now convinced, was in some way involved in the Pendero case. The last thing she wanted, the day before she rode Shine On, was to be drawn back into the past. There were questions she needed to ask Butler, but not yet, not now and not here.

'You look after yourself, y'hear,' McCray was saying. 'You know what Jack's like with the ladies.'

That was the worst of it. In spite of herself, Kelly felt a quickening of the heart, that she was going to sit

next to Jack Butler – bookmaker, bastard, crook –
and she couldn't wait.

'Thanks, Cy,' she said quietly.

Kelly had expected that Jack Butler would live up to
the image she had painted of him in her mind. A wide
boy on the make, a rake of the Silver Ring – vulgar,
randy, pleased with himself. But he wasn't like that
at all, in fact. He appeared almost shy among the
other party-goers, a little boy let loose in the big
playground, nervously looking about him. As Ibn
Fayoud's guests took their seats for dinner, he introduced himself to Kelly with edgy formality. This was
not the Romeo she had expected.

'Kelly Connor?' It was almost a mutter. 'I'm your
dinner partner. Jack Butler.'

Kelly shook Jack's hand and felt a shiver of
excitement run through her body as they touched.
His manner was polite but his handshake held an
unmistakable invitation. He was taller than she
expected and wore a well-cut dinner jacket that con-
trasted with the eccentric fancy-dress of some of the
other diners. She was about to say something when he
turned away to introduce himself to the girl on his
right.

A goofy individual in a Batman cape distracted
her attention by falling into the seat to her left, spilling some champagne in the process. 'I'm Johnny
Prescott.'

Kelly smiled politely as the man tried to focus his
eyes on her.

Prescott shook his head slowly. 'God, you're
lovely,' he said. 'Haven't we met at Tokyo Joe's?'

'I don't think so.' Kelly was annoyed with herself for feeling a pang of jealousy that Jack Butler was now deep in conversation with the girl on his right. A waiter brought smoked salmon. Kelly turned back to the partner on her left. 'Tell me all about yourself, Johnny,' she said with an interested, dinner-party smile.

It took Prescott a good ten minutes to describe the full pointlessness of his life as a stockbroker and man-about-town before the combined effects of drink and sustaining a conversation took their toll and he declined into a glazed, sullen silence.

Jack Butler's conversation with the girl on his right seemed to have dried up too. 'Dear, oh dear,' he said, almost to himself. 'I think I've enjoyed myself more after the housewife's choice has just won the Grand National.'

Kelly laughed. 'So why did you come?'

'I like to do a bit for charity now and then.' When Kelly raised a sceptical eyebrow, he added, 'Even bookmakers have hearts, you know.'

'It's hardly your image.'

Jack shrugged. 'Journos,' he said. 'What do they know?'

'And presumably you didn't want to disappoint Ibn Fayoud.'

Jack Butler glanced across the table to their host who was listening with rapt attention to a woman dressed as a schoolgirl. 'He bets with me now and then, nothing special. Tell me, why are you here? You don't look the charity ball type.'

He was looking at her now, not with the leer of a

natural lecher, nor with the beady eye of a professional digging for information, but with polite, sympathetic curiosity. Jack Butler was not at all what
she'd expected.

'Ibn Fayoud is an owner,' she explained.

'But he doesn't own you.'

Kelly smiled. 'These days jockeys have to be diplomats.' As she spoke, Jack moved his hand gently on
to hers and asked for the salt. Again she felt the same
shiver down her back like an electric current.

Eating smoked salmon while talking to Johnny
Prescott had seemed to last a lifetime. The two subsequent courses, passed in conversation with Jack
Butler, took no time at all. He kept Kelly amused with
a string of stories about his life as a bookmaker, and
then surprised her with his knowledge concerning the
world's fifteen million refugees. Kelly found herself
fascinated by him.

'You'll be doing a runner on me in a minute, won't
you?' he said. 'You're not here at all. You're at York
racecourse already. I doubt you'll even stay for the
dancing.'

'I'm here all right.' Kelly smiled. 'Just one dance.'

'Great,' Butler seemed genuinely pleased. 'I'm
getting myself a cognac from the bar. What d'you
fancy?' He stood up.

'A port please,' she said.

Across the room, amid a throng of guests, Jack
Butler was given two drinks by a nun. 'Half will be
enough,' she said quietly. 'All of it and we'll be
laughing.'

Jack looked uneasy. 'I don't know,' he said. 'I'm

not sure about this. She's not like I expected.'

'I'm sure we could find another volunteer.' The nun's eyes were cold, glittering. 'Our little friend appears to have plenty of admirers.'

Jack thought of the job in hand.

'Leave it to me,' he said reluctantly, and made his way back to Kelly.

Across the table from Kelly, Annie and Bill were engaged in a silent battle of wills. Chin set in a parody of male stubbornness, Bill was attempting to convey to his wife his urgent need to get away from this madness and return to the house where they were staying. With equal determination, Annie was making it clear by chatting away happily to Ibn Fayoud and his schoolgirl friend that it would be rude to leave before the dancing had been under way for half an hour or so.

To Kelly, watching them as she sipped her port, it was clear who was going to win. On training matters, Annie deferred to her husband; on everything else, she had the last word.

'We'd better have that dance,' she said to Jack Butler. 'I get the feeling that my boss and his wife will be out of here before long. They're driving me home.'

'You don't have to go with them.'

'Yes, I do. I'm riding tomorrow.'

'The dedicated professional.' Jack made the remark without a hint of sarcasm, taking the glass out of Kelly's hand and getting to his feet. 'Maybe we could meet when you're not riding the next day.' He held out his arm in a surprisingly old-fashioned gesture.

Not a chance, thought Kelly, and then found herself saying, 'That would be lovely.'

Normally, at charity functions run by Henry, the Marquess of Flaxton, the music was loud and contemporary. Tonight, in a rare moment of good judgement, he had hired a big band whose music would not drive his older guests out into the night. When Jack and Kelly joined the dancers, they were playing a waltz.

'How are you feeling?' Jack said quietly as they danced.

'Good,' said Kelly.

And she did feel good. Was it because the man who held her in his arms was a confident and easy dancer? Or that she had drunk one glass too many? Her anxieties, her tension, her thoughts about racing tomorrow had never seemed so distant. She felt light-headed, idiotically, illogically happy. The music stopped, but she stayed in Jack's arms. The next dance was a foxtrot, but they continued to dance slowly.

It must have been several dances later that she noticed Annie standing on the edge of the dance floor. It seemed to Kelly that she was trying to catch her eye for some reason. Eventually, between dances, she came over.

'We're off,' she said in a voice which seemed oddly distant. 'Are you coming?'

Kelly found it hilariously difficult to concentrate. 'I think . . .' she said. 'I think I'll get a lift with Cy McCray, if you don't mind. He's staying in the same hotel.'

Annie looked concerned. There was something about the way Kelly was speaking that seemed unlike her. And she was normally keen to get an early night before a race. 'Are you sure?' she asked.

'Absolutely. I'll be home soon. Drive carefully.'

After Annie had left, Kelly realized that she hadn't asked Cy for a lift home. She certainly wasn't going to drive herself home. For all she knew, he might have gone already. 'Got to find Cy,' she murmured. Suddenly the idea of tearing herself away from Jack's warm, firm body, even for a minute, seemed heartbreaking. She looked across the dance floor and for a moment lost her balance. The band, dressed all in white, seemed miles away. The dancers were no longer people but there was something hostile, dangerous about them. Kelly swallowed hard, and closed her eyes. She felt cold and slightly sick. Behind her, she heard a voice. Snapping open her eyes, she realized that everyone was staring at her, everyone was talking about her, everyone knew that she was about to—

'You all right, Kelly?'

With staring, dilated eyes, Kelly looked up at the man who held her. His gentleness was fake, she knew that now, his face distorted as she looked at him. Jack Butler, the wolf; there was no escaping him. 'Let me go, let me go,' she whispered, discovering her helplessness too late. 'What have you done to me? What have you given me?'

'Is something the matter with her?'

It was a nun, who now stood beside Jack. Both of them looked at her with apparent concern but Kelly

123

knew with utter certainty that they were together in
this.

'I think she's had a spot too much to drink,' said
the nun. 'I'll just take her to the ladies'.' She took
Kelly by the arm; terrified, Kelly allowed herself to be
led away like a little girl. The world was staring at her.
She looked back at Jack in wordless supplication. As
the nun passed Kelly's table, she knocked the remains
of a glass of port on to the ground.

Kelly's scream echoed silently within her as, like
something out of a distant dream, the band played on.

She must have lost consciousness. For a moment
Kelly thought that she had been buried alive. Afraid
to move, she became aware that she was in a strange
room, in a bed. Her black dress, her underclothes
were hung over a chair. Was it morning? Where was
she? Had she had a fall? Was she meant to be racing
somewhere? She tried to sit up but a wave of nausea
engulfed her and, with a sob, she fell back on her
pillow.

The door opened, slowly at first. She could see the
figure of a man in the shadows. Jack Butler. He
looked down at her, like a surgeon before an operation. She could see his mouth moving but the words
were strange, alien. 'Worry . . . don't worry . . . all
right . . . all right?' He took off his jacket. Was he
going to cover her up? She was so cold now. Her
shoulder ached. Slowly, he undid his bow tie, pulled it
off. He was unbuttoning his shirt.

Kelly looked away and drifted off once more into a
hallucinogenic nightmare.

*   *   *

Behind the mirror was a nun with a camera. Breathing heavily, she occasionally brushed the sweat from her eyes as she photographed the scene in the next room.

'Oh, Jack,' whispered Margaret Stanhope to the whirr and the click of the camera. 'Oh Jack, you bastard.'

Chapter 7

An early morning mist hung over York racecourse, gift-wrapping it for the fine autumn day's racing that lay ahead. In the stables, the horses on whom thousands of pounds would be won and lost that afternoon stirred as their lads unlocked their boxes, brought them their feed. Kevin Briley, whose favourite horse Shine On was to run in the big handicap, talked to his charge as he mucked him out. He told him how much of his pay he had saved up for today, how he would personally kick him all the way back to Newmarket if he didn't win, how he was a big beautiful bastard that couldn't fucking lose, could he? Shine On, who knew Kevin well, concentrated on his breakfast.

Damien Gould walked briskly from his BMW towards the stables. Three rides he had today, for three different trainers, and not one of them had a squeak. To make it worse, the Connor bitch was on a fancied runner in the big race. The idea of her succeeding annoyed him. She was everything he wasn't. Young, charming, talented; she was also more resilient than he had anticipated. She must be screwing either Bill Templeman or that Arab bastard. Probably both. That would be a good rumour to start. He could maybe wind her up a bit if he had the chance. A thin smile, like a scar, spread across his face. Perhaps today was going to be all right after all.

At the York Hotel, a phone rang in Room 3012. It was Kelly Connor's early morning call. After two minutes, it stopped ringing.

Roddy Chalmers lifted his head from a table at Flaxton Hall, tried unsuccessfully to focus on his surroundings, and belched. His brain, never an overactive organ even on those rare moments when it wasn't pickled in alcohol, grappled with the fact that he appeared to be in some sort of tent before triumphantly reaching the conclusion that he was at a party. That was it, Henry's charity ball. Christ, it had been one hell of a thrash, an absolute bloody classic.

Roddy shifted his eighteen-stone frame and looked about him. Although it was light outside the tent, music was still blaring from a disco in the corner and Henry was dancing about the floor, ashen-faced and wide-eyed. When Roddy had last been conscious – about an hour ago, maybe two – he had seen Henry playing hunt the little white worm with a straw and a hand mirror. Snort, dance, bonk, snort some more – bloody good value, old Henry. Right now he was groping Joanna who had taken her top off, as she always did on these occasions. You could tell how a party was going by the number of items of

Jo-Jo's clothing scattered about the dance floor.

There was a glass in front of Roddy which he drained. It was time for kip. Thank God he was staying with Henry. He thought he could just about make it up the stairs. At the third attempt, he managed to stand up. He staggered out of the marquee in search of his bedroom.

It was a dream.

Kelly was in a large room she had never seen before, lying alone, naked under a sheet. She felt heavy-lidded and drowsy, as if she had been asleep for a week. Through the heavy curtains, a shaft of sunlight cut through the gloom. It revealed, at the foot of the bed, a fat man taking off his trousers and mumbling to himself. As she stirred, the man seemed to become aware of her presence. 'Well,' he said, trying to focus on her. 'Well, well.' A drunken grin spread across his flushed, porcine features. Kelly pulled the sheet to her. As she moved, her body ached as if she had been in a fight.

It wasn't a dream.

'Girl in my bed,' the man was muttering incredulously. 'Got a girl in my bed.'

Kelly could see her clothes in the corner across the room, but she needed to get to them without being jumped by this barrel of lard. She said nervously, 'Would you mind . . .'

The man held up a finger, as if he had remembered something very important. 'Better freshen up,' he said, wheeling round and staggering into a bathroom next door. Kelly heard a tap running. She leapt out of bed, shut the bathroom door, ramming a chair under the door handle. Trying to ignore the buzzing in her head, which was like a badly-tuned radio, she scrambled into her clothes.

Seconds later, there was an elephantine thud from the bathroom as the man tried the door. 'Cheeky,' he was chuckling drunkenly. 'Saucy little minx.' There was another thud. Kelly made her escape.

What the hell had happened? As she hurried down a long corridor, her mind groped backwards over the events of the previous night. She remembered dinner, then dancing with Jack Butler, Annie saying something to her, a nun taking her by the arm. After that, there was a series of horrific, shaming cameos that could only have come from the unconscious.

Downstairs, it was like a battlefield in which the only victors were excess and decadence. Champagne bottles were strewn about the floor. In the hall, a woman gloomily collecting dirty plates and ashtrays looked up as Kelly appeared. She had seen it all before – last night's high spirits turned to this morning's hangover, last night's gay blades to green-faced ghosts, last night's belles of the ball to tousled tarts with smudged lipstick and laddered tights. Kelly paused and looked about her.

'Where are the coats?' she asked the woman.

The maid smiled. By the look of this young girl in black, she'd have some explaining to do to someone. Serve her right.

'Cloakroom's over there,' she said, pointing. Kelly found her coat without too much difficulty.

'What's the time?' Kelly asked.

Time you knew better, young lady. That was what she wanted to say. 'Ten past seven,' she muttered.

Thank God. Kelly walked quickly through the marquee where her host Henry was dancing with a girl dressed only in black knickers.

Shivering in the morning chill, Kelly got into her car and started the engine. Bill expected her to be at York racecourse to ride out at eight – if she put her foot down, she could just about make it. Her head was clearing now but she still felt strange, drowsy. If it hadn't been for her fat friend, she would have overslept.

Something odd had happened to her last night. She must have passed out, but then she had drunk so little. It was just possible that the painkillers she had taken for her shoulder had reacted with the alcohol, but it seemed unlikely.

She was back at the hotel by 7.45. As the man at reception gave her the key to her room with a knowing look, Kelly reflected that she hadn't felt so guilty since her teenage party days. Her head pounding, she took the stairs to the second floor two at a time. The phone was ringing as she entered the room.

It was Annie.

'Thank God,' she said, when Kelly picked up the phone. 'I thought something had happened to you. Where have you been? Or shouldn't I ask?'

Briefly it occurred to Kelly that it would be sensible to lie. Apprentices do not wake up in strange beds the night before an important ride and then tell all to the boss's wife. But Annie was a friend.

'I'll explain later,' she said. 'Why didn't you bring me home like you promised?'

131

'Bloody hell,' Annie said loudly. 'You must have been in a bad way. I tried to drag you away but you were too engrossed in the Butler man to pay any attention.'

'*What?* I can't remember—'

'I'm sure you can't,' Annie said sarcastically. 'If I were you I'd get down to the racecourse pronto.'

'Annie. I must speak to you about this.' Kelly thought fast. 'Could we meet downstairs later, after I come back from the course?'

'Come on, Kelly, for God's sake. You're meant to be thinking about your big ride not a married man.' Annie sighed. 'All right,' she said reluctantly. 'Can't have our star apprentice worried on the day of a race, can we? I'll see you at ten.' She hung up.

A married man? Kelly held her head. Right now she needed about a million cups of coffee.

If she had any doubts that Shine On was good enough to win that afternoon, they were dispelled by the way he felt during his early-morning pipe-opener. The way he worked upsides her other ride, Spooked, showed that Bill had trained him to perfection. Today was Shine On's day, given a bit of luck and a decent run.

And a jockey who felt more alive than dead. The exertion and fresh air had done nothing to ease the pain Kelly felt in her head, the weakness in her muscles. Shine On took no hold at all, yet she had difficulty in pulling him up.

After the gallop, Bill was his usual communicative self. He looked the two horses over, then glanced up at Kelly. 'What's the matter with you? You looked like a wet rag coming up there.'

Kelly felt her face turn red with embarrassment. Bill missed nothing. 'I feel fine,' she bluffed. She always said she felt fine when asked, no matter what state she was in.

Bill looked as if he had something else to say. 'Just pretend he's Jack Butler or something,' he muttered loudly.

Kelly felt sick. It must have looked bad last night for Bill to say anything. Worse, his remark had been heard by Dennis, who was riding Spooked. By this afternoon, the events of last night, or Dennis's lurid version of them, would be common knowledge on the racing gossip circuit.

'Jack Butler, eh?' Dennis winked unpleasantly as they walked back to the stables. 'You little raver, you.'

The low murmur of conversation in the hotel's sun lounge was like the crashing of waves to Kelly as she entered to see Annie at a corner table. It was true, as Annie had said, that now was hardly the time to talk about dances, drugs and Jack Butler but it was important for Kelly to talk to her. Something strange had happened last night, she was sure of that. As far as Annie was concerned, Kelly had drunk too much, slept with Jack Butler and put her rides on Shine On and Spooked at risk. Trainer's wife, best friend – either way, she had to be told the truth.

'This had better be convincing,' she said frostily after they had ordered coffees.

'If our friendship means anything,' Kelly said, 'you're going to have to believe me.'

She described the events of the evening slowly, as if afraid that one word out of place would make Annie more sceptical than ever. Yes, she had spent a lot of time with Jack Butler and, yes, she had found him interesting, attractive even. She would have danced with him anyway. But it was the events after dinner that defied explanation.

'I can't remember anything clearly after that first dance,' she said. 'Maybe I heard you when you told me you were going home, but I was miles away. It was as if I couldn't act on my own behalf. I was suddenly . . .' The memory of how she felt made Kelly feel sick once more. 'Helpless.'

'Or legless.'

'I swear I had had one bucks fizz and half a glass of port. It wasn't like drunkenness anyway.'

'So it was the painkillers. You should have known better.'

Kelly shook her head and winced. It was like running razors through the brain. 'I don't think so,' she said. 'I took two pills that evening – they've never affected me like that before.'

'So what are you saying?' Annie sipped her coffee thoughtfully. 'That you were drugged? Who by? And why?'

'I think I'd better tell you about what happened after you left,' Kelly said quietly. Haltingly, she spoke about her sudden irrational terror on the dance floor, the nun leading her away, how she found herself in a bedroom with Jack Butler. Tears filled her eyes as she described seeing him looking down on her.

'Did anything happen?'

Kelly shook her head. 'I'm not sure,' she said. 'It was all hazy. I remember him getting into bed with me. Then I must have lost consciousness.'

Annie smiled humourlessly. 'Something happened,' she said. 'I rather doubt if Jack Butler would climb into bed with you to keep warm.'

The two women sat in silence for a moment. 'D'you believe me?' Kelly asked.

'Even if it's true and not some sort of dream, what can you do about it?'

'But why?' Kelly's question came out as a loud protest. A couple of middle-aged women at a nearby table turned to look at her disapprovingly. 'Why should he do that?'

Annie shrugged. 'The usual reason. What else?'

'Pendero.'

Annie struck her forehead in exasperation. 'For God's sake, Kelly. You're becoming obsessed by—'

'Listen.' Kelly lowered her voice. 'The big gamble on Pendero was by Ibn Fayoud – Harry Short told me that. The person who stood to gain most from Pendero losing the race was Jack Butler. After the race, Ibn Fayoud moves all his horses to Bill and suddenly he's big buddies with Butler. Why?'

'Racing's a small world.'

'And was it just coincidence that I get invited to the Flaxton dance, that I'm seated next to him? There's something going on, I'm sure of it.'

Annie sighed wearily. 'It sounds a little elaborate as an excuse for getting yourself laid,' she said half-jokingly. 'And at the moment, one of your villains, Ibn Fayoud, is your best owner. Bill's been told to enter his horses in several races abroad, with you riding.'

'Why abroad?'

'I suppose he has ambitions to be a great international racing owner like his dad. Or more likely it's a good excuse for a party abroad.'

Kelly shook her head gloomily. 'Everything seems to be going wrong at the moment.'

Annie drained her coffee and stood up. 'Here's what you do,' she said briskly. 'You ride horses. You mind your own business. You stay clear of Jack Butler – that's for certain. And you don't drink port.'

'You're right.'

'And you can do something for me.' For the first time Annie smiled with genuine warmth.

'What's that?'

'Win on Shine On.'

Kelly nodded. The razors leapt in her brain. 'Piece of cake,' she said weakly.

Later, much later, Kelly was to reflect on how lucky she had been that day. There was the fat man who had woken her up, Annie who had at least made her feel slightly better, and then Cy McCray and his diet pills.

She had just walked the course and was making her way to the weighing room before the first race when she heard the familiar Bronx accent behind her.

'How ya doin', sweetheart?'

Kelly turned and gave McCray a wan smile. 'OK,' she said.

Cy looked at her more closely. 'Jeez,' he said. 'You look like shit.'

'Thanks, Cy. I feel better already.'

'What's the problem?'

For a moment, Kelly considered telling him about the dance, but then she thought better of it. 'I had a hard night,' she said. 'I think something disagreed with my painkillers. I feel terrible.'

'You mean I might win this afternoon? With Shine On being ridden by a hospital case, my horse could have a chance.'

Kelly didn't laugh.

'Hey.' Cy reached inside his jacket pocket and took out a phial of pills. 'I wouldn't do this for anybody else, but take these,' he shook out three yellow capsules, 'and you'll be OK. They're great for tiredness, flu, hangovers.'

'What are they?'

'Diet pills.' He winked. 'On three of those, you'll be flying.

Trust no one. Kelly remembered her father's words. Cy was riding against her this afternoon. It was a risk, and she'd already made one monumental error of character judgement.

She decided she couldn't be so wrong twice in as many days. 'Thanks. I'll take them.'

'Their only disadvantage is that you can't take the painkillers with them. You'll be in agony but you'll feel so good you won't care.'

'As long as they get me past the post.'

'In second place.'

'First,' said Kelly. She glanced at her watch.

Spooked was running in the second race. It was time to get changed. As she walked to the weighing room, she gulped down the three pills.

Two hours later, Kelly sat on the scales, reflecting that Cy had been right. Her collarbone felt as if it were about to burst through her skin but her head had cleared and she felt strong.

'Thank you.' She alighted from the scales.

She'd just ridden Spooked like her old self and the horse had run above himself, finishing third in a field of twenty. In the enclosure afterwards, Bill Templeman had grunted in a way that suggested satisfaction with her. Standing behind him, Annie had shaken her head as if disbelieving the race Kelly had ridden after the excesses of the previous night.

Thank God for Cy and his pills. If she'd cocked up a second race, Bill would have jocked her off Shine On, whatever Ibn Fayoud said.

Cy emerged carrying a saddle, ready to weigh out for the next race. He winked conspiratorially at Kelly.

'They say they're dope-testing jockeys of the first three,' he muttered out of the side of his mouth.

Kelly laughed. 'They're not addictive are they, those things?'

'Not if you keep taking them,' said McCray. 'Catch ya later.'

Bob Collins didn't like it when the past came knocking at his door. It was ten years since he came north, married a young Indian model called Raksha and went straight. Now he lived in a neat semi-detached on the outskirts of Bradford with his wife

and three lovely kids, earning a comfortable, respect-
able living doing weddings, portraits, the odd news
pic for the local paper. It was a long way from Brewer
Street.

Not that he had regrets. If it weren't for his days at
the mucky end of the trade, he would never have
earned enough to buy a house and he wouldn't have
met Raksha who had been doing a bit of topless work
to supplement her salary as a nurse. He had learnt his
craft the hard way; after you had shot an Ibizan beach
orgy sequence in a studio in Soho on a cold January
morning with a load of complaining bimbos and a gay
black man coked out of his brains, any other gig was a
breeze.

The only time that he wished he hadn't been quite
so deeply involved in the skin trade was when the past
came to visit. Like two days ago. Margaret Stanhope.
A posh secretarial voice on the phone.

'Who?'

'Margaret Stanhope.' A pause, a sigh. 'Maggie.'

Oh my Gawd. Maggie. Mad Maggie. Do-anything-
if-the-cash-is-right Maggie. Quite a little cracker in
her day, she must have been in her late thirties now.
God knows what kind of seedy cinematic productions
she was involved in these days.

'Hullo, Maggie.' Bob had dropped his voice so that
Raksha in the next room wouldn't hear. She didn't
like the past any more than he did. 'What are you up
to then?'

'I'm a bit like you, Bob,' she said. 'I've gone legit.'
She gave him a brief, sanitized account of her life as
Margaret.

'And now you want something from me.' Bob knew that, whether she called herself Mad Maggie or Margaret Stanhope, friendship came at a price.

'Just a little favour,' she said. She gave him the details, sparing him time, place, names.

Bob leant against the wall and rubbed his eyes wearily. 'And that's what you call legit, is it?' he said.

'Bob.'

He knew that tone of voice. This was one dangerous bitch if you crossed her. So he agreed to give her the camera, show her how to use it; he'd make sure the family were out the afternoon she came round to get the film developed.

At least, looking on the bright side, he didn't have to take the shots himself. 'No, I want to do that,' she had said. Mad Maggie. She always was a weird one.

Now she was here and it was just like old times: in the darkroom with Maggie, working on filthy pictures. With the other girls, it had been simple: morning, darling, a quick strip, a bit of pout, grunt and groan under the studio lights, then off they went to the next job. Mad Maggie was different. She liked to stick around, see the results, maybe enjoy some off-camera larks in the back office. Not that there was the slightest danger of Bob getting into that these days, thank you very much. At least not on his home ground.

'Not bad.' Bob took the first contact sheet from the developing fluid and hung it up. 'You did a good job here, Maggie. Apart from a spot of camera shake.'

'It's Margaret,' she said, pushing him aside. 'Never

mind the photographic quality. Can you see the faces?'

Bob Collins looked at the contact sheet through a magnifying glass.

'Hope you're not going to try and sell these,' he said. 'She looks as if she's asleep and he doesn't seem to be having much fun either.'

The second contact sheet was ready. Margaret inspected it and asked for a number of prints to be made.

As he worked, Harry muttered, 'If I didn't know better, I'd say that was your Mr Butler on the bed there.'

Margaret was examining the prints, absorbed. Now as she looked up at Bob Collins, the smile left her face. 'One word of this and I tell your local rags where you learnt your craft.'

Harry shrugged. 'My mistake,' he said. 'Must be a Jack Butler lookalike.'

'Let me have an extra copy of these ones.' Margaret gave the photographer three prints in which her boss's face was clearly visible. The show had been set up for the little jockey but maybe, at some time in the future, Mrs Butler would be interested.

Two birds with one stone. Margaret Stanhope smiled.

Driving back to Leeds, Margaret tuned her car radio to the commentary from the York races. Personally, she couldn't stand horses but these days Jack's interests were her interests. After all, she was his personal assistant.

'Shine On has drifted slightly in the betting,' the

commentator was saying. *'He's now 4–1 third favour-ite behind the Irish challenger Breakdancer and The Guppy.'*

Drifted. Margaret laughed softly. The punters had probably caught a glimpse of Shine On's jockey. You wouldn't want to lay the family heirloom on a horse ridden by a zombie, would you? In fact, it was amazing the Connor girl could even find her way to the racecourse the way she must be feeling today.

'. . . while there's a slight question mark over Shine On's ability to stay this distance and of course it's a big test for his rider Kelly Connor, who's having her first ride in a listed race. Kelly, of course, is the daugh-ter of the great Irish jockey Frank Connor who died so tragically last month. They're all in now . . .'

Frankly Margaret couldn't give a toss. She'd feel a little sorry for the little girl if she blacked out in the race and fell under all those hooves. After all, it hadn't really been her fault that she became mixed up in Jack's business affairs. A bit nosey, that was all, and Margaret understood what it was like to be nosey.

The commentator was reeling off horses' names like an auctioneer, mentioning Shine On only occa-sionally. Bringing up the rear. Backmarker. Making no impression . . . Silly sport it was. Making horses run faster than they wanted to. And they always let you down when you least expected it. The things she had heard Jack say after a favourite that he had care-fully arranged to get well stuffed, as he put it, promptly went and won. Secretly Margaret thought he'd be better out of the racing business. Show busi-ness, boxing, snooker – that was where the money was. She'd tell him that when they were together at last. Maybe over dinner one night.

'. . . *as they pass the three-furlong marker, it's still The Guppy, who's made every yard of the running, behind him a group of horses led by the grey Prince Charming, Cy McCray has yet to move on Breakdancer, Shine On has an awful lot still to do . . .*'

Jack would be going all pale and intense now. Margaret smiled affectionately. She had seen him surrounded by people shouting and screaming, 'Go on, my son', not one of them down to lose or win as much as Jack, and he'd just stand there like a beautiful, pale statue. Involuntarily, Margaret thought of Jack's muscular body last night. She hardly heard the growing excitement in the commentator's voice.

'. . . *into the last furlong, and The Guppy looks beaten, Breakdancer takes up the running with Prince Charming on the stands side – it looks to be between these two – but now Shine On's absolutely flying on the outside, a terrific challenge, the three locked together, Breakdancer and Shine On stride for stride, at the line it's very close but I think it's Shine On who gets it on the nod. There'll be a photograph but there's not much doubt about the winner. Shine On ridden with breathtaking confidence by the young apprentice Kelly Connor who got up in the last stride to—*'

'She didn't look so breathtakingly confident last night, darling,' Margaret Stanhope said to the radio set. 'She was more like something out of *The Night of the Living Dead*.'

Switching to a music channel, Margaret wondered how Jack would be feeling right now. Pleased that his little doll had won? Surprised that she had the energy? Pissed off? Personally, she thought it was fair enough if Connor had a small moment of glory before Jack, armed with the material in the briefcase beside her, hauled her in and finished her little investigation for good and all.

'Yeah,' Margaret muttered. 'Good for Kelly, that's what I say.'

After all, the higher she was riding, the further she had to fall.

Within Kelly's body there was a war going on. Her collarbone was ambushing her with surprise guerrilla raids of searing pain while her head was screaming revenge for the ordeals it had undergone during the past twelve hours. Don't do drugs, Kelly. Nix those narcotics. She felt like a government health warning, but the sheer pleasure of having won her first big race made up for it all. If only her father had been there to see it.

Wincing, she eased on her coat, picked up her bag and saddle and walked slowly out of the weighing room. Ibn Fayoud would be celebrating in the bar and Annie had urged her to join them, but there was only one place Kelly wanted to be – home, in her bed, lying there reliving today's race.

It was the last time she was going to take diet pills before a race, that was for sure. They had made her feel so confident that, from the moment Shine On had jumped off, she had been utterly convinced that she would win. Even when she passed the two-furlong pole, some five lengths off the leaders, she knew she had them; but if the post had come ten yards earlier, she would never have got up. Those pills were lethal.

'How d'you ride on these things?' she had asked Cy as, pulling up, he shook her hand in congratulation. 'Doesn't your judgement go?'

'Sure.' He smiled across at her. 'I wouldn't dream of taking them before a race.'

Kelly's head was swimming as she left the race-course. She hardly had the energy to acknowledge the odd 'Well done, Kelly' she heard as she walked slowly towards the car park. She would be mad to drive home tonight, she decided. She would book in for another night at the hotel and leave in the early morning.

She glanced at the winners' enclosure. It had been a great moment. A tremendous reception. Ibn Fayoud and his blonde of the day; Annie, hardly able to conceal her astonishment at the way Kelly had been able to ride after the events of the previous night; Bill himself, flushed and more inarticulate than ever. 'Never do that to me again, Kelly,' he had muttered. 'My heart couldn't stand the strain.' It was as near to a compliment as he could manage.

'Two winners in twenty-four hours, eh sexy?'

The unmistakable tones of Damien Gould interrupted her thoughts as Kelly was putting her bag and saddle into the boot of her car.

She turned to see him standing ten yards away.

'Just the one, Damien,' she said quietly. 'One more than you, I think.'

'No, surely.' Damien scratched his head, frowning. 'There was that Shine On this afternoon then . . . what was it?'

Kelly knew what was coming. All afternoon she had been waiting for evidence of the racing rumour-machine at work. Even a loser like Dennis would know how to get word around. There was an angry throbbing in her head as she walked slowly towards him.

'Or maybe . . .' Damien assumed a smug little smile. 'Maybe it wasn't you who rode the winner but – yes, that's it, the winner rode you.'

Kelly found her breath was coming thick and fast. There was a tight knot of anger in her stomach. Damien paused to savour the moment as fully as possible.

'Go on, Damien.' Kelly's voice was almost a whisper. At another time and in another place, it could have been almost seductive. 'Say it.'

'You *know*, sexy.' Damien was truculent now, leering. 'Your boyfriend Jack—'

The blow from Kelly's right fist brought blood spurting from his nose and sent a searing pain up her arm which she refused to show on her face.

'Bitch,' he hissed, trying to staunch the blood which flowed from his left nostril.

'Yes, and you're just a chippy little has-been.'

Booking into the hotel for another night, Kelly was told that someone had been trying to call her. Nick Morley – it must have been. Although he had declined to leave a name, he must have hoped to catch her before she returned south. She smiled. After the madness of the last twenty-four hours, he'd be a welcome relief.

'Oh, and Miss Connor,' the receptionist called out as she made for the stairs, 'there was a delivery for you this afternoon.' The woman disappeared into a back office and returned with a bunch of ten red roses. She looked surprised when Kelly seemed reluctant to take them.

With a sense of foreboding, she read the note attached to one of the stems. It read, 'We'll be paying out a fortune on Shine On but you were brilliant. Congratulations. Thinking of you. Love, Jack.'

Kelly groaned. She tore the note off and gave the roses back to the receptionist.

'Keep them,' she said with a grim smile. 'I'm allergic to roses. They make me sick.'

After last night, she never wanted to see him again. Maybe, briefly, he had awakened in her a craving for the wild, the dangerous, the forbidden, but whatever had happened later had cured her of that. More than ever she needed to talk to Nick.

Anyway who needed danger if you were a jockey?

Jack Butler stared morosely at the large white television in his modern penthouse flat in the centre of Leeds. Nothing could lift his mood – not the fact that his supplier had managed to get his hands on a pirate video of the new Schwarzenegger, nor the really quite healthy profit he had made on the afternoon's racing at York, nor even the fat Havana cigar to which he had treated himself.

It wasn't despair. Jack had no time for the dark night of the soul. It wasn't the sort of long-term depression that had settled on him when his wife persuaded him to take her on holiday to Marbella. But it was bad all the same. At this particular moment, Jack didn't like himself, and popularity among people that mattered – and who mattered more than himself? – was very important to him.

'Shit,' he said, pressing the remote control, plunging Arnold into darkness mid-massacre.

He stood up, wandered over to the cocktail bar in the corner and poured himself another cognac. He stood by the large window, looking down on the lights of Leeds. Normally he enjoyed staying over at the firm's northern hospitality suite which was situated above their offices – bloody hell, he had treated a few girls to his own style of hospitality there enough times – but tonight it was all wrong. He didn't feel like company, however blonde, young or willing. For a moment, he almost wished he were at home, but then he shook his head as if to rid himself of the thought. Home, with Charmaine and her hurt, resentful eyes, her domestic conversation, her irritating attempts to keep their marriage alive.

'Jesus.' Jack shuddered. He felt bad, but not that bad.

Kelly Connor had probably received the flowers by now. He had spent ages trying to get the words right on his note but somehow it all came out wrong. He was genuinely delighted that, in spite of last night, she had won the big race. But what exactly do you say to that special someone whom you drugged to get into bed? It wasn't the sort of situation the etiquette books catered for.

He picked up the phone. He'd call her. Not to apologize – that would be asking for explanations he wasn't able to give right now – but to see that she was all right. Frankly, it had amazed him that she had been able to ride at all that afternoon, given how wasted she was the previous night, but then she was quite a determined little thing. Too determined for her own good really, which was why he had had to agree to last night in the first place.

Her line was engaged. Jack put down the receiver. Perhaps that was a good thing. He didn't know what was the matter with him.

The phone rang. He picked it up with a quiet 'Yeah?'

'I have something to show you.' It was the last person in the world he wanted to talk to, apart from Charmaine.

'Not now, Margaret.'

'I really think you should see these. After all the trouble we've taken.'

Jack sighed. He couldn't stand Margaret when she was in one of her perky moods. Normally, he'd slap her down but, right now, he didn't have the energy. 'I'll give you five minutes,' he said wearily.

There was something unfamiliar about Margaret Stanhope as, moments later, she entered her employer's hospitality suite, brushing past him, a triumphant smile on her face. She threw the black leather briefcase on to the sofa and said briskly, 'Gin and It for me, please, Jack.' It was almost as if she were in charge.

Setting it all up so beautifully, manipulating Jack
and the girl into the most compromising of positions
had done her self-confidence a power of good. She
looked at Jack now as, sulkily, he fetched her a drink.
A fine figure of a man, even finer without his
clothes – Margaret had no complaints there – but
not quite as strong as he made out. It was like a trick, a
game she had played. Strip Jack Naked. Now that she
had stripped Jack naked, she felt stronger. This was
one game she was going to win.

'About last night.' Jack handed her a drink.

Margaret held up a hand, her eyes twinkling with
amusement. 'About last night, you need have no
worries.' She picked up the briefcase. 'No one need
know about your first-night nerves.'

Butler looked at her coldly. He hadn't anticipated
this change in Margaret. It made him feel even worse
than before. 'Cut the crap and show me the pics,' he
said. 'I'm not in the mood.'

Margaret laughed lightly. 'When *are* you in the
mood, Jack?' She pulled out two contact sheets from
the briefcase. 'Only kidding, love,' she added with
unwelcome intimacy.

Sighing, Jack glanced at the first sheet. He and
Kelly had only been together five minutes but the
photographs brought back the full nightmarish shame
of it all. She had stared at him wide-eyed, unseeing,
and any desire that he might have felt had died in that
instant. He may have the morals of an alley cat but
raping a semi-comatose girl was beyond him. She was
so out of it that it would have been like making it with
a corpse.

Butler threw the sheet on the sofa. He was paler than Margaret had ever seen him. 'They make me feel sick,' he murmured.

'Of course, we need to get rid of the shots that look obviously posed.' Margaret pored over the sheet as if they were wedding photographs. 'But these two here look very natural. Almost as if you were—'

'Keep a couple, destroy the rest. And all the negatives, OK?'

'Anything you say, Jack.' Margaret closed the briefcase with a click, like someone who has just completed a sale. She sighed thoughtfully. 'If only you'd let her finish her drink before dancing with her. That was Ecstasy crossed with smack. Good stuff, too. The whole glass and she'd have been climbing the walls – just how you like—'

Jack walked quickly over to the door. He held it open. 'Get the fuck out of here,' he muttered.

Margaret shrugged and sauntered through the door. She smiled at Jack. He would be better in the morning. Then he would realize what a good girl she had been, how she had helped him. It had been difficult, of course, but the experience would bring them closer together. After all, what other personal assistant would have done what she had?

Jack Butler closed the door, turned and leant against it, as if afraid that she might suddenly return with more horrors. He covered his face with his hands and groaned.

Chapter 8

A vixen barked in the woods behind Dermot Kinane's cottage, breaking the early evening silence with its plaintive cry of love and need. Kelly Connor sat on an old garden bench in Dermot's orchard thinking of her father and the past. They had always spent a few weeks every year in Ireland, relaxing and visiting old friends. When she had been a child, those holidays had seemed magical, a time when everyday concerns were put in perspective by the rhythm of village life. At church, at the pub, or sitting by Dermot's roaring peat fire, she would catch a glimpse of her father as he once was, before his life turned sour – expansive, smiling, good-humoured.

Now, without him, she was back, taking stock of her life.

She had loved both her parents. Her mother had filled her early childhood with wonderful memories of picnics and riding ponies and of a stream of smiling schoolfriends who were always made welcome, but it was her father to whom she'd felt closest. Somehow he'd always been much more sensitive to her feelings. He could judge her mood almost before she was aware of it herself. After her mother had died, and despite his own grief, he'd done everything possible to help her forget. They had little money to spend once he'd given up riding altogether but they shared love in abundance. Kelly smiled as she thought of his early attempts at cooking and the hours he'd spent coaching and encouraging her while she'd practised riding a finish on the back of the sofa.

The racing world was more fickle than any other she knew of. After Shine On had won at York, the papers had sung her praises. Kelly, our most promising apprentice. Connor turns tragedy into triumph. Will Kelly Connor be the first woman champion jockey? The phone at the flat rang constantly. Spare rides. Requests for interviews. Old friends who had forgotten her during the hard times. During the subsequent week, she had ridden three winners, only one of which was for Bill Templeman. There was talk in the racing press of her being retained by one of the country's top trainers for next season, but that was the first she'd heard about it.

At York, she had ridden no better than she had ever ridden before. It was a bigger race, she was on a better horse, maybe she had ridden with more coolness than usual thanks to the emergency prescription of Dr Cy McCray. But what racing could give after one good day, it could take away after a bad one. Nothing had changed. Now, there were two days on which the only race meetings were in the north; Kelly

154

had asked Bill for time off and he had agreed.

It was as if events had conspired to make her forget Ascot, Pendero, the fact that the most important person in her world had been clubbed to death because he wanted to save her from the fate that he had suffered. Kelly was ambitious: there was almost nothing she wanted more than to ride winners, to be next year's champion apprentice, to make it. She had the ability and now she had had the break. Her moment had come.

Almost nothing. She knew what the sensible course of action was. Make racing the reason for your existence, your religion, forget the outside world. All that happened out there – love, life, death, murder even – they could wait until the day you hung up your saddle and retired rich, successful, envied.

Almost. Her father would have had words with her about that. The idea that she should risk her future by dwelling in the past, raking over the cooling embers of his life in order to discover who killed him and why would have enraged him. Even now, she felt his silent reproval from the grave. Don't let them hook you. Don't get involved in corruption even if it's on the side of the angels. Do your best at the work you've chosen. Ride winners.

'Just listen to her, will you?' Dermot Kinane appeared out of the gloom and sat beside Kelly. She had been so caught up in her memories that she hadn't heard him approaching. He nodded in the direction of the woods from where, every few seconds, the thin cry of the vixen could be heard. 'It's like she's laughing at us.'

Kelly smiled. 'She's calling for her mate.'

Dermot Kinane took a tin of tobacco from the pocket of his old tweed coat and rolled a cigarette.

'Last week that little bitch broke into my hen house. Ten bantams she killed.' The flare of the match lit up his thin, craggy face. 'She's reminding us who's boss.'

'She won't be so noisy when the hounds come. The hunting season starts soon, doesn't it?'

Kinane nodded. Now in his sixties, he still rode out with the Black and Tans, as wild and fearless as ever. He had broken more bones in his body riding horses that anyone she knew, yet he lived for his hunting. He'd probably die for it in the end.

'Makes no difference,' he said. 'She'll be back. Or if they get her, one of her cubs will be back. We can chase her across fields, lock away our birds every night, protect them with wire and all sorts of nonsense but, when we're dead and gone, a fox will still be coming back. She'll have the last word because she has nature on her side.'

Kelly laughed softly. 'You make it sound like a war,' she said.

'Not at all, not at all. It's a game. The day after she came I put up another roll of chicken wire.'

For a moment, they sat in silence, Kinane puffing at his cigarette, the pungent smell of cheap, strong tobacco wafting across to Kelly.

'What should I do, Dermot?' she said eventually. 'What should I do about Dad?'

Kinane looked at her tenderly. 'It wasn't thieves, was it, that killed him?' he said.

'No.' Kelly shook her head. 'He had been told to stop me winning at Ascot. He didn't.'

'Poor old Frank. Always was the pig-headed one.'

'I've found out who wanted Pendero not to win. There was a big gamble on him. A bookmaker paid Damien Gould to take some lead from my weight cloth while a journalist distracted me.'

'You know this, or are you guessing?'

'I found the journalist but the day he was going to talk to me he was killed by a hit-and-run driver. Gould virtually admitted it the other day.'

'So someone tried to stop you. It happens all the time. How d'you know it had anything to do with Frank's death?'

'The letter. Then, as soon as I started asking questions, they tried to stop me. There were threatening calls to the Templemans and—' Kelly decided to spare Kinane details of the death of her cat '—to me. They were prepared to kill the journalist Broom-Parker rather than let him talk to me. And I think they tried to drug me the night before I rode Shine On at York.'

'Why? What do they care if you ride winners?'

Kelly stared out into the darkness. 'That's what I don't understand. Shine On's owner was the man who had the big gamble on Pendero, and Jack Butler, the bookie, was the one who slipped me the drug. They're up to something, but I don't know what. It doesn't make sense.'

Kinane stared at Kelly in the evening gloom. He had known her since she was a baby. Even then, she had been wilful, determined. Today her soft, dark features concealed a tough obstinacy. That was why she was making the grade as a jockey. And that was why she was allowing herself to become sucked into a whirlpool of corruption which could destroy her career, or worse.

'Does the term "conspiracy theory" mean anything to you?' he asked softly.

Kelly looked surprised. 'You mean, as in "it wasn't a lone lunatic who killed Kennedy but the Mafia working in collusion with the Russians who had a deal with the FBI" – that kind of conspiracy?'

'Precisely. Look at a crime closely enough and everything becomes significant. Accidents, coincidences, ordinary everyday events are all part of a great plot and—'

'Thanks, Dermot,' Kelly interrupted. 'You don't have to explain. You think I'm inventing all this, seeing shadows behind every door, right?'

The fox was barking more closely now. Kinane stood up. 'Let's go and look at that henhouse. I can do without losing any more bantams.'

They walked in silence to a gate at the end of the orchard and into a farmyard. Beyond some stables, there was a chicken run. Kinane opened the door.

'Eejits,' he said quietly, as he looked at the bantams roosting on a low perch. 'Mrs Charlie's at their front door and they still don't get out of her reach.' One by one, he put the drowsy birds on to the top perch.

'Sure, you're as bad as your father,' he said, as he worked. 'You can't leave well alone.' A black bantam squawked in surprise as he picked her up. 'As it happens, I believe you. I'm sure the people who murdered your father are up to something.' He turned to Kelly.

'But so what? People are always up to something. They're like that vixen. There's nothing you can do about it.'

'Listen, Dermot, there's a reason for everything. The reason that vixen killed your bantams is because it's nature. Maybe she wasn't even hungry but it's in her to kill. I want to know the reason why someone killed Dad.'

'That's what the authorities are there to find out. The best way you can repay your debt to your father is to be a success as a jockey.' Gently, he lifted the last bantam to the top perch.

'So you won't help me?'

'Me?' Kinane looked round as he closed the hen-house door behind him, bolting it twice. 'What could I do?'

'You know everyone in racing. You could ask around about Jack Butler, Ibn Fayoud, Dad's dodgy contacts from his riding days. No one would be suspicious of you.'

Dermot Kinane took Kelly's arm as they walked back towards his cottage. 'D'you know what I think? It's not racing at all. I'll bet you it goes outside the business.'

They walked on in silence. 'Here's what I'll do,' Kinane said eventually. 'I'll talk to some friends of mine if you promise to tell what you know to the Jockey Club. Officially.'

'I've already done that. I've told them everything that I've told the police, but nothing's happening.'

Kinane stopped and looked at her, a deep serious-ness in his eyes. 'Well, give them time.

'And promise me it's no more Kelly Connor, private detective, all right?'

Kelly nodded. 'Promise,' she said.

Reg Butler sat beside a roaring gas log fire, smoking a fat cigar and wondering when he was going to be able to retire, relax, play golf, take in the odd West End show like other successful men of seventy-two. The dreams of his youth, when he was a tough, small-time bookie around the dog tracks of London, had long since come true. He had his luxury mock-Tudor mansion in Purley, his holiday home in Tenerife. He had a young wife who, although she was thirty years his junior, loved him dearly or, at any rate, behaved as if she did. He had a bank balance that a senior merchant banker would not be ashamed of. He had a son, running the family business for him.

He sucked greedily on the cigar, like a heart patient needing oxygen. Ah, that Jack. What a problem he was. A chip off the old block he was not. Bright, yes. Motivated, yes. But tough? Dream on. Young Jack thought he was hard, thought that having a few blondes and getting a few legs broken made you a man, but underneath it all he was soft, a little boy. If Jack had had to protect his pitch at Dagenham and White City in the days when men were men, he wouldn't have survived until the third race.

Not for the first time, Reg Butler tried to analyse what was wrong with his son and the way he ran the business. First of all, he appeared on television like he was some kind of game-show berk, not a businessman. Reg didn't like that. Bookmakers had no place in front of the cameras. Then he wanted to stay with the horses. He just would not diversify, that boy. And what was the point of ambition if it was limited? If Reg Butler hadn't looked beyond the horizon, he'd still be a one-pitch loser down the dogs. He'd had it too easy, Jack. That's what Reg had told his mother, God rest her soul, and he'd been right.

Soft. That was Jack. Soft-centred. He had two fundamental weak spots. One was situated behind his fly-buttons; greed was good in Reg's book, but sexual greed was dangerous when it interfered with business. The other was in his heart. That was the problem, Reg smiled grimly. His son had a heart, the stupid, randy little bastard, and what good were brains and charm if you had a heart?

Butler stubbed out his cigar in an ashtray and reached for a telephone on the table beside him.

'Jack?'

'Hello, Dad.'

The voice was weary, as if this was the fourth time he'd been called by his father that evening. Which it was.

'You set it up yet?'

'I told you. I'm just putting the finishing touches on. The Arab's cutting up rough.'

'Pull him in then. He owes us a fucking million quid, don't he? Squeeze the bastard.'

'Leave it to me, Dad.'

Leave it to him. Reg Butler felt a tightening in his chest. Leave it to Jacko. That would be the day.

'What about the girl?'

A pause. 'She's a problem. I think we'll send

someone else to Tokyo. Someone like McCray. She's trouble, that one.'

See? Heart. And probably fly-buttons too.

'Send her, Jack. She's better in than out.'

'Dad, I've told you. Don't worry about Kelly Connor. She's in.'

'You've spoken to her? She agreed?'

'Not exactly. But she'll do what she's told. We've got her.'

Reg Butler hung up. The boy was talking riddles. In? Got her? What half-arsed plot was that berk hatching now? Don't worry, he'd said. Some fucking chance.

It wasn't meant to happen. Kelly had called Nick Morley from Ireland and had arranged to visit Jockey Club headquarters in Portman Square when she returned. It was to be a formal, confidential statement, she had said. Nick had seemed concerned and had agreed at once to convene the security subcommittee. After the meeting, she would drive back to Newmarket. It was never meant to become complicated.

Kelly felt quite calm as she entered the large committee room. Before her, across a large mahogany table, were three stewards, two of whom she knew. To Nick's left sat Colonel Beamish who was looking as sceptical and impatient as he had in the stewards' room at Ascot, and Lord Chester, a wealthy landowner who had ridden as an amateur until recently. At the end of the table, a middle-aged woman stenographer sat impassively with her notebook in front of her.

It was a more sympathetic hearing than Ascot. Nick introduced her to the panel and explained the background to her visit. He was so candid that, for a moment, Kelly expected him to reveal that they had had dinner together, but with the slightest hint of a cautionary glance in her direction, he merely referred to 'a follow-up meeting away from the office'.

Carefully, soberly, Kelly told them everything she knew. It was like a confession, a purging, except that her only sin had been an over-zealous curiosity, a need to discover who killed her father. It was easier than she had anticipated. The three men listened to her without interrupting. Every name she mentioned was noted down, not only by the stenographer, but by Beamish. Short. Ibn Fayoud. Broom-Parker. Gould. Butler. Kelly held only one detail back. Although convinced that she had been drugged before the race at York, she had little chance of persuading three Jockey Club stewards that she had not been drunk, out of her depth, hysterical, and she didn't want Nick to know either. The rest of her story was too important to take the risk.

When she finished, Nick had a few muttered words with his colleagues before asking her one or two questions, mostly concerning times, places and names. If the events outlined by Kelly came as a shock or a surprise, he concealed it in his calm measured tones. He might have been asking her about the traffic on the way in from the airport. It was almost as if he and his committee dealt with murder and corruption every day of the week.

'We shall, of course, look into these allegations,' Nick concluded, winding up the hearing. 'It would be helpful to know if you wish to be kept in touch with developments.'

'Yes, of course I do,' Kelly said quietly.

Colonel Beamish gave a wintry smile. 'Naturally, if there are legal proceedings, you may be required to testify as a witness here, or even in a court of law.'

'I understand.'

'Thank you for bringing this to our attention, Miss Connor,' Nick said, standing up. 'I'll show you out.'

It was as he escorted her through the hall that he quietly suggested a drink after work. Kelly agreed. She had made up her mind to put the past behind her. Now would be a good time to start. She wanted to talk about something other than death and danger. Racing perhaps, or even life.

Nick didn't send any shivers through her the way Jack Butler had but after he'd kissed her softly good-bye and she was walking through Portman Square, she found herself looking forward to seeing him later.

He took her to a club in Camden Town, a dark cellar where a jazz quintet played hypnotic Chicago blues and where the pale faces of London's night people were lit by candles as they drank, smoked and laughed. Some of them looked as if they had only just risen from their beds, as if this was breakfast time to them; others had the look of people who hadn't slept for a week.

Kelly was glad of the anonymous atmosphere. She was still in the dark coat and dress she had selected for the Jockey Club hearing and Nick was in pinstripes. A spotlight on them in this company and they would feel like tax inspectors. But it was a good place to unwind; the chance of either of them being recognized was remote.

Kelly smiled at him. His hair was tousled, his tie at half-mast.

'How d'you know this place?' she asked. 'It hardly seems your style.'

'I love this music. Sometimes I come here by myself, just to relax, think things over. They know me here.'

'By yourself?' Kelly narrowed her eyes with mock suspicion. 'The eligible bachelor on the pull?'

Nick didn't smile. 'I rather think my pulling days are done. And anyway,' he nodded in the direction of the dance floor where a young girl in a T-shirt and torn jeans was entwined in the arms of a dreadlocked Rastafarian, 'I'm not quite the type for the regulars here.'

There was something sad about him, Kelly realized. It was as if there were no place where he quite belonged. On the racecourse, in Portman Square, he was treated with the wary politeness reserved for outsiders. Here he was a punter, a champagne Charlie, dossing with the underclass. Briefly, he reminded Kelly of her father. Once Frank Connor had left the certainties of life in County Limerick, he always seemed like an actor who had wandered into the wrong play. Frank Connor and Nick Morley, they were both uneasy with their surroundings, out of context.

'I brought my wife here once,' Nick said suddenly. 'We lasted half an hour. She said a black man had made an obscene suggestion to her outside the ladies' loo.' He smiled as Kelly burst out laughing. 'She was easily shocked, my wife.'

'Bet she loved it really.'

'No.' Nick frowned and looked at his glass. 'Her

niceness wasn't just on the surface. She was nice all through. One hundred per cent nice. That was probably why I married her. Everybody liked Sarah. My parents thought my marriage was the first sensible thing I'd ever done. But she turned out to be too nice for me.' He raised a glass to Kelly. 'Down with niceness,' he said.

A waitress brought them a bottle of champagne. 'With the manager's compliments,' she said. Nick looked across the room to where a fat man in jeans stood by the bar and ticked the side of his forehead like a taxi driver acknowledging a tip. The man gave a portly little bow and smiled.

'I knew him in the army,' he said simply. 'We've kept in touch.

Kelly sensed a strange vulnerability in this man. She asked him about his parents, how he became involved in racing.

'My father's a lawyer,' he began, sipping at his champagne, adding quietly, 'In fact, he's a judge. Very successful. My mother,' he smiled wryly, 'is a successful lawyer's wife.'

'They must be proud of you.'

Nick shook his head. 'They expected me to be a lawyer too. Join Daddy's chambers. So I went into the army. Looking back on it, I realize it was some sort of act of rebellion. Then, just to make it worse, I went into the SAS. Ireland. Anti-terrorist stuff. Intelligence.' He smiled distantly. 'Father hated it.'

'Why did you leave?'

'I got married. Sarah disliked the idea of being an army wife. The only other thing I knew about was racing so I went into bloodstock.'

'And the rest is history.' Kelly smiled. It was reassuring to hear of another life that had gone wrong, to be reminded that, however successful a person might seem, things weren't always easy. Nick reached across the table, took her hand and held it for a moment. He looked into her eyes, and she knew she was lost. It wasn't exactly love, but it was close enough to love not to matter.

'Stay with me tonight,' he said.

'I've got to work in the morning.' Kelly cursed her job, thinking how nice it would be to have someone she trusted holding her.

'Leave early.'

'I'll see,' she said. But she'd already made up her mind.

The flat in Pimlico was much as Kelly had expected. Spacious, tidy, decorated with old-fashioned, bachelor good taste. 'Night cap?' Nick asked as they walked into the drawing room. He fetched some chilled white wine from the fridge.

They stood in the middle of the room, chinked glasses and kissed.

'Shall we take our drinks to the bedroom?' she said softly.

Nick smiled and took her hand.

It surprised Kelly how much she wanted him. She wasn't drunk. She wasn't like some of her friends who needed sex like they needed food and drink. It had been almost a year since she had found herself alone with a man in a bedroom, voluntarily, at least. It had been a tearful last time with Jonathan, her boyfriend of the time – but casual sex had never been among her hobbies. She watched him as he switched on the light by the bed and drew the curtains. No, it wasn't love. Reassurance, warmth, sanity after the craziness and sadness of the past few weeks.

Nick stood by the bed, smiling, sipping his wine.

'This is mad,' she smiled. She reached behind her neck and undid the clasp. Her dress fell obediently to the floor around her ankles. Standing semi-naked in the bedroom of a Jockey Club steward. Yes, it was mad.

'More,' said Nick with some difficulty.

Kelly hooked her thumbs in the tops of her pants. 'Turn the light off,' she said.

He was a good lover, slow, gentle, aware of Kelly's needs almost before she was aware of them herself. Once, feeling herself slipping away dangerously into another land, a land of sweet warmth, desire and sensation, she opened her eyes to see him watching her and, for a moment, Kelly felt uneasy, almost manipulated. But then he whispered, 'All right?' and touched her again. She closed her eyes, bit her lip and nodded.

Yes, she was all right.

Afterwards, they slept. At three or four in the morning the telephone beside the bed rang shrilly. Nick picked up the receiver and listened for a moment, before muttering 'Wrong number' and hanging up. He turned to Kelly, smiled and kissed her softly, and then with renewed desire.

Kelly laughed softly. 'Thank you, wrong number,' she whispered.

* * *

It should have been a new beginning, a clean slate but, as she rode out the following morning, her head clouded from lack of sleep, Kelly knew that life was never that easy. A rest in Ireland, a confession before the Jockey Club, possibly a new relationship – it all should have signified a break with the past, particularly the recent, unhappy past, but history can't be discarded like an old coat.

As soon as first lot pulled out that morning, she sensed that something had changed. The lads were as cheerful as ever but guarded, like the possessors of unwelcome news. Then there were the riding arrangements: she was on a four-year-old called Captive Audience. Dennis was riding Shine On. Today was to be his last serious gallop before Tokyo.

'He's a lovely little ride, that one,' Dennis called out to her as they rode along in the string. 'Doesn't pull too hard. You can place him just where you want him.'

Kelly looked at him. Now she knew she was in for an unpleasant surprise. It was never good news when Dennis was happy.

'I know,' she said. 'I've ridden him before.'

'By heck,' Dennis slapped Shine On's neck. 'This one's been going well. I reckon he'll win in Tokyo.'

It was true that Shine On looked magnificent. He had lost a bit of weight after the race at York but now seemed stronger, harder.

'Are you riding him work?' Kelly was unable to resist asking the question.

Dennis frowned, as if he weren't sure quite what was happening that morning. 'No,' he said. 'I don't think I am.'

The string was walking round in a circle at the end of the gallops when Bill's Audi drew up. A small figure was seated beside the trainer and it was only when the two men got out of the car and walked briskly towards them that Kelly saw that it was Cy McCray.

'Oh yes,' said Dennis, enjoying every moment. 'Now I remember who's riding Shine On. It's Cy. D'you know him? Good jockey.'

Bill and Cy were now standing a few yards from the string. The trainer called Dennis over. Jauntily, he slipped off Shine On's back and gave Cy a leg up. 'Let's have Captive Audience over here then.' Bill's voice gave nothing away but Kelly noticed that he avoided looking at her as he gave them their orders.

'Thanks, Cy.' Kelly looked straight ahead as they cantered down to the start of the gallop.

'Hey, Kelly, I'm sorry, all right?' The American sounded sincere. 'Bill called me a couple of days ago. What could I say?'

They pulled up at the end of the gallop.

'Are you riding him in Tokyo?'

Cy shrugged. 'Guess so.' He busied himself adjusting his leathers. He glanced up. 'It's a tough break, Kelly. I'm sorry it had to be me. If I'd said no, he'd have booked somebody else.'

Kelly tried to smile gamely. 'That's racing,' she said. 'Ready when you are.' Cy nodded.

Bill's orders had been for Captive Audience to lead Shine On at racing speed over six furlongs, then for them both to stride out for home over the last two furlongs.

That's racing. Kelly jumped Captive Audience off

smartly, glancing back to check that Shine On was with her. Cy had him handily tucked in a couple of lengths behind her. How many times had she heard the phrase that she had just used so easily. Get robbed of a race in the weighing room, smash your shoulder up in a gallop – that's racing. The wind whistled in her face bringing tears to her eyes. Captive Audience was going easily but Kelly knew that behind her, Cy would be swinging off Shine On, who was in a different class to her horse. Ride a big winner, hit the headlines – that's racing. The six-furlong pole approached and Kelly heard Shine On moving closer to her. His head was nodding beside her left boot. Lose a ride to one of your best friends, on the horse people had said you rode better than anyone else – that too was racing. Shine On was upsides her now. She saw Cy change his grip on the reins; Shine On effortlessly moved into overdrive and, in a matter of yards, was well clear of her. Captive Audience was tiring. She rode him out over the last furlong and finished some six lengths behind Shine On. Yes, that was racing.

'Nice horse, isn't he?' she said to Cy as they pulled up.

'Sure is.' Cy nodded. 'He's a fucking flying machine.'

Bill was not one for lengthy explanations. Standing in the middle of the yard, he called Kelly over after first lot had returned.

'Captive Audience runs at Sandown on Saturday in the lads' race,' he said.

'Right,' said Kelly. She could see Dennis watching

them from one of the stables behind Bill. 'And Cy rides Shine On in Tokyo,' she said as casually as she could manage.

Bill looked embarrassed. 'Sorry, I've been meaning to tell you. Owner's orders.'

'I thought Ibn Fayoud liked the way I rode.'

'He did.' Bill looked down. 'It appears that he's changed his mind.'

'And you?'

'You know what I'd prefer but the man's got nine horses with me now.'

Behind him, Dennis smirked. He might not ride winners these days, but just now and then all the disappointment of his life in racing was forgotten for one sweet moment. She had it coming to her, that girl.

'Come and have breakfast.' Bill felt like a weight had been taken from him now that he'd told her. 'Cy's in the house.'

Kelly smiled politely. Just this once, she would risk being considered a bad loser. 'No thanks,' she said. 'I have a couple of things to do.'

It was nine thirty when Kelly rang Nick's number. As she had anticipated, he was out.

She left a message on his answering machine: 'Nick, I wanted to thank you for last night. For everything you said and for listening and for—' She paused. 'For everything. I have a busy schedule for the next few days, so I may not be in touch. Perhaps I'll see you racing. Hope so anyway. 'Bye.'

It wasn't perfect, she reflected after she had put down the telephone, but it wasn't bad. Friendly, open, but containing an unspoken message that Nick would hear. Last night was last night; today's different. Let's take this one day at a time.

Kelly sighed and looked at her watch. It was time for second lot.

When in doubt, keep going. That was what her father used to say. Don't look to the right, to the left, or over your shoulder, but concentrate on where you're going. Kelly sat in the jockeys' stand at Sandown and gave a quiet laugh. Where the hell was she going? She was no longer sure, but at least she had a job and was offered rides. That was something. Keep going.

Half an hour previously, Captive Audience had run to the best of his ability in the lads' race, plugging on one-paced up the Sandown hill to take second place. It had been a rough race and Kelly had been glad that she had elected to be among the leaders throughout. By the sound of it, World War III was breaking out behind her and after the race there had been a stewards' inquiry. The last thing she needed right now was another confrontation with the bowler-hat brigade.

She was offered a spare ride in the last race, a two-year-old trained by Ian Gardem, for whom she had never ridden before. She had time to kill before then. As she looked down from the stand, the horses for the third race, a handicap over six furlongs, were filing out on to the racecourse. Cy McCray was riding one of the joint favourites and, somewhat to her surprise, Harry Short had retained Damien Gould to ride Heraldic, a three-year-old with negligible form.

'What's Harry doing bringing that yoke down to

Sandown?' one of the jockeys sitting behind Kelly asked.

'Spare place in the box, I suppose,' his companion muttered. 'He's got a horse running in the big race, hasn't he?'

'It's a right camel, that horse. Pulls like a train. I saw it pissing off with an apprentice on the way down to the start at Chester. He'd done a couple of circuits before they stopped. That's probably why Damien's riding it and not his retained jockey. That's the only type of animal he gets to ride these days.'

The two jockeys laughed. Yes, Kelly reflected, there was something odd about it. Harry Short rarely brought his horses south when they had no chance of winning and, on all known form, Heraldic was outclassed in this race. And why put Gould up? After Pendero's race, the trainer would hardly speak to him. What was Short up to? In spite of her determination to leave the past to look after itself, Kelly found herself speculating as to where the fat trainer fitted in with Jack Butler and Ibn Fayoud.

'There he goes,' one of the jockeys laughed. Even by the standards of Harry's yard, Heraldic was no looker, a great, gangling colt with a head and neck that seemed to have been added to his body as an afterthought. As his lad let him go, he set off towards the start flat out with his mouth open and his nose in the air. For a brief moment, Kelly felt almost sorry for Damien Gould.

'Christ!' Both jockeys were staring horror-struck out on to the course.

Kelly looked up to see Heraldic bolting towards the

174

start with Damien clinging vainly upside down round his neck.

There was a gasp from spectators and a solitary scream as Damien fell towards the fast-moving ground, but instead of lying there he was yanked mercilessly forward as it became obvious that his foot had slipped through the iron and he was hung up. Panicked, the horse dragged Damien along under its flailing legs towards the steeplechase fence, bumping his body like a yo-yo as it went.

'Oh my God.' Kelly covered her face with her hands. It was a jockey's nightmare, being dragged under a horse's feet, held by a leather that won't break. Damien's body appeared to be twisting and writhing like a fish on a line but there was no escape for him. A groundsman ran on to the course waving his arms in a vain attempt to head the horse off but Heraldic was panicking even more now. Maddened by the limp rag doll banging against his legs, he veered to the left.

Kelly could feel her stomach turning. 'Why doesn't the leather break?' she muttered as the horse continued its terrifying charge downhill.

And then suddenly it was all over as Damien's body smashed with a sickening thud into the solid frame of the fence. A stunned silence fell over the racecourse as he lay motionless in the grass while Heraldic galloped on. Kelly's eyes flicked from the body on the ground to the horse, trampling the saddle beneath its unfeeling hoofs. Then she strained her eyes. There was something else. As she realized what it was, she turned and threw up. Damien's left leg was still in the iron.

A sense that what had just happened involved her in

some way made her pull herself together and run down on to the course where racecourse attendants were already putting up a screen.

It was no accident, she thought as she ran. It was too much of a coincidence.

She hurried across the course and pushed through a knot of ghoulish spectators who were standing gloomily by the area which had been cordoned off. She walked round the ambulance. The stretcher holding Damien's inert body was just being lifted into it. An ambulanceman held out an arm. 'Sorry, love,' he said. 'We've got to get him to hospital.'

The man pulled himself in after the stretcher, the doors were closed and the ambulance began to move off, its siren wailing mournfully. Kelly headed back towards the stand.

Heraldic had finally pulled himself up at the start. He was being led back by his lad who held the saddle under one arm. Kelly stared at it and the lad hurried on.

Someone touched her arm. 'Cup of tea?'

'No,' she muttered. 'That was no accident.' She turned to walk to the weighing room. She had a horse to ride in the last.

Chapter 9

'So it's another winner for the girl wonder?'

Dermot Kinane liked to bring a ray of sunshine wherever he went. If someone had told him a nuclear bomb was targeted on County Limerick, he'd be delighted that his heating bills would be reduced. But that Sunday morning, Kelly was in no mood for optimism.

'Yes,' she said unenthusiastically. 'It was a nice little horse. Gardem says he'll be offering me more rides.' She held the phone to her ear with her shoulder and sat up in bed, pushing the newspapers on to the floor. Normally, Sunday breakfast time spent reading the papers in bed was one of Kelly's favourite moments, but not today. The news on the radio had seen to that. Damien Gould had died during the night.

'Sure, you'll be first jockey to a big stable within the next couple of seasons,' Kinane was saying. 'What did I always—?'

177

'You heard about Damien Gould?' Kelly interrupted.

There was a pause. 'Yes,' Dermot said quietly. 'Poor bastard. Horrible thing to happen.'

'It didn't just happen, Dermot. I think it was murder.'

'Ah, Kelly,' he sighed. 'What did we agree when you were over here? No more conspiracy theories, wasn't it?'

'Dermot, I saw the saddle when the lad brought the horse back. At the time I thought something must have been tampered with. It wasn't until later that I realised what it was. I'd seen it but it hadn't sunk in. The irons were much too big. More like hunting irons. But when I went back to have another look they'd been changed. The lad must have done it. It's a terrible thing to say, but I think the lad may have pulled the iron over Damien's foot as he let him go.'

'Jesus.'

'If I'd only realized sooner—'

'Kelly, I know it doesn't look good but for God's sake, leave it be.' Dermot's voice took on a new urgency. 'Tell your friends at the Jockey Club. Leave it to the experts.'

A vision of Colonel Beamish, listening to her with undisguised scepticism, loomed before her.

'Experts?' She laughed bitterly. 'Two days after I tell them about Damien Gould, he's dead. That's where their discreet inquiries have led.' A thought occurred to Kelly. 'Anyway, what about your part of the deal? Did you find out anything about Ibn Fayoud or Butler?'

'I think Jack Butler's the most likely of the two. They say he's a hard bastard, like his dad. There's rumours that he's involved in some sort of organized crime caper outside racing, but it's difficult to find out more. He doesn't like gossip, our Jack. Those who gossip about him tend to meet with nasty accidents.'

'Like Damien Gould.'

'Could be. There was one other thing. Before your time, during the sixties, there were finance restrictions in the UK. It was made very difficult for businessmen to ship money abroad.'

'You think Butler was involved?'

'Not so far as I know. It was the method used for smuggling that interested me. Bloodstock, mares, stallions, used to travel abroad loaded up with notes. For some reason, the Customs inspectors never suspected horses as smugglers.'

'You mean Ibn Fayoud might be entering his horses abroad as part of some sort of smuggling operation?'

'It's a thought. He needs the money. The word is that Ibn Fayoud's in Jack Butler's pocket. So you watch yourself in Tokyo.'

Kelly smiled wryly. 'That's one thing I don't have to worry about,' she said. 'I've been jocked off. Cy McCray's riding Shine On.'

'Why's that?' Dermot sounded almost as angry as Kelly had felt when she'd heard the news.

'It's the owner's decision.'

'Bastard.' Then his voice lifted. 'Oh well, maybe it's for the best.'

After she had put down the phone, Kelly sat deep in

thought. It was almost as if someone were keeping her away from trouble. There was no other explanation for Ibn Fayoud's insisting that she shouldn't ride Shine On.

Maybe Dermot was right. She should leave it to the Jockey Club, suggest to Nick that he take a closer look at Harry's yard for a start. He seemed to be up to his fat neck in this.

There were some aspects of her job that Margaret Stanhope really did not like, and spending every other Sunday in bed with Reg Butler was one of them. All right, it was at the Sheraton Park and there was champagne and chocolates and the odd item of expensive jewellery, but then there was also Reg Butler.

Margaret looked across at him as he checked his pools in the *News of the World*. He was not one for the romantic niceties, was Reg. Do it, read the papers. Maybe do it again, order up a bit of nosh and champagne. Talk a bit of business. Then it was 'Fuckin' 'ell, is that the time?', back into the vulgar check suit and home to his little wife, who had been told that he had a business meeting in the City. Not that she believed him. She knew her Reg. She was probably delighted that someone else had to submit to his unsavoury needs now and then.

Seventy-two, and getting filthier by the minute, Reg Butler had sex like other men of his age spent Sundays digging their vegetable patch down at the allotment. It got him out of the house, gave him a bit of exercise, kept him young. The only difference between them was that the bloke on the allotment was probably more careful when he prepared the soil, gentler when he started digging.

'Reg?' Margaret Stanhope saw by the watch that never left his wrist that their unromantic interlude would soon be drawing to a close.

'In a minute.' Reg Butler frowned as he read the newspaper. He was on the racing page now. His reading routine was always the same. Pools. Racing. Bonk stories.

'Shame about the Gould feller,' he muttered. 'Nasty accident, that.'

'Reg, it's about Jack.'

'I said,' Reg Butler looked up from his newspaper, 'in a minute.'

Margaret sighed. What she put up with. She couldn't nag because Reg said he got enough of that at home. And she knew she was expendable; one word out of place and he would find another Sunday partner. In fact, it was only because he was chronically mean that she had lasted this long. 'Reg Butler was never a fuckin' punter,' he had once said. 'Never will be.' And, frankly, who else would do this for free? Since the age of seventeen, Margaret had regarded her body as a tradeable commodity; she saw a fortnightly meeting between the sheets with an elderly bookmaker as an investment, a means to an end. It helped, albeit in an unpleasant way, in her campaign to become the next Mrs Jack Butler.

'It's just that he looks like bottling the Tokyo job,' she said quietly.

Reg Butler took a long drag on his cigar and glanced up from his newspaper. 'You what?' he said, expelling a cloud of smoke in her direction.

Margaret stifled a cough. 'He's pulled that little girl jockey off the job. Says he doesn't trust her. She's too nosey.'

'He told me. All the more reason to send her out there, I said. If it goes wrong, she's in the shit with Ibn Fayoud. We can't lose either way.'

'That's what I said to Jack.'

'And?' Margaret was pleased to see that she now had Reg's full attention.

'And he still got Ibn Fayoud to jock her off. Some Yank's riding now.'

'Fuckin' useless, that boy,' Reg said, as if none of this came as a surprise to him.

'I think he likes her.'

'Jesus.'

'But I've got an idea, Reg. A little plan.'

Reg Butler swept the *News of the World* off the bed. This was one evil woman, no doubt about it, but she knew how to do it. These days he liked a woman who knew how to do it.

'Later,' he said, resting his cigar carefully in an ashtray. He stroked Margaret's hair. 'What *is* the problem with that son of mine?'

'He's soft, isn't he?'

Reg Butler took her hand, kissed the palm and pushed it downwards. 'Not like his old dad, eh?'

Margaret smiled professionally. 'No, Reg,' she said. 'Not at all like his old dad.'

Nick Morley had said he'd be visiting the Whetstone Park Stud that Sunday afternoon. There had been talk of meeting for a drink in the evening, but the talk had taken place at five in the morning as Kelly was hurriedly slipping into her clothes and now Nick seemed to have forgotten. There was no answer from his London flat or from his car. The Damien Gould business couldn't wait. On an impulse, Kelly decided to drive to the stud and catch him there.

Charles Caldecott, who owned the Whetstone Park Stud, was an odd character whom Kelly had met a couple of times and had never really taken to. He had been an unsuccessful amateur jockey some fifteen years ago and had then been assistant to a leading jump trainer in Lambourn. He had been a flop there too because, after a couple of years, he had left amidst rumours of misconduct. Some said Charles had been having an affair with an owner's wife, others that he was involved in some gambling scam. Whatever the reason, no other reputable yard would touch him and for a while Charles drifted about on the fringe of racing. He ran a transport company, sold insurance schemes to jockeys, worked for a dodgy outfit that specialized in horse tonics. Among racing people, Charles Caldecott was something of a joke.

Then he got lucky. His father died. The family money, acquired from mining interests in South Africa, was divided between his brother, a rather dim stockbroker, and Charles. He invested in a stud. To everyone's astonishment – after all, Caldecott's knowledge of bloodstock could be summarized on the back of postage stamp – it prospered. There were still rumours that the Caldecott business methods were not above suspicion, but he became part of the establishment. His yearlings sold for astonishing sums. The Arabs liked him. Charles had made it.

All the same, it was surprising that Nick dealt with him, Kelly thought to herself as she drove her car down the drive of the Stud. They seemed so different; Caldecott was the epitome of the public school chump that Nick detested.

They were sitting together in the garden, their backs to the gate through which Kelly appeared. For a moment, she hesitated. She hated arriving at places unannounced and, although Charles Caldecott had always been at his most ingratiating when he met her, that had been on social occasions. The two men sat with catalogues in front of them, deep in conversation. Then she remembered Damien. The stirrup. Nick had always said that his Jockey Club duties came before his business. She would take him at his word.

Caldecott saw her first.

'Why, er, Kelly,' he said, standing up. 'What a lovely surprise.'

'I'm sorry to turn up without warning like this,' Kelly said. 'I was told that Mr Morley was here and I just needed a brief word.'

Nick was standing too, smiling, holding the catalogue under his arm. He was pleased to see her. 'Kelly, I'm sorry, I meant to phone you. Whatever are you doing here?'

'There's something you ought to know and it couldn't wait.'

'Of course it couldn't,' Charles Caldecott said heartily.

'I'll get you a cup and saucer and you can join us

for tea.' He walked off briskly towards the house.

'Nick, I'm sorry, just turning up unannounced. But I had to talk to you today.'

'That's OK. Charles is the biggest gossip in racing but I don't mind people talking about us,' said Nick, grinning slightly.

'It's not about us. It's about Damien Gould.' She told him what she had seen at Sandown.

He appeared to be only half listening. 'Kelly, it sounds implausible,' he said finally. 'And anyway, what am I meant to do on a Sunday?'

Kelly glanced towards the house. Charles Caldecott was returning, a cup and saucer in his hand.

'You could go and see Harry Short and ask him why Damien was riding his horse,' she said sharply.

'Of course.' Nick looked contrite. 'You're right. I'll ring you later.'

'Now,' said Caldecott. 'Shall I be mother and pour or d'you want me to disappear while you two talk Jockey Club business.'

'That's fine, Charles,' Nick smiled. The colour had returned to his cheeks. 'We've sorted it all out.'

'A steward's work is never done, eh?' Caldecott laughed with hearty insincerity. He turned to Kelly. 'By jove, that was a nice winner you rode for Gardem yesterday. Are you going to be first jockey for him next year?'

Kelly smiled. 'Hardly,' she said.

The three of them talked politely about horses and racing for a few minutes, before Kelly decided it was time to leave. She had done what she could.

'Thank you for the tea,' she said, rising to her

feet. The two men stood up and said goodbye.

'Goodness,' she heard Caldecott say as she walked across the lawn towards her car. 'What a little popsy that girl is.'

'I'm sorry I was a bit short with you this afternoon,' Nick said when he rang Kelly later that night. 'It was just that I had other things on my mind. Anyway, I got one of my lads to go up and see Harry Short.'

'And?'

'He's just phoned from the car to say that as far as he could tell Harry had nothing to do with it. He seemed genuinely upset that the boy had been killed. Apparently he'd rung up for the ride. It wasn't Harry who'd booked him. He said he'd been pleased because his own jockey hated the horse.'

'And what about the lad who led the horse up?' Kelly asked.

'He's only been working for Harry for a few weeks. Came from a yard in the south. My lad said he was still suffering from the shock of seeing Gould's leg in the iron.'

'Maybe he never meant Damien to end up dead, but I'm certain he had something to do with it.'

'Well, let's hope we find out. The investigation is still going on.'

'A steward's work is never done,' Kelly quipped.

'Precisely,' said Nick seriously. 'Precisely.'

It was just like old times. Annie and Kelly sat drinking sweet tea in a noisy café in the centre of Newmarket. It had been an uneventful morning, apart from the trainer behaving with more surliness than usual, and Kelly needed to talk to Annie. Catch up on the gossip, she said. Girl talk. She managed to guide the conversation round to Ibn Fayoud. Lightly, she asked Annie why Bill Templeman had booked Cy McCray for Shine On in the Japan Cup.

Annie sighed. 'It's like Bill told you,' she said quietly. 'Ibn Fayoud wanted experience.'

'Listen, Annie, you can't tell lies to old liars.' Kelly sipped her tea. She had been friends with Annie long enough to know when she was holding back on her. 'What really happened?'

'All right.' Annie gave up. 'Ibn Fayoud rang late at night. Eleven thirty. You can imagine Bill's reaction.'

'I'm amazed he answered it even!'

'There was something about Ibn Fayoud's voice, he told me. Something . . .'

'Wired?'

Annie laughed. 'Yes, he was probably on something. But Bill said he seemed frightened. Like a little boy. Almost pleading.'

'So he listened.'

'Right. Ibn Fayoud talked and talked. He seemed to think that the Tokyo race was particularly important. He said that his future plans as an owner were very uncertain at the moment.'

'Meaning?'

'Bill took it to mean that he might have to pull out of the yard or even out of racing altogether.'

'Which still doesn't explain why he dumped the one person who knows how to ride Shine On.' Kelly pushed her cup of tea away from her. None of it made any sense.

'That part of what Bill told you was true. Ibn Fayoud said that the stakes were too high to risk using an apprentice.'

'D'you think McCray had got at him?'

Annie shook her head. 'No,' she said. 'It was Bill who suggested Cy when it was clear that Ibn Fayoud would take his horses away from the yard rather than use you.'

'Nice, isn't it? After the winner I rode for him at York.'

'There's something odd about it.'

Kelly thought for a moment. 'I was really looking forward to the trip, too. Maybe—' She didn't like play-acting for her friend, pretending that the thought had just occurred to her, but this was important. 'Maybe I could go anyway. As a lad.'

'You'd do that?' Annie looked surprised.

'Of course. It's all experience. And I'd like to see how Shine On goes. Would Bill agree?'

'Why not?' Annie smiled. 'You could keep your old friend Dennis in line. And we've got to pick up a mare that Ibn Fayoud's bought out there. I'll talk to him.'

'Promise?'

'Trust me.'

It was as they left the café that Kelly noticed a Lamborghini, bearing the number plate FAY 1, badly parked outside a chemist's shop on the High Street. She told Annie that she had to do some shopping, then doubled back and waited. It was too good an opportunity to miss.

*　　*　　*

Ibn Fayoud didn't like mornings and he didn't like country air. Right now, he was overdosing on both. That was why he needed a hit of Valium before he headed back to London, to his bed. Sometimes being a racehorse owner was tough on the nerves.

Ibn Fayoud wasn't a normal user. He needed to come down from a greater height than most. Last night, he must have done about three grams of the white stuff, plus cognac to stop the shakes, plus not going to bed all night, plus having to behave like a serious grown-up with his trainer and make sure his horses were going to the right races in the right countries at the right time, plus a screaming anxiety attack about his father and Butler and the mess his life was in, plus the horrific combined effects of the morning and the country air. Now *that* was stress.

'Are you sure this is right?' The small grey-haired chemist returned from the back of the shop, still bearing Ibn Fayoud's prescription. 'The quantity seems—'

'It's correct,' Ibn Fayoud interrupted through clenched teeth. He fixed the man with his cold black eyes. 'And it's urgent.'

The man went off, muttering to himself. Ibn Fayoud clenched his fists to stop himself trembling. Country bumpkin. Racist. They didn't know what it was like, these people.

'Looks more like a horse prescription to me,' the man said gloomily when he returned with a phial of pills.

Ibn Fayoud, holding out his hand, flashed him a gleaming, insincere smile. 'They're for my wife. And she's not a horse.'

189

Emerging from the chemist, he winced as the morning sun danced around his brain. He walked quickly towards his car, got in, and fumbled with the bottle of pills. He was just cursing the child lock which his sweating, trembling hands were unable to work when he noticed the girl jockey walking towards his car. Shit. There was no way to avoid her. She was smiling at him. It was instinct – the natural reaction of a predatory male – that made Ibn Fayoud smile back and press down the automatic window beside him.

'Hello there,' he said. His mouth felt dry. His body was screaming for relief.

'Morning, sir.' Kelly Connor gave a polite little bow, glancing at the phial of pills in his hand. 'Everything sorted out with Mr Templeman?'

'Absolutely fine.' The girl was leaning on the car door, her face unnervingly close to his. Within Ibn Fayoud's racked, confused person, there was a moment of conflict. His body, out of sheer force of sexual habit, wanted her; his brain, despite the ravages of the previous night, was sending out warning signals.

'Cy riding the horses everywhere, is he?'

Ibn Fayoud looked uneasy. 'Not at all,' he said. 'I hope you'll be riding for me again soon. Now I must—'

'Me too,' Kelly interrupted with a sweet smile. It was true what they said about Ibn Fayoud. The sweat was pouring down his forehead. The man was a serious user. 'Especially after York,' she added conversationally.

'York?' Ibn Fayoud managed to say. 'That was a social thing. This is business.'

'Oh, I didn't mean the Flaxton dance with Jack

Butler.' Kelly was amused to see the Arab flinch at the name. 'I meant York races.'

Ibn Fayoud smiled and glanced at his watch. The pills rattled in his hand.

'Better be going,' he said almost imploringly.

'Are you all right, sir?' Kelly looked at him more closely. 'You don't seem quite yourself.'

'Fine. I'm fine.'

Kelly made no move. 'If you happen to see Mr Butler, you can tell him I'll be going to Tokyo anyway.' Ibn Fayoud half closed his eyes as if someone had turned a knife in his guts. 'I just want to see how things go.'

'Things?' Ibn Fayoud fiddled with the car keys and eventually managed to start the engine.

Kelly stood back. 'Goodbye, sir,' she said, smiling as the Lamborghini drew away. Ibn Fayoud was in control of nothing, least of all himself. The user used. But if he was the puppet, who was pulling the strings and to what dance?

Jack Butler really didn't like the idea that he had been nobbled and worse than that, nobbled by a girl. On the surface, his routine had changed little: travelling around the country, shaking hands, keeping his staff in order, checking his contacts were behaving themselves, sleeping with his girlfriends. But he was more withdrawn, tetchy.

His father was on his back night and day. Do this, do that. However bent, however evil Jack was, it was never bad enough for his father. One spark of decency and Jack was going soft. A hint of humanity and he was a disgrace to the family name. Deep down Jack Butler was a simple man – give him a couple of Jaguars, a regular income pushing the half mill, a half-dozen talented sack-artists, preferably blond, and he'd be happy. But Reg wanted more. For Reg, book-making was a mere step along the road to riches and power on the grand scale. In a rare moment of fatherly frankness, he had once told Jack of his dreams of floating the company on the stock market, of the Reg Butler (Entertainments) Corporation being a name in the City, of maybe even being Lord Reg one day. For services to industry.

Moodily, Jack stabbed the intercom on his desk. 'Get me General Winstanley,' he said. Services to industry? Services to brutality and corruption, more like. Services to keeping the National Health supplied with patients. Services to giving his only son more grief than any mortal should have to bear.

There was a polite 'beep' from the intercom.

'He's out for a walk at present, Jack. He'll call you when he gets in. Should be a few minutes.'

That was another one. Margaret Stanhope. Jesus, that woman had turned out to be the biggest mistake of his life. All right, so she was an adequate fixer, she helped him cut corners, smoothed out the rougher edges of his life. But these days she was stepping way out of line, coming on like she had something on him, like she was something more than a two-bit secretary. Ever since York.

She knew too much to be fired and she refused to be bought out with money or offers of promotion. All she wanted was to be by his side. What had happened?

How come Jack Butler was no longer in charge? How come, all of a sudden, everything was out of control?

Ever since York. That was the worst. Wanting someone, like he wanted Kelly Connor, was no novelty to Jack – hardly a day passed when it didn't happen to him – but a quick telephone call and a Suzi or a Debra, one of his sexual Samaritans, would be there to make it feel better. This was different. Thanks to Margaret, her box of drugs and her camera, Kelly was beyond his reach probably for ever.

Jack leant back in his chair, put his feet on the desk and stared out of the window. Was that all? The fact that she was unavailable? That she was virtually unique in that she would say no to Jack Butler? He sighed. Hardly. He found that he wanted the sort of things girls, his wife even, demanded from him – chat, company, sharing.

Not just need, but affection. It was like discovering an old trick, something he hadn't done for years and had thought was dead – unnerving but not entirely unpleasurable.

Jack Butler had discovered he could still love. Shit. That was all he needed.

The intercom sounded once more.

'General Winstanley for you,' said Margaret.

Jack picked up the phone. 'Put him on.' He rubbed his eyes as if to rid himself of thoughts of Kelly Connor.

'David,' he said with a dangerous, false heartiness. 'How ya doin'? Good.' He interrupted the small talk. 'Then you can do something for me.'

The truth was that General Winstanley did quite a

lot for Jack. He told him which of his fellow owners were open to a spot of friendly blackmail, when they had a horse running that stood to lose the firm a lot of money. He put in a good word for him at meetings of the Jockey Club. He landed him invitations to society dances where Jack would normally have been lucky to be collecting coats at the door. Poor old General David Winstanley. His weakness for girls from an escort agency run by an old friend of Jack's had cost him dear over the years.

Mind you, he was never Mr Co-Operative. Even before Jack had given him his instructions he was moaning, silly old bastard.

'Shut up, General,' said Jack, suddenly losing patience. 'It's a simple job. Any of your horses running next week? Well, they are now. I want Marking Time and that three-year-old filly of yours to run at Kempton on Saturday. Of course they're ready to fucking run. Otherwise your trainer wouldn't have entered them. And get him to book Kelly Connor.'

There were sounds of protest from the other end of the telephone.

'Bollocks to the stable jockey. Bollocks to what your poxy trainer wants. You tell them. You're a general, right. Give them their marching orders. Otherwise I'll give you yours. If I don't see their names in the overnight declarations on Friday afternoon, I'll be on the blower to the *News of the World* before you can say "flagellation", right? Right.'

He slammed the phone down and allowed himself a small smile. He liked dealing with army types. They understood orders.

Predictably, Margaret Stanhope found an excuse to interrupt his thoughts within moments of his conversation with the general.

'Just a couple of letters to sign, Jack,' she said lightly. As he glanced over his correspondence, she muttered, 'You'll do anything to help that little jockey, won't you?'

Jack looked up sharply. 'I've told you about listening to my calls. What I do about Tokyo is my business.'

'Your business is my—'

'Close the fucking door behind you.'

The look of hurt astonishment which crossed Margaret's face pleased Jack. He hadn't talked to her like that for ages. It felt good. Maybe everything was going to be all right. This time he would do it himself, without Margaret, without any of her pet goons who could be guaranteed to get it wrong – to maim when they were meant to frighten, to kill when they were meant to maim. Jack sighed. If you wanted something done, you just had to do it yourself. You couldn't get the staff these days.

For Kelly, it was just like it used to be. The early-morning call, then down to the yard to get the horses ready for their big day. She hadn't been a lad for a couple of years now, but she knew the routine. Shine On had to be at the airport by ten. The four o'clock call would give her enough time to make it with ease.

She smiled as she sipped her coffee. It was the one part of the job her father had hated. Getting up early, making time, punctuality. He would doubtless disapprove of what Kelly was doing. Turning down two good, last-minute rides at Kempton in order to be a lad. But she needed to know. She had gone too far towards discovering who killed her father to turn back now.

She set the answering machine, grabbed her bag and locked up the flat. Travelling with Dennis was hardly going to be a delight, but it would be worth it. Tokyo was not just about Shine On winning a big international race and collecting a top breeding mare, she was sure of it.

Minutes later, she was down in the yard, unlocking the feed shed in the morning darkness. She'd agreed with the head lad that there was no need for him to get up extra early, but he'd insisted on leaving Shine On's feed already made up. She walked across the yard to check Shine On. As soon as Dennis arrived, she would bandage him up and they would be on their way by five thirty. She glanced at her watch. It was unusual for Dennis to be late.

It was as she approached Shine On's box that she noticed a torch light in the tack room.

'Dennis?' she said quietly. The light was snuffed out. Kelly walked over quickly to Shine On's box to check that he was unharmed. Switching on the light, she saw that he was fine.

She turned out the light and reaching for a pitchfork crept towards the tack room. It was unlocked and in darkness. When Kelly turned the light on, there was no one to be seen and nothing seemed to have been moved.

From beyond the other end of the yard, she heard

the distant whistling of Dennis, getting closer. She turned. Perhaps he would have an explanation.

She was just about to call out when she felt the iron grip of an arm clasped round her throat. Before she could scream a damp rag had been clamped over her mouth, and suddenly there was pain behind her eyes and all was darkness.

The man carried the limp body to where the Saab was parked. Expertly, he tied her hands behind her back, felt inside her pockets and took out a key. He unlocked the boot and, almost tenderly, lifted the body into it.

He looked at her for a moment. She would be out for an hour. He would have to lock the boot but he would leave the key in the ignition. By the time she was discovered, it would be too late for her to catch the plane.

The man paused before closing the boot. Her face looked calm and beautiful as it slept its enforced slumber, the lips slightly parted, the dark curls spilling over a pale cheek. Please God, she'd never discover who had done this to her. She hated him enough already. First drugs and now chloroform. It was no way to start a relationship.

The man closed the boot quietly and put the key into the ignition of the Saab.

He was whispering something, repeating it, like a chant, a mantra, a magic spell to make everything better.

'You always,' he said, swaying slightly in the darkness. 'You always hurt the one you love.'

Chapter 10

Shine On travelled so well it might have been a trip to Yarmouth. He took the long air journey and everything else in his stride like an old police horse. The high-rise stable block next to the racecourse, the lift which took him to and from his quarters with an eerie, high-tech smoothness, the canned music which wafted over the looseboxes from seven in the morning to nine at night, the noisy chatter of the Japanese stable lads – none of it concerned him. He had travelled well, lost not an ounce of weight, and eaten up since his arrival as if he were at home.

'You're a professional, that's what you are.'

Kelly patted Shine On's neck and scratched behind his ears. They had been in Tokyo for two days now and she had seen little of the sights beyond the stable block and the racecourse where the horses exercised. This evening she had agreed to look after him while Dennis explored the back streets of the city in search of Eastern decadence. It was no good telling him that one red-light district was very much like another, that there was little or nothing here that couldn't be found on a quiet night in Greek Street. Dennis had seen the films, read the magazines. The East was the place where young beauties did weird and wonderful things on stage. Bangkok, Hong Kong, Tokyo – to Dennis they were the ultimate in sleaze and kinkiness. As far as he was concerned, if Kelly wanted to turn her virginal little nose up at the idea of a good time, that was her problem.

As it happened, all Kelly could think of was the following day's big race, the one in which she should be riding but wasn't. She drained the automatic trough in Shine On's box and measured in a small amount of fresh water. Of course there would be other races, other class horses to ride but getting jocked off hurt as much as being dumped by a lover. Perhaps, after all, it had been a mistake to travel here as a stable lad. If he won, it could only add to the pain.

A Japanese stable lad walked past Shine On's box and made a clicking sound with his teeth. Kelly wasn't sure whether the greeting was lewd or merely polite, or indeed whether it was intended for her or the horse, so she smiled coolly.

No, she had been right to come. Her suspicion that there was something odd about the trip to Tokyo had been confirmed on the morning of their departure. Someone didn't want her to make the trip, and was determined enough to knock her out with chloroform and then lock her in a car to make certain that she didn't. If it hadn't been for a lad who had come to work early and a go-slow by the handling staff at the airport, they would have succeeded. She couldn't have afforded to buy her own ticket. After rushing down the M11 and round the M25, she had finally caught up with Dennis and Shine On as they waited in the horsebox on the tarmac.

She looked up at the red eye of the stables' camera as it ranged over the looseboxes. The Japanese left nothing to chance. If a horse was going to be doped, it wouldn't be from within the racecourse stables: twenty-four-hour surveillance protected every one of the runners in the big race tomorrow.

It wasn't a question of doping, almost certainly. There were too many inponderables in an international race for it to be the subject of a major gamble, with or without narcotic assistance. Not only was the form of horses from different countries difficult to equate, but there was the toll of travelling to consider, the vagaries of a foreign racetrack. Shine On was among the favourites but, Kelly was almost sure, the danger was not to him.

She locked the stable door and walked towards the lads' room, deep in thought.

'Wanna game, Kelly-san?' An Australian stable lad, playing cards with three Japanese boys, looked up and smiled at her. He was only eighteen but what he lacked in years he made up for in confidence. Ever since they had met, he had joked and flirted with Kelly, putting on an absurd Nippon accent, as if she were only holding out against his pint-sized Australian charm as a matter of form.

'No thanks, Craig,' she smiled.

'Drink? Take in a club? Tonight's the night, eh?'

'No, Craig, tonight's not the night. Stick with your game. It's all you're likely to win out here.'

'Ah, lighten up, you frigid pommie.' Kelly closed the door to the sound of male laughter. The Japanese lads spoke little English but they could recognize an exchange of small-arms fire in the international battle of the sexes, and they knew which side they were on.

Kelly used the second pass-key she had been given to check the storeroom where all the runners' tack and spare rugs were kept. The locker marked '31. SHINE ON (Brit)' was as tidy and ordered as any of them. Dennis may have been a jerk in his private life but at least he knew his job. She closed the door and locked it.

Why her? Why did someone want to stop her coming to Tokyo? Kelly pressed the button for the lift which would take her to the top floor where her sleeping quarters were. First of all, she had been jocked off Shine On, then locked in her car on the day she was meant to fly out. Why?

By some miracle, the ubiquitous canned music failed to reach the inside of the lift. Kelly leaned against the side with her head back and enjoyed a few seconds without a distant, sanitized version of a Beatles hit.

Her room was at one end of a long corridor and was the ultimate in Japanese economy. Somehow, all the basic requirements of an overnight guest – bed, table, shower, cupboard – had been compressed into a room with as much space as a British Rail toilet. Craig had told her that the men's bedrooms were spacious and airy, but Kelly was not tempted to check his claim at first hand.

She dialled a number. 'Cy?'

'Who's this?'

'This is your stable lad speaking. I was just checking that you were getting an early night.'

Cy laughed. 'I've just had dinner with the Templemans,' he said. 'Trying to make conversation with Bill as he complains about having to eat raw fish would make anyone tired.'

'Cy, don't get me wrong here, but have you time for a nightcap? I need to talk.'

There was a pause from the other end of the telephone. Cy McCray was a charming, straightforward guy but he was a man of the world. When an attractive, single woman rang you in your hotel room and suggested a nightcap, it could only mean one thing.

'Sure,' he said. 'I've got a bottle in my room.'

'I think the hotel bar would be a better idea.'

'You mean,' Cy allowed incredulity to enter his voice, 'nightcap as in drink?'

'Of course.' Kelly laughed. 'What else?'

'Nothing.' He sighed. 'Anyway, I never do it the night before a race.'

'Cy, you're a liar. You'd do it down at the start given half a chance. The Hilton bar in ten minutes, OK?'

'Sure. I'll be there.'

Ibn Fayoud bit his nails as he paced the length of his suite at the Tokyo Hilton and swore. It was eleven o'clock in the evening. He was in an exotic Eastern city. There were girls out there, clubs, interesting local drug cocktails, and he was alone, sober, in a hotel room. It was unnatural.

Ten forty-five, Butler had said, and the shifty son-of-a-bitch was late. Fifteen minutes was nothing to Jack Butler but to Ibn Fayoud, fifteen minutes without laughter, fawning waitresses, the pop of champagne corks, the flash of tanned female flesh, the breathtaking sensation of his brain humming into life under the influence of that sweet white powder – fifteen minutes without all that seemed like an eternity of deprivation.

The phone rang. Ibn Fayoud brought his hand down on the receiver like a man swatting a fly. 'Yes?' Jack's voice sounded drowsy, laconic.

'Everything in order?'

'Of course.'

'Horse all right, is it?'

'Sure. Look, could you make this quick. I have . . . people to see.'

'You're alone there, are you?'

'Of course I'm alone. What d'you think I am? Stupid?'

There was an eloquent silence from the other end of the telephone. 'We're green,' Jack said eventually. 'Go for it.'

'Fine. I'll see you in London.'

Ibn Fayoud hung up, ran a comb through his dark hair, grabbed his wallet and made for the door. At this particular moment, it didn't bother him that tomorrow his fortune would be made or broken, that his partner Jack Butler had seemed weary, almost regretful, now that there was no going back. At this particular moment, only one thing mattered to Ibn Fayoud. At last, it was playtime.

'No.' Cy sat back at a corner table in the Hilton bar and shook his head. 'To me, there's nothing odd about my being booked for tomorrow. I've ridden for Bill before, and I've ridden here before. You know yourself what an advantage it is to have ridden round a course beforehand. It's experience, that's all,' he said sympathetically. 'Your time will come.'

Kelly smiled. She knew McCray well enough to be all but certain that he was not involved with Ibn Fayoud or Butler. Maybe in the past he had tried a little less hard than was strictly ethical on a horse that, once it was down in the handicap, would be the medium of a hefty gamble, perhaps he was on rather more friendly terms with certain bookmakers than professional jockeys were meant to be, but so what? That wasn't corruption. That was racing.

Kelly put her drink down. 'I think,' she dropped her voice, 'I think there's some kind of smuggling ring that Ibn Fayoud's part of.'

'Oh yeah? What about Jack Butler?' Cy was unable to conceal his scepticism. 'I think you might be getting a little paranoid here.'

'Ibn Fayoud owes Jack Butler a fortune. That's why Pendero was stopped at Ascot. From then on, Ibn Fayoud was in his pocket.'

'And how exactly does this involve you and the ride on Shine On?'

Kelly told him of the events at the Templeman

stable on the morning of their departure for Tokyo.

'Why?' The American looked confused. 'I still don't see why they wanted to stop you coming out here.'

She shrugged. 'I can't work it out either but I'm certain it's all got something to do with my father's death. Think about it. Broom-Parker. Gould.'

'Who else knows about this?'

'Just an old friend back in Ireland and the Jockey Club. And the police, of course.'

'They believe you?'

'Who knows.'

'And now you think it was these guys who gave you chloroform and locked you in the boot of a car. Sounds more like the Boy Scouts than the international Mafia.'

Kelly sighed. Certainly, it was odd that the attempt to stop her travelling to Tokyo had been so uncharacteristically half-hearted. After all, these were the people who had clubbed her father to death, run down Broom-Parker, engineered the bloody demise of Damien Gould. She remembered the grip round her neck. Firm, determined, professional. He could have killed her, or at least put her out for a long time. Then he could have driven the car to a deserted spot and thrown away the key. But he didn't.

'Of course, it might not have been what I knew that bothered them.' Kelly muttered the words, as if talking to herself.

'Mmm?' The American's eye had been caught by a Japanese girl, sitting by herself at the bar. 'Put me to bed, Kelly,' he said quietly. 'Get me outa here or I'll blow my winnings before I've won.'

'It might have been just to get me out of the way, to

save me from something.' Kelly remembered how Jack Butler had looked at her across the table at the Flaxton dance. 'To protect me.'

Cy was raising his glass to the girl, who lowered her eyes in a parody of girlish modesty while crossing her legs. 'Jesus,' he said. 'I think I've seen heaven.'

'Cy?' Kelly touched his arm. She glanced in the direction in which he was staring and sighed. 'Thanks, Cy,' she said. 'You've been a great help.' She stood up, taking him by the arm.

'Maybe,' he said, resisting, 'maybe I'll just stay down for another nightcap.'

'What about your never-before-a-big-race rule?'

Cy smiled and looked back at the girl who had now abandoned all pretence to innocence and was staring hopefully in his direction.

He looked sheepish. 'I guess that must have been a lie.'

Like racing all around the world, Japanese racing is run on class lines. Racecourses are divided between the heaving populace, the punters, and the enclosures where the sport's aristocrats – owners, administrators, trainers, the established jockeys – can roam in relative space and comfort. At the lowest end of the social scale were stable lads.

Kelly had agreed that, if Bill allowed her to come to Tokyo as a stable lad, she would play the part. There would be no dinners with owners and trainers, no chats with Ibn Fayoud. Like Dennis, she was there to look after Shine On. The fact that, at another time on another continent, she had been his jockey was entirely irrelevant.

Now, as she stood in the ill-appointed section of the stand at Tokyo racecourse reserved for stable lads, she felt apart from the excitement all around her. She wanted Shine On to win – for Bill and Annie, for the horse itself, even for Cy McCray – and yet she was helpless against the feeling of anger at the circumstances which had led to her being in the stand looking down on the crowded racecourse rather than on Shine On's back. There was more than a part of her that dearly wanted him to run badly.

Dennis had insisted on leading the horse up, which had left Kelly free to wander the racecourse while the runners were in the paddock. She had looked at the electric board showing the ever-changing odds on the runners. An American horse Carpetbagger was the firm favourite with three other horses – Shine On, a French filly called My Ninette, and a local horse, Driver – all around the 3–1 mark.

Kelly had tried to get to the paddock but the crowd had been such that she had only been able to catch a glimpse of Shine On before she left for the stand. Despite the noise and the heat, he had seemed remarkably calm, but the French filly was black with sweat. Still, some horses didn't run their best unless they were on their toes.

Looking down from the multi-storey grandstand, Kelly watched the runners filing out on to the racecourse, and then made her move. The horses would parade in front of the stand before turning at the end of the straight and making their way to the stalls on the far side of the course. She had ten minutes before the race started.

Pushing her way through the crowd, she took the down escalator and made her way into the underpass leading to the racecourse stables. It was only a hunch, but she wanted to check Shine On's box while all eyes were on the big race.

'You all right, Kelly-san?' One of the friendlier Japanese lads was walking a horse due to run in the next race round the outer paddock as she hurried past.

'Fine, thanks,' she said.

She held up her pass to the security guard at the entrance to the stables. He eyed her suspiciously before nodding and opening the gate.

Apart from the commentator's voice which had replaced the jangling monotone of canned music, all was silence on the floor where the foreign horses were kept. The lads who were not involved in the Japan Cup would be up in the stands watching it or, like the lad outside, preparing their horses for the next race.

As casually as she was able, Kelly opened the door to the lads' room. The television was turned on, but without the sound, and there was no one watching. On the screen, the runners for the Japan Cup were cantering down to the start. She closed the door and walked past several empty looseboxes to where Shine On was kept. She could feel her pulse quickening as she got closer and told herself not to be ridiculous. All she was going to do was look inside a stable that she had every right to.

She pushed open the door and went in, kicking the sawdust on the floor. Looking for what? Kelly smiled. A large hypodermic syringe? A packet of diamonds? A shopping bag full of heroin? She moved every piece of bedding, but there was nothing. Maybe Cy was right. She was paranoid.

On the other hand, Cy had too much on his mind last night to pay attention to her suspicions. Winning the Japan Cup in the morning. Pulling the girl at the bar. It would have taken a lot more than her conspiracy theories to distract his attention from his own immediate needs and concerns.

Kelly looked at her watch. It was almost time to return to the stand. She'd just take a quick look inside the storeroom. She paused briefly at the large mahogany door. As she reached for her key, she noticed it was ajar. Senses on red alert, she slowly pushed it open – and smiled.

An old man pushing a trolley was muttering to himself. With typical hospitality, the racecourse was giving uniform, emblazoned rugs and beautifully made wooden travelling trunks to the foreign runners so that, as they returned home, they would be walking advertisements for the glories of racing in Tokyo. The man looked up at her in surprise and said something in Japanese.

'Excuse me.' Kelly shrugged apologetically and pretended to be looking for something in Shine On's locker. His new rug and bandages were already neatly placed on top of the trunk which had been hand-painted with Bill's name, round which, in much larger letters arranged in the shape of a horseshoe, were the words JAPAN CUP. Dennis would be thrilled.

The trunk was large enough to hold almost everything needed to travel one horse, and inside, next to the section which had been specially designed to hold a saddle, was an expensively made anti-cast roller. Hand-stitched in leather, with brass buckles, it was about five inches wide and went right round the horse's middle. Something similar to the roll-over bar fitted to rally cars was attached across its top. The idea of it was to prevent the horse from being able to roll right over in its stable and risk getting its legs caught in something.

'Nice,' Kelly said politely.

The old man shrugged and shuffled on with his job.

Kelly had seen enough. She turned and ran back towards the grandstand.

The lads' section was packed by the time she reached the stand and it was only with the help of Craig who, with much unnecessary touching and squeezing, found her a place beside him, that she was able to see anything.

The start was halfway up the straight. Just a short run, and then one complete circuit. A huge roar went up from the crowd as the stalls flew open. All thoughts of wrongdoing and criminality disappeared from Kelly's mind.

When the runners were some distance away, Kelly switched her focus to the enormous TV screen in front of the stands. It was nothing like those she'd seen on occasions in England where the picture looked as if it was being filmed underwater. This one was as clear as the set in her living room.

Kelly picked out the red-white colours of Ibn Fayoud tucked in behind Driver as the runners settled down some ten lengths adrift of the leader.

It had irritated Kelly that Cy hadn't asked her how to ride Shine On. Somehow, if he had it would have made her feel slightly more part of the team, but he'd seemed embarrassed whenever the horse's name was mentioned. Eventually it was a sheepish-looking Bill who had asked her to have a word with the American and she'd done it the evening before at the Hilton. Hold him up and don't hit the front too soon, she'd told him, or he'll think he's won and pull himself up. With the distraction of the girl at the bar, Kelly wondered just how much he'd taken in.

As the field raced past the stands, Kelly stood on tiptoe, holding on to Craig's shoulder, to get a better look.

'Don't worry, he's still there.' Craig put his arm round her waist. Kelly thanked him as she firmly took his hand out of her jeans pocket.

As the field turned away from the stands and Kelly switched her focus back to the screen, the leading horse slowly began to lose his position. His jockey, realizing his chance had gone, eased off the rails to let My Ninette through. The French filly was still pulling hard and quickly opened up a gap of three or four lengths from the others. One furlong later a huge roar went up as the local horse Gyroscope went after her.

Kelly's eyes were fixed on Shine On. Cy waited and waited. Then, as the jockey in front of him made his move on Driver, Cy followed. Slowly but surely, and with neither jockey appearing to move a muscle, the two cruised round the outside of three or four beaten horses and began closing on the leaders. Kelly's eyes darted from the screen to the course and then back again. The French filly was tough as nails and as Gyroscope went to tackle her as they straightened up for home, she laid her ears back and fought like a terrier to stay in front. At the two-furlong pole and with both jockeys going for their lives, the local horse got his head in front. The cheering from the partisan crowd became a deafening roar as they sensed victory.

Driver, his jockey hunched up his neck American-style, whip held upright like a cavalryman with a sword, had now gone in hot pursuit with Shine On still glued to his tail.

'Not yet, Cy,' Kelly whispered, but as she spoke the American pulled his horse out of Driver's slipstream and set sail for home. His electric change of pace made the two horses in front of him look ordinary as he swept past them, with a furlong left to run.

'You've won,' muttered Craig beside her.

A handful of different emotions jostled for Kelly's attention all at once. Pleasure that the horse she loved was going to win, bitterness that she wasn't riding him, sadness for her father, loneliness. She'd barely managed to isolate one of them when she noticed Shine On prick his ears. Driver and My Ninette had shot their bolt but the locals were still cheering Gyroscope who, under the frenzied driving of his jockey, had not yet given in.

'I don't think so,' said Kelly, almost afraid to watch the last few yards of the race. Shine On's concentration seemed to waver as he hit the wall of sound coming from the stands. He changed legs and, too late, Cy went for his whip. As Shine On and

Gyroscope flashed past the post, the crowd near the winning post were in no doubt that their favourite had got up on the line. Cy's head dropped as Gyroscope's jockey punched the air. A photograph was announced but the result was a formality.

'Needs blinkers.' Craig shook his head wisely. Like most stable lads, he could ride a great race from the safety of the stands. 'Good try, though.'

Kelly managed a smile as the crowd pushed past her on the way to the winners' enclosure. Second, against an international field, having travelled halfway round the world. It wasn't bad. The English contingent in the crowd would be celebrating, the travelling British journalists would be polishing up the old so-near-yet-so-far clichés, but there were a few who would be more subdued. Bill and Annie, Dennis, even Cy McCray. Above all, Cy. They all knew that Shine On should have won. Kelly hated herself for it, but deep in her heart she was glad Shine On had been beaten. There was still some justice left in the world. She decided not to watch them coming in.

It was hardly a night for celebration, but the plane home left in the morning and Kelly had yet to see more of Japan than Tokyo racecourse. She had wanted to spend the evening having a look round the city with Annie but she was due to play dutiful trainer's wife at a reception given by the Japanese Jockey Club.

Craig had made one last attempt to win her heart. 'Wanna go out, catch a skin show, then mebbe come back to my room and fool around a bit, darling?'

'In a word, Craig, no.'

He'd asked the next girl passing by the same question.

Dennis was still researching bizarre sexual practices of the Orient, and Cy had a date at the Hilton.

'With the love of your life?' Kelly asked as they stood by the paddock shortly after the last race. Cy had given her a subdued account of his ride on Shine On and was clearly in no mood for further postmortems.

'Right,' he said gloomily. 'With the love of my life. Suki. That's her working name anyway.'

'You don't exactly sound like love's young dream. I thought you had seen heaven.'

'Yeah, yeah.' Cy inhaled deeply on a cigarette. 'I've been to heaven and back. Lost more weight in one night than I would have in a sauna.'

'Where from? Your body or your wallet?'

He shrugged. 'Heaven doesn't come cheap. She wants to be taken out to dinner tonight.'

'Romantic.'

'Expensive.'

Kelly smiled. 'So Cy McCray's in lust with a Japanese hooker. I guess I'll just have to eat alone tonight. So much for friendship.'

Cy shot her a look of embarrassed reproach. 'If it hadn't been for you and your nightcap, I never would have met her.'

'Call me Cupid,' said Kelly. 'I'll see you tomorrow.' As he walked away, she couldn't resist calling after him, 'Hey, Cy, I hope for Suki's sake you don't come as soon as you did on Shine On.' The American put two fingers in the air and kept walking.

Back in her room, the light on Kelly's telephone was flashing. She rang down to reception.

'Two messages for Miss Connor,' the sing-song voice of the receptionist told her. 'Please to ring Mr Morley in London, any time OK. And Ibn Fayoud ring from Tokyo Hilton. He says having party at Club Joey tonight. Can you please go?'

'Club Joey?' Kelly frowned as she noted down the address. 'What's it like?'

There was a pause from the receptionist. 'Smart,' she said. 'Very funky, you know?'

Typical. Kelly smiled grimly to herself as she waited for the international operator to put her through to Nick in London. The man she most wanted to see was on the other side of the world and her only chance of seeing the bright lights of Tokyo was playing bimbo to a playboy cokehead in a funky club, whatever that was.

'Yes.' Nick's voice had an early-morning croak to it.

'Nick, it's Kelly. Sorry to wake you. I just got in.'

'How are you?'

'Fine.' Kelly was going to add that she was missing him but knew that at that moment she was probably just missing company.

'How did he go?'

Kelly took him through the race that afternoon. It was good not to have to fake an enthusiasm she didn't feel. Of all people, with the possible exception of Annie, Nick understood her disappointment.

'What about the other stuff?' he asked. 'Are you still convinced that Ibn Fayoud's up to something?'

'If he is, he's playing it cool. I've just been invited to one of his parties.' Across the thousands of miles, Kelly sensed his disapproval. 'I doubt if I'll go,' she added.

'No,' he said finally. 'I think you should. We've had a whisper that something's going on. From the Drug Squad. Maybe you can find something out, or just make a note of who he's with.'

'OK. What's been happening at home? Did either of those horses of General Winstanley's win at Kempton?'

'I don't know. I've been busy.' Kelly thought he sounded distracted.

'Are you all right?'

'Yes, it's just that I wish I were there with you.' He seemed embarrassed at what he'd said and continued quickly, 'Don't go asking questions but listen out for anything he might say. I'll see you at the airport tomorrow evening.'

'The airport?' Kelly was surprised. She would have to take Shine On and the mare back to the Templemans, so there was no question of his collecting her.

'Yes. I told the police I'd be there. Just in case.'

'Fine.' Perhaps it was the distance between them, but Kelly felt uneasy. The tone in Nick's voice as he'd spoken that last sentence was brisk, almost military. 'I'll look forward to seeing you there,' she said.

'Yes.' Nick, ever the Englishman, sounded embarrassed. 'Yes, me too.'

There were few bright lights at the Club Joey. It was a private club, situated in one of Tokyo's few quiet back streets. Kelly had not been encouraged by the appraising way the taxi driver had looked at her as he

217

took her fare at the door, nor by the knowing smile of the doorman who allowed her in almost before she had mentioned Ibn Fayoud's name. She could sense the pair of them wondering how much she charged for her services.

She was escorted by a young French waiter across a dark basement, past low tables where guests, many of them Westerners, sat on cushions. Most had a geisha girl seated beside them. There was a small dance floor with multi-coloured lights flashing from a mirrored dome, and a couple were swaying to a disco beat. Beyond them was a darker section of the club, which seemed less populated.

A fat American looked up and muttered something lewdly appreciative as she walked by.

'What goes on at the back?' she asked the waiter.

He gave a knowing little smile. 'Private rooms,' he said. 'You maybe see them later.'

So that was it. A private club with rooms at the back. Very funky. She saw Ibn Fayoud's party in a corner and was relieved to see that there were more women than men. If Ibn Fayoud had her marked as his geisha for the night, he had a shock coming. But it was too late to escape now.

'Miss Connor, you look divine.' Ibn Fayoud extended his arms as he stood up to greet her. He was wearing silk robes and his dark eyes shone.

'Sir.' Kelly held out a hand for a formal handshake. The Arab took it as if it were a precious jewel and, gently caressing the fingers, held it to his lips. Briefly, she remembered the last time they had spoken, the chill morning in Newmarket, the pinched face and sallow skin of a man coming down from a long and high narcotic journey. From the look of him, he was airborne now, any disappointment at his horse's defeat that afternoon forgotten.

A waiter brought a small silk cushion and placed it beside Ibn Fayoud as Kelly was introduced to his other guests. A couple of the men she had seen with him in England; the rest were instantly recognizable as members of his branch of the international jet set. Heavy jewellery, impeccably cut suits, vacant expressions on their well-tanned faces. Jet set? Jerk set more like.

'Kelly is the best apprentice in England, the best by far, and she rides all my horses in England,' Ibn Fayoud was saying, the words tumbling from him as if his lips could scarcely keep pace with the speed of his thoughts. She shrugged modestly, noting with some satisfaction that, even in her simple blue silk dress, she had attracted the attention of all male eyes round the table.

'Yes, sir. I'm so good that this afternoon you got someone else to ride for you.'

Ibn Fayoud was in no state to appreciate irony. He laughed loudly. 'My dear Kelly,' he trilled. 'My close friends call me Ib.'

The girls around the table laughed dutifully. In addition to the streak-haired model types without whom no Ibn Fayoud party would be complete, there was a tall black girl with a severe haircut and a dark lace dress that just failed to cover her perfect breasts, and two fragile, young Japanese girls who smiled beautifully and said little.

For a time Kelly sat quietly, trying to look interested as mindless conversation of last night's parties eddied around her, but it was difficult, particularly since the right hand of her host frequently brushed her bare knee. Sitting on the floor, she discovered, posed certain problems of etiquette.

Suddenly, he raised his voice and changed the subject, looking deeply into her eyes. 'Let me tell you all about my guests.' Kelly tuned out as he put names and uncensored biographies to the vacant faces round the table. Only the geisha girls escaped this treatment. 'They're just here for fun, aren't you, girls?' he said. The two girls averted their eyes shyly, like Cy's Hilton Suki had. Girlish modesty seemed to be big in Tokyo.

One of the blonde models stood up, affording the other guests a full view of the length of her tanned thighs.

'Well, I need to go to the girls' room,' she piped. She giggled unsteadily and tapped the side of her nose. 'I need to powder my nose.' She looked across at Kelly. 'D'you want to powder your nose, Kelly?' It was more like a challenge than an invitation.

'I'm all right, thank you,' she said coolly. It had definitely been a mistake to accept Ibn Fayoud's invitation.

'What about you, Ib? Are you—' the model allowed a sneer, directed at Kelly, to enter her voice '—all right too?'

Ibn Fayoud got to his feet and, placing a confident, proprietorial hand on the girl's right buttock, walked with her in the direction of the back rooms.

'Never says no to a spot of nose-powdering, does

220

Ib.' The man on her right, a blow-dried Italian, winked at Kelly.

'Is that what goes on at the back?'

The man gave her a gleaming smile. 'Everything goes on at the back. Would you like me to show you?'

'No thanks,' Kelly smiled. 'Doesn't he worry about his reputation? He's a member of the Qatar royal family.'

'Precisely. And he's an accredited diplomat. He has diplomatic immunity. He could roll up a fifty pound note and do a line of coke on this table and he wouldn't be arrested.' The man winked. 'But he likes the back room. He says that he can get any girl once she's done half a gram in the back room with him. That's probably why you're here.'

'You reckon?' Kelly had heard enough. She stood up, saying, 'Maybe I will powder my nose, after all.' The men round the table leered knowingly. Good old Ib had done it again.

'Room Thirty,' her Italian neighbour said. 'You'll just be in time for the party.'

Kelly walked swiftly towards the back room. She brushed past a curtain into a dark hall, with rooms on each side. There was a small peephole in each door which, she noticed from one of the rooms that had been left open, could be covered from the inside. Room Thirty was halfway down the hall.

Ibn Fayoud and his friend had not bothered to close the peephole. She remembered the Italian's words. Diplomatic immunity. Ibn Fayoud al Hassan could do anything he wanted. And right now he was. At a glass-topped dressing table he sat crouched over a line of powder, a small ivory tube up his nose. The model knelt at his feet and was attending to his other needs with her mouth.

Kelly was about to leave when she became aware that she was no longer alone.

'You like to watch?' The Italian must have followed her. His mouth was close to her right ear and a hand cupped her breast. 'Want to find another room?' The hand began a slow but determined progress across her stomach.

Kelly grabbed his index finger and, in one fluid movement, whirled round, twisting it painfully. The man gasped and fell to one knee in front of her.

'Not tonight, thanks, Julio,' she said, pushing him backwards on to the floor. The man lay, nursing his finger and looking after her in astonishment as she walked briskly towards the exit.

'Please tell Ibn Fayoud I had a migraine,' she told the doorman, taking her coat. 'I'm sure he'll understand.'

Chapter 11

Even by the standards of a British airport, it had been an unusually long delay. The deep-bellied jet, carrying six horses and their handlers, had landed an hour previously. It had taxied into a bay by the Customs building, cut its engines and now waited in silence to be unloaded.

'Some sort of Customs hold-up, I believe,' a steward with carefully coiffed hair and an unnatural tan had told Kelly. The steward had long since shed his air of courtly politeness. They were on the ground. He was doing Miami tomorrow. His boyfriend would be ready and waiting for him in Putney. Frankly, the last thing he needed was some check-up by the drugs boys.

'Can't we just transfer the horses?' Dennis had seemed distinctly edgy during the flight. Now he was fumbling with a packet of duty-free cigarettes.

'Not until we're given the green light,' said the steward tetchily. 'In the meantime, there's still no smoking, please.'

Dennis sat back in his seat and closed his eyes with a martyred sigh. 'British fucking Airways,' he muttered.

'*This is Captain Briggs again.*' The intercom crackled into life as if in reply. '*I apologize for the delay. Our colleagues in Customs wish to make a routine, on-board check-up and are apparently involved in a situation involving an earlier flight.*'

'Bureaucratic bastards,' said Dennis.

'*I'm told that they will be attending to us in a matter of moments.*'

An earlier flight. Kelly found herself wondering whether it was the one taken out of Tokyo by the Templemans and Cy McCray. Bill and Annie had sped off to the airport as soon as they had seen Shine On and Ibn Fayoud's new mare, who had arrived at the racecourse stables the previous night, safely on their way. Kelly had called Cy at seven thirty to check that he had survived his night in heaven. He had, at considerable cost to his wallet. According to Cy, the trip to Tokyo had turned out to be one of his more expensive jaunts; all he had gained was a Tokyo Jockey Club tie and an ornate courtesy suitcase they liked to give visiting jockeys. That, and a few tender memories, Kelly had said. Cy had laughed, wincing at the memory. Tender was right.

'Uh-oh, here come the marines.' The airline steward hurried by them with a tight little smile on his face. As soon as the Drugs Squad people were on board, he would be on his way. Kelly looked out of the window. Ground staff were pushing mobile steps towards the front of the aircraft as a van approached.

The driver opened the back door and two men with golden retrievers jumped out. Dennis stared straight ahead like a man who had just been given a death sentence. 'Sniffers,' he whispered.

Four men, including the two with dogs, entered the passenger cabin with a grim, purposeful air. One of the men spoke to the passengers one by one as the sniffer dogs worked their way down each side of the aisle, tails wagging in anticipation.

Dennis gripped the side of his seat as a dog approached. It yelped as it reached his carrier bag.

'Excuse me, sir.' The Customs officer reached down for the bag. He spilt the contents on to a vacant seat. A number of magazines and various plastic sex aids fell out.

'Had a good holiday, did you, sir?'

The man smiled nastily at Dennis who shrugged and muttered, 'Free country, innit?'

The Customs officer turned the bag upside down and unzipped a small pocket underneath it. 'What's this?' he said, pulling out a bag of white powder.

'Oh, Dennis,' Kelly groaned as the Customs man recited his rights.

'Never seen it before in my life,' he said unconvincingly.

After they had completed their search, one of the men escorted Dennis down the steps. The other three stayed on board.

'We'd like to see the horses now, please, miss,' one of them said to Kelly.

She took them through to the back of the aircraft. Shine On and the mare seemed unworried by the delay.

'Quiet, are they?' one of the men asked her as he untied one of the hay nets and began methodically pulling out the hay.

Kelly nodded. 'They're all right.'

The dogs were excitedly wagging their tails, oblivious of the horses. The senior Customs man patted Shine On and felt his rug. He then prodded the new anti-cast roller. He looked significantly at Kelly before pulling a penknife from his pocket. Moving close to Shine On, he cut into the stitching. White powder spilled from it on to the sawdust. One of the sniffer dogs barked ecstatically.

Kelly stood and watched in shock. She cursed herself for being so stupid as she thought back to the old man in the storeroom. 'Of course,' she said. 'It had to be.'

'Yes.' The Customs officer stood up, licked a finger covered in powder and walked slowly towards her. 'It had to be, didn't it?' he said knowingly. 'So what's a nice girl like you doing smuggling high-grade smack into the country, eh?'

She should have been an actress. The show that Margaret Stanhope put on in the arrivals lounge was worthy of the West End. They were her friends, she told the young man with spots who was doing duty on the information desk. Flying in from Tokyo. Her lips quivered, her hand fluttered at her breast. If they didn't arrive she didn't know where she would stay tonight since she had just flown in herself from Scotland. The young man, who had heard about situations like this from the older hands, was soon caught up in the drama. It was more than his job was worth, he said, as he rang through to Customs.

Eventually the word came through. Four passengers from two different flights from Tokyo had been detained in Customs. He gave her the names. Before he could suggest that maybe, since his shift ended in half an hour, he could help her in some way, Margaret had turned on her heel and was on her way. Within moments, a couple of Drugs Squad officers hurried through to the information desk, but it was too late. All they found was a disappointed young man with spots.

Margaret gunned her Golf out of the short-term car park.

So Templeman was delayed in Customs. McCray was nicked. So was the stable lad. In fact, the only bit of good news was that the Kelly woman had been nabbed too.

Jack had done it, the righteous bastard. Pulled the plug on the whole operation. It was time for her to teach him a lesson.

And she knew just where to find him.

It was the longest three hours of Kelly's life. Three hours of questioning in an airless room lit by bright strip-lighting. Three hours in the company of two detectives who, like an alternative comedy double act, took turns at asking her the same questions in different ways. Who had she met in Tokyo? Where had the rugs come from? What was the name of her contact in England? Why did she do it? Money? Love? A ruthless boy friend? She could tell them. They were her friends. If she was a good girl, they'd see her all right when it came to court. Why not save everybody a load of bother and tell the truth? That's what the others were doing. Jim and John took turns to keep up the barrage of questions. Fat, threatening Jim who reeked of aftershave, and soft-voiced, wheedling John. Once, they both left her, doubtless in order to discuss their tactics. The woman police constable had been friendly, almost human, before she too started on the questions.

For a while, Kelly had tried to interest them in the events leading up to the trip to Tokyo, but the policemen made it clear that they were only interested in the truth and not some clever smokescreen. Tokyo was what they were interested in. She told them about the day of the race, the old man with the rugs, the call to Nick Morley.

'Is he here?' she asked. At first, she had assumed that Nick would see that she was released quickly. Out of an obscure sense of loyalty, she had sensed that it would be unwise to bandy his name about.

John glanced at Jim, who said, 'We're the ones asking the questions around here, Miss Connor.'

'But I was the one who tipped him off, for God's sake,' said Kelly with a flash of anger. 'He said he'd meet me at the airport.'

After another few minutes of questioning, both men left her alone once again with the woman police constable. Five minutes later, Nick was at the door.

'Sorry I've been so long,' he said. 'I was helping down the passage. They've charged McCray and Bill, I'm afraid.'

She'd hoped for an embrace or some sign of pleasure from him at seeing her. But he sounded as if he was forcing himself to be polite.

'It's crazy.' For the first time, Kelly was unable to keep a crack of emotion from entering her voice. The two policemen appeared in the doorway behind Nick. 'Tell them about Ibn Fayoud.'

'I have. He's seeing business contacts in Hong Kong. They'll be talking to him when he flies in.'

The smaller of the two policemen stepped forward and said with an ingratiating smile, 'We'll probably be needing you as a witness when your friends come to court. In the meantime, Miss Connor, you're free to go. Thank you for your co-operation.'

Nick smiled and took her bag as they emerged at last into the arrivals hall. He seemed more like his old self. 'Drink?'

'Yes, I'd love one, but not here. I never want to see an airport again in my life.'

'You'd better stay with me. You look too tired to get home and the horses have been collected.'

'What about Dennis?'

'He was released an hour ago. They tested the stuff they found in his bag and discovered it was talcum cut with bleach. Apparently some sex shop had sold it to him as an aphrodisiac. The airport police knew that no one that stupid could be a smuggler and they let him go.'

For the first time in several hours, Kelly laughed.

If anybody could take Jack Butler's mind off his troubles, it was Roseanne. Eighteen, a fresh-faced natural

blonde with a perfect face and a flawless body, she
had been hired as a teller in the Dagenham shop. One
look at her – a look she had returned with interest –
had been enough to convince Jack that she was too
good to be stuck behind a counter; she had the potential to go places. Like to central office, where she
worked in accounts, to clubs where she discovered
that, after a few glasses of champagne, she could
forget that Jack reminded her of her father, and to his
London flat which she visited whenever Jack asked
her. Which was quite often these days.

But this afternoon, not even Roseanne could shake
him out of it. Her flawless body, now stretched care-
lessly across the bed, meant nothing to Jack; her
perfect face, smiling sympathetically, was almost
irritating. Relax, she said, we don't have to do anything. She giggled. 'Sex isn't compulsory, you know.
We can just talk.'

'Talk?' Jack muttered. Christ, he felt old. 'Yeah,
there's always that.' And what exactly, he reflected
grimly, could they talk about? Smuggling maybe?
Drugs? How, with one simple call, he had put an end
to his father's grandiose plans? Or the future, now
that Jack had pulled back at the moment of truth?
Maybe they could talk about that.

'You. Me.' Roseanne laid her head on Jack's shoulder and ran her nails gently through the hairs on his
chest. 'Us.'

'Mm?' Right now Jack could think only of himself
and things he could never tell Roseanne, or any of the
other Roseannes. Jack Butler. Formerly as in Jack the
Lad. Now as in Jacked It In.

'Doesn't matter,' she was saying. 'This often happens.'

'To men of my age?' He put his hand on hers. He really didn't feel like being touched right now.

'No.' It was a squeak of protest. 'To anyone. You've got a lot on your mind, haven't you? The business. Your marriage.'

Jack glanced down at her. What the fuck had his marriage got to do with this? 'Oh yeah,' he said eventually, with a convincing sigh. 'It gets to you after a while.'

'Love you, Jack, you know that.'

'I love you too, doll.'

For a moment, they lay there on the bed. She was thinking of what her parents would say when she broke it to them that Jack Butler – the Jack Butler – was leaving his wife for her, and he was wondering whether they would keep Kelly Connor in custody. Then the doorbell rang.

Jack closed his eyes wearily. It couldn't be the police, or his father, or his wife, none of whom were aware of the existence of this flat. There was only one person who knew where he would be this afternoon.

The bell rang again, more insistently this time.

He extricated himself from Roseanne, slipped on a silk dressing gown and walked into the next room. 'Yeah,' he said into the intercom.

'Jack. Sorry. It's urgent. Must see you.' Margaret Stanhope's voice lost none of its sharpness over the intercom.

'I'll ring you later. I've got business right now.'

'She can wait.' It was odd how imperious Margaret

had become of late. Sometimes she behaved as if he were the hired hand, not her. 'I need five minutes right now,' she said.

Sighing, Jack pressed a button to let her in.

'Sorry, darling,' he said to Roseanne. 'Duty calls.'

'Nanny Margaret?'

He smiled at the nickname Roseanne liked to use. 'Right first time. I'll get rid of her as quick as I can.' He closed the bedroom door.

Margaret was standing outside the front door to the flat when he opened it. She looked at him, standing there in his dressing gown and bare feet, with undisguised disapproval.

'I told you never to—'

'Shut it,' said Margaret, brushing by him and making straight for the cocktail bar in the corner. There was a time when she had fantasized about afternoons spent in this flat with Jack Butler, but not any more. She had grown up. As she poured herself a whisky on the rocks, she nodded in the direction of the bedroom. 'Who is it?'

'Mind your own fucking business.'

'It's your fucking business I'm more concerned about. Can she hear us?'

Jack walked over to a sound stack in the corner and pressed a button. The sound of Jason Donovan, Roseanne's favourite, filled the room. 'No,' he said.

Margaret sat on the sofa and took a swig of whisky. 'Presumably you know that we've been busted,' she said.

'What exactly are you talking about?' Suddenly Jack looked absurd in his silk dressing gown, old even.

'Someone blew the whistle on Tokyo. Templeman, McCray, one of the stable lads and your little friend have been arrested.'

Jack tried a smile. 'Well, none of them can point the finger at us. What about Ibn Fayoud?'

'He's in Hong Kong. They're looking for him.'

'They're not the only ones, I shouldn't wonder. There was half a million quid's worth in that shipment. His contacts are not going to be at all pleased.'

'His contacts? And what about us?'

'Oh, we're clean.' Jack opened a box of cigars on the cocktail bar and lit up. 'I've covered our tracks completely.'

'You know what I think, Jack?' Margaret leant back in the chair and crossed her legs. 'You set it up. You've been unhappy about the way Reg was expanding the business and this was your way of getting out. Jack Butler goes straight. You bottled it.' There was contempt in her voice. 'Because all Jack Butler really wants is to be a little bookmaker who appears on telly and gets to take young girls to bed when the fancy moves him.'

She had to go. Jack looked at the woman who had once made his job so easy and was now making it so impossible. Not just out of this flat, but out of his life.

'Thank you, Margaret,' he said quietly. 'Now would you be so kind as to get the fuck out of here?'

She stood up, ambled over to him and fingered the collar of his dressing gown thoughtfully.

'I've done a lot for you, Jack, over the past few years. I've sold my soul for you. I really don't know what I'd do if you went straight on me. I've outgrown the loyal secretary lark.'

'I've told you. I'll promote you.'

'But I don't want promotion, Jack.' Margaret leant against him. She could smell his body now. 'I don't want money. I want to run the business. Run it my way. Jack and Margaret. You front it with your famous personality and I deal with the mucky bits behind the scenes. It's a simple dream, I know, but I really do want it, Jack.'

'You are one mad bitch,' he said uneasily. 'And what about my father?'

'I can handle Reg,' she said dismissively.

'No.' Butler stepped back. 'I've had enough of the deception, the lies, the cheating.' He shrugged. 'I'm through with our dealing friends. You've got the choice. You can stick with me and go straight or go paddle your own canoe.'

'Deception? Lies? Cheating?' Margaret spat the words out. 'What the fuck d'you call this flat? You want me to tell Charmaine what you get up to?'

'She's too sensible to believe a vicious bitch like you.'

'Unless—' Margaret walked quickly to the sofa, picked up her bag and reached inside it. 'Unless she saw these.' She threw some photographs on the sofa. 'What do you think?'

Jack looked down at the prints. He recognized them instantly.

'Some racing snaps,' Margaret said. 'A famous young jockey offering a spare ride. Kelly Connor, Jack Butler up.' She looked at one of the prints and smiled coldly. 'Or almost up anyway.'

She gathered up the photographs and put them into her bag which she snapped shut.

'Think about it,' she said, glancing at Jack who stood immobile in the middle of the room. 'Sorry to interrupt.'

Gently, sarcastically, she closed the door as she left.

The Foreign Office exists to avoid unpleasantness, to camouflage the unpleasantness of Us and to neutralize the unpleasantness of Them. As far as Mark Fowler and his colleagues in the FO's Arab Section were concerned, the Emirate of Qatar counted as Us, and the events set in motion by the indiscretion of one Ibn Fayoud al Hassan were no more than a routine exercise in damage limitation.

Yet another indiscretion caused by one Ibn Fayoud. Fowler had been in the job almost twenty years and was no stranger to the waywardness of certain Arab diplomatic staff – shop-lifting princesses, gun-running naval attachés, the occasional attempt to smuggle schoolgirls out of the country in a diplomatic bag – they all ended up on his desk, but Ibn Fayoud's behaviour had tested his patience before. The man was becoming a monumental pain. It would be good to send him packing once and for all.

Gatwick and Heathrow were well trained these days. Before some noddy appeared in front of a press conference to crow triumphantly about another battle won in the war against the international drug barons, they would put a call through to Fowler's office just to check that none of the said international drug barons were in fact friends of HMG. Or friends of friends of HMG. Or even HMG itself.

Within an hour of discovering that certain high-class nags were carrying a few kilo overweight in the form of heroin, Mark Fowler had been made aware that the incident had a diplomatic dimension. The horses, and quite possibly their illegal cargo, belonged to Ibn Fayoud. By some miracle of good fortune – knowing the man, it would have nothing to do with judgement – Ibn Fayoud was wandering about the Far East, which would make Fowler's task a good deal easier.

He called an old friend at the Consulate of Qatar to express his concern. The man promised to talk to Sheikh al Hassan and ring Mark back.

With Ibn Fayoud temporarily in 'Pending', Fowler moved on to his next problem. A member of the Omani diplomatic staff had been caught in the bushes of St James's Park with a Guardsman. Ye gods and little fishes. Fowler wearily dialled another number. What a way to earn a living.

Sheikh al Hassan had been having a particularly difficult day when the news of his son's latest misfortune reached him. If his son had been in his office with him, the Sheikh might have been tempted to raise his voice, even to direct one of the weighty ivory ornaments on his desk at the young fool's head. But, fortunately for him, the boy was away on a business trip. Sheikh al Hassan pressed a button on his desk and asked his secretary to summon Simon Brompton-Smiley to his office. The days of Ibn Fayoud's business trips were drawing to a close.

Ten minutes later, the Sheikh's international racing manager was ushered in.

'I'll spare you the details, Simon.' Doubtless, Brompton-Smiley would find out through his normal contacts the precise details of Ibn Fayoud's indiscretion. At the moment, something approaching embarrassment constrained the Sheikh from confiding in him. 'Suffice to say that my son has, over the past few days, gone too far.'

'Too far, sir?' Brompton-Smiley looked puzzled.

'Yes. Too far.' Sheikh al Hassan sat back in his chair, rolling his worry beads. The occasional nonsense with drugs, or money, or women, he could understand, but smuggling – yes, that was certainly going too far. His oldest son had shamed the family name. Sheikh al Hassan felt the deep tiredness of a disappointed parent. He wanted to get rid of this silly, frowning Englishman as soon as possible. He needed to be alone.

'He will be returned home for an indefinite period. I shall take over his racing and breeding interests until the end of the season, at which point I shall sell his horses and move mine to France as we have discussed. This shall be announced in due course but you are to tell no one until I give the word. Merely inform the Jockey Club that the ownership of all my son's horses has been transferred to me.'

'Yes, sir.' Brompton-Smiley nodded thoughtfully. He looked forward to the moment when he could break the news to Nick Morley. 'Would you like the horses with Templeman to be moved to Gardem's yard.'

'No,' the Sheikh said absently. 'Let them stay there for the moment.'

Brompton-Smiley, aware that his audience with his employer was over, stood up. 'I'm very sorry, sir. If there's anything else I can do—'

'No, thank you, Simon,' said Sheikh al Hassan. 'That will be all.'

Alone again, the Sheikh put through a call to the Embassy.

It had all been quite civilized, Mark Fowler reflected when confirmation came through from the Consulate that Ibn Fayoud would be met at Heathrow the following day and put straight on a private jet bound for Doha. Naturally, the Drugs Squad boys would want their pound of flesh and, at some stage, would be allowed to refer to 'an unnamed diplomat who has since been expelled'. At some point, too, over the next few days, the Qatari Consul would be requested to visit the Foreign Office for a cup of tea and a chat which would later be described as a 'formal protest'. It would all take its course in the normal way of things. In the unlikely event of the press taking an interest, it was always sensible to show that the proprieties had been observed in these cases. It was something of an arse-covering exercise, of course. Mark Fowler smiled as he put his report on the Ibn Fayoud incident into the out tray. But then even plump, pinstriped Foreign Office arses needed to be covered sometimes.

Nick Morley believed in the curative powers of strong drink. He gave Kelly an exotic version of a brandy mix which almost lifted the top of her head off. It was just what she needed.

At first, when he had brought her back here from the airport, her anger at what had happened had spilt out in a torrent of words. Nick had put a call through to Gatwick airport and discovered that Bill and Cy McCray were to be detained overnight in the local police station, Bill because they'd found drugs hidden inside the travelling trunk, and McCray because the suitcase he had been given in Tokyo was sealed with yet more heroin.

Now, as the brandy did its work, Kelly needed to know more about what had happened.

'Bill's not involved in this,' she said quietly, cupping the glass in her hands. 'It's the last thing he'd do, however much he needed the money. He was the one who didn't want Ibn Fayoud entering his horses in different races around the world, or trading in foreign mares.'

Nick sat across the room in a deep leather chair, his legs crossed and his tie half undone.

'You and I know that,' he said. 'But try convincing the police. There's just no proof.'

'And how about Cy? It could destroy his career.'

'It might have been worse. What if you had been riding Shine On?'

Kelly shook her head. The brandy cocktail was reacting with her jet lag, making it difficult to think straight.

'If someone didn't want me riding in Tokyo and was even prepared to knock me out to prevent me getting to the airport, they must have known that something was likely to go wrong.'

'It could be. D'you have friends in the drug-dealing community?' Nick smiled questioningly.

'Jack Butler maybe.' Kelly still found it hard to associate the man she had met at York with drugs and violence, but that's how it looked. Perhaps that night was all a figment of her imagination. Nothing seemed certain any more.

'What about Ibn Fayoud himself?' Morley stood up and walked over to the telephone. 'He needed the money desperately enough.'

'No.' Kelly remembered the last time she had seen him, hunched in a back room of the Club Joey, helplessly indulging his favourite habits. A pathetic figure. 'I think he was being used too.'

Nick was dialling a number. 'Indian?' He smiled. 'You must be hungry. They deliver to the door.'

Kelly nodded gratefully. He had his life organized to perfection. Nick Morley, the perfect bachelor. Maybe the perfect husband? She had her doubts. He could be as caring as anyone she'd ever met, but his time in the army had left its mark, or perhaps it was his childhood. There'd been a brief moment at the airport when she'd detected a frightening coldness about him. Now, while they waited for the take-away to arrive, his mind seemed to be not on her but on other matters. Then suddenly he snapped his attention back to their conversation, and she saw it again, a determined, almost fanatical side to him as he went over the evidence with her again and again.

'We're as bad as each other,' she said at one point. 'I'm obsessed with my father's death. You're obsessed with cleaning up racing.' She rubbed her eyes. 'And they'll probably beat us both in the end.'

He looked at her sharply. 'What gives you that idea?'

'There are always more where the Butlers and Ibn Fayouds come from. More plausible villains. More weak-willed playboys. There's a waiting list to get into crime.'

'We can win the battle but they will win the war,' Nick Morley said bitterly, almost to himself. 'You know where I last heard that? Northern Ireland. In the SAS. Every time we dropped a Paddy, discovered an arms cache, took out an IRA hit team, there was some professional wetback who'd come out with it.'

'This isn't quite the same, is it?'

Nick smiled, but his eyes spoke of past horrors committed in the name of winning the battle, or the war, or just winning. 'For me it is,' he said quietly.

He stood up, then knelt before Kelly. He took her chin, lifting her face towards his, and looked into her eyes. The iciness was leaving him now and he sounded almost triumphant. 'Come to bed?'

Kelly shook her head. Somewhere in her body she could feel a guard going up against him. 'I'll stay here,' she said. 'Tonight I need to sleep alone.' She kissed him chastely on the cheek.

He stood up and looked down on her and, for a moment, she felt uneasy, like a spoil of war.

'Of course,' he said, and smiled.

It was twenty-four hours since the Tokyo operation had hit the rocks, twenty-four hours in which Margaret Stanhope had been busy regrouping, planning, making moves to sort out the mess that others, softer and less determined than her, had left behind them. A plume of smoke rose from the cigarette in her hand as she sat in her car, waiting on a side street in Newmarket. She narrowed her eyes. She hadn't had much sleep last night, but then she didn't have time for sleep right now. She was good in a crisis; she acted while others considered their position. By the time the rest of the world caught up with her, it was too late. Margaret Stanhope was in control.

'Come on, little girl.' Margaret inhaled deeply on her cigarette. 'I haven't got all day.' She smoothed the photograph that lay on her lap with a slow caress. There were other shots of Jack, but this was the one she kept with her at all times. She looked at his naked, muscular shoulders, his neat, almost girlish waist, his broad back. He wasn't as tough as he liked to make out. She knew that now, as surely as she knew that she had manoeuvred him into a position where he'd welcome the future that she offered, welcome it with open arms. Margaret clenched her teeth as her body trembled with a passing spasm of desire.

Ambition. Love. The need for security. It was all wrapped up in Jack Butler's perfect frame. It didn't matter that he had proved to be a touch soft at the edges. She liked sensitive men. And she was tough enough for both of them.

The lights in Kelly Connor's flat were still on. Margaret picked up the car phone. She'd call the girl, summon her to meet her destiny.

No. That would be a mistake. Get her on the wrong foot, take her by surprise, that was the way.

Margaret dialled another number. There was no reply from Jack's flat. She tried the number in his car.

'Shit,' she said, as it rang unanswered. She really wanted to talk to Jack right now.

When she rang his home, it was the squeaky voice of his wife that answered.

'Oh hi, Margaret, hold on a minute.' It was one of Charmaine's many affectations that she liked to give the illusion that every call to her had interrupted some astonishingly important task. Like leafing through a magazine. Or arranging an appointment with a hairdresser. Or heaving a large glass of sherry to her cute little lips. ' 'Fraid he's not here at present. Said he had to go on a trip.'

A trip? What the fuck?

'I'm surprised that you didn't know.' Charmaine gave a nervous laugh.

'Yes, of course. I knew that he had to go on a trip. I thought it was tomorrow. When is he due back? I don't have his diary with me.'

'That's just it.' Charmaine sounded puzzled. 'He said he didn't know. He said it was . . . open-ended.'

'Of course. It would be.'

'Is he all right? He sounded a bit out of sorts on the phone. Like he had something on his mind.'

'I'm sure he's fine, Charmaine. I'll just call our Bradford office. They'll know where he is.'

'Honestly, men. One moment they're . . .'

Margaret held the phone loosely in her hand. She had heard the Charmaine Butler theory of life, love and the universe before. That bastard. Where the hell had he gone? And which of his many bimbos did he have in tow?

'Better run now, Charmaine,' she said lightly, hanging up with a suitably girlish farewell.

Open-ended? She'd give him open-ended when she found him. As slippery as eels, those Butlers.

Glancing up at Kelly Connor's flat where the lights still shone brightly, Margaret reflected on her call to Reg last night.

The old man had been curiously cool when she had told him that Jack had blown the whistle on the Tokyo run. That's a pity, was all he said as if he'd known for ages. She'd added that Jack seemed to have gone cold on the whole idea of expansion. Must be mid-life crisis, he said, as if his son were indulging in some piddling eccentricity rather than putting all her plans – all Reg's plans – in jeopardy. Can you talk? she had asked. Not exactly, Reg muttered, but she hadn't believed him because, when Reg Butler had private business to discuss on the phone, he merely told his wife to fuck off to another room. He was no New Man, was Reg. Sunday, as usual? No, said Reg. That's not convenient. Leave this one with me and I'll get right back to you.

Leave it with him. He must be joking. Margaret hadn't got where she was today by trusting men like Reg Butler, or his shifty son, or anyone else for that matter.

She stubbed out a cigarette as the light in Kelly's window was switched off. Picking up her favourite, slightly dog-eared photograph of her naked employer, she took out of her bag an envelope with two other prints in it and put it on the dashboard.

The girl appeared in jeans and sweater at her front door. She looked good, Margaret thought as she approached; not as cute as the last time she had seen her but not bad considering she had clothes on.

'Kelly Connor?'

The girl turned from fumbling with the lock. 'Yes?' she said warily.

'Jill Turnbull, Reuters. I wonder if I could have a brief word with you.'

Kelly Connor looked pale and distracted. 'It's not a good moment,' she said crisply.

'I know it isn't.' Margaret smiled. 'But, believe me, it would be in your very best interests to give me just two minutes. We could talk in my car over there.'

Kelly looked uncertain.

'It's not about Gatwick,' Margaret added.

There was something about the way the woman threw 'Gatwick' into the conversation that alarmed Kelly. It was the first that she had heard about the press getting hold of the story. 'Two minutes,' she said and walked purposefully towards Margaret's Golf.

'Cigarette?' Margaret was keen not to hurry this. She looked at the Connor girl as she sat uneasily in the passenger seat of the car. Yes, she really was quite appealing; on this occasion, there had been nothing wrong with Jack's taste.

'Thanks, no. How can I help you?'

Margaret lit up, filling the car with smoke. She was going to enjoy this.

'My people have been sent some material about

245

you, Miss Connor,' she said slowly, as if weighing up her words carefully. 'Rather sensitive material, as it happens. Drugs, betting—' She paused for effect. '—sex. The feeling among my people is that it will make quite a story.'

Kelly looked across sharply. 'I can't think what you're talking about,' she said.

'No, I'm sure you can't. My people, most of whom are rather disgusting middle-aged men, seem a lot more interested in the more intimate side of the story than anything else. You see,' Margaret pursed her lips as if embarrassed by the task she had to perform, 'we know all about you and Jack Butler.'

'What?' Kelly gave a nervous laugh. 'I've only met the man once.'

'Well, once would certainly seem to be enough for you. Under the circumstances.'

The woman's confidence unnerved Kelly. 'What circumstances?'

Margaret reached for the envelope on the dashboard and, with a reluctant shrug, passed it across. Kelly opened it slowly, took one look at the top photograph and gave a little gasp of disbelief. She covered it with her hands and sat with her eyes closed for a moment.

'They're fakes,' she said eventually.

'My people say they're genuine. Girl jockey in sex romps with TV bookie. It won't look good, will it?'

'I was drugged.'

'Fortunately all is not lost. I have a friend who's marginally involved in this business. The details are unimportant, but it really would help this friend of mine if you spoke to the police.'

Kelly had opened her eyes, and stared straight ahead of her. 'Go on,' she whispered.

'I think I can persuade my people to destroy the negatives if you just explained to the law how Ibn Fayoud approached you and persuaded you to bring his horses back from Tokyo with their special little packages.' Margaret held up her hand as Kelly tried to interrupt. 'You didn't know that drugs or smuggling were involved, of course. But it was Ibn Fayoud who was behind it all. Ibn Fayoud and no one else.'

'You're not a journalist, are you?' A harshness had entered Kelly's voice. 'You work for them.'

'Who I am is not your problem.' Margaret lightly touched Kelly's hand which still covered the photographs. 'But these are.'

Kelly withdrew her hand sharply, and Margaret picked up the photographs. She looked, almost tenderly, at the top print, which had been smudged by Kelly's damp palm.

'Why can't you just leave me alone?' Kelly said.

'But I will. When you've spoken to the police. I'll call you later to check that everything's all right.'

Like a zombie, Kelly Connor opened the car door and stepped out. She felt sick.

The car started and Margaret gave a chummy wave before driving away at speed, leaving Kelly standing at the side of road, wondering whether her life could get any worse.

Jack Butler had never done this before. All his life, he had ducked and dived, but he had never turned his back on the other side, however tough things were, never turned tail. He looked across at Roseanne who was singing tunelessly to a tape on the car cassette. It was a big adventure to her. Jack was a wild, romantic hero who had swept her off her feet like some knight in shining armour. He clutched the driving wheel and stared at the motorway ahead of him. Why had he involved this little girl? What was he, afraid to face them alone? In need of blonde company, even at this desperate stage? He smiled palely as she turned and touched his thigh.

Some knight in fucking armour. Up to his neck in it, sweating with fear, out of control and driving, fuck knows where, just driving. Running.

Chapter 12

Over the next few days she was haunted by the pictures. Her mind continuously flashed up the images of Jack Butler's naked body leaning over her. She felt physically sick every time it happened.

The rest of the time she thought of her father. The time when he had been there, advising and encouraging her, seemed now to belong to a distant, innocent age when life was harsh but simple. Since his death, she had ridden winners – no one who saw her on Shine On at York or in subsequent races could doubt that she had the ability and strength to make it to the top – but now that golden future was under a dark cloud of uncertainty. Violence, blackmail and corruption seemed to be following her every footstep.

The worst of it was that Kelly knew she had brought it on herself. If she had listened to the advice of Annie and others, the nightmare of the past few days would never have happened, or at least it would have happened to someone else rather than to her and those who worked with her. Kelly thought of Bill and Cy, bystanders struck down by events that crashed forward heedlessly, like a freight train on which the brakes had failed.

Once the press had picked up the story of Shine On's eventful return from Tokyo, the careers of the two seemed doomed. Both men protested their innocence at a magistrates' court and were committed for trial in a month's time at the Old Bailey. In the meantime, they were released on bail and, it was announced by the Jockey Club, were 'entirely free to pursue their careers until charges against them have been proved'.

Fortunately for Bill the majority of his owners were unwavering in their belief in him. Apart from the change of ownership to Ibn Fayoud's horses, which wouldn't affect him until the following season, there were no dramatic changes in the yard. Annie became more involved in the horses' training than ever before, partly because Bill was too preoccupied to do the job properly and partly through a discreet, unpublicized agreement between them that, should he be found guilty at the Old Bailey, she would immediately apply for a trainer's licence and continue to run the yard. Fiercely loyal to their employer, the lads found no difficulty in taking their instructions from the guv'nor's wife; in fact, some of them claimed that the horses were going better under the changed regime.

It was tougher for Cy. A freelance jockey, however senior, depends on good will; there's no room for sentiment or loyalty in his life. Some trainers neglected to book him because, they said, he had too much on his mind to ride at his best. Others claimed that their owners were unhappy to be employing a man suspected of smuggling drugs. But most of them didn't bother with excuses. McCray was out. Next season maybe, if he was given a clean bill of health by the beak at the Old Bailey, it could be a different matter. Until then, it was like he had the plague.

Kelly took to calling him most evenings. At first, he would answer the telephone eagerly, managing to conceal his disappointment that the call was not from one of his trainers offering him a ride. In those early days, he was like a man caught up in a nightmare, convinced that one morning he would wake up and find that his life had returned to normal. But gradually, the hope in his voice faded. Frequently, Kelly noticed a slurring incoherence which suggested that Cy was taking something to help him through the bad times – Valium perhaps, or grass, or even good old-fashioned alcohol. Whatever the drug was, it was changing him. He became surly, cynical, defeatist.

Just ride the horses. That was what Frank Connor would have said. They may be cussed and unpredictable but, compared to life outside racing, they were simplicity itself. His advice would have meant nothing to Cy, who had become obsessed with the cruel hand fate had dealt him and whose rides were now restricted to the occasional no-hoper, but it kept Kelly going through the dark days.

She also thought about Nick. She hadn't seen him since the day he'd collected her from the airport. He'd phoned a couple of times asking her out to dinner but she'd put him off. She still felt slightly uneasy about him, though she knew that it was thanks to him that she had not been implicated in the Tokyo scandal. As a result, she continued to receive offers of spare rides.

There was a hard, driven quality to the way she rode these days; the conviction that, sooner rather than later, her world, like Cy's and Bill's, would come crashing about her ears lent a recklessness to her race riding. Nothing mattered any more, only winning, only proving that she could do it before it was all taken away from her.

She won several races and, as the flat season drew to a close, she finally became a fully-fledged jockey, losing her claim. But she realized that she too, was running on a drug.

The drug was anger. In the weighing room, in the paddock, at the start, even during a race, images would flash before her eyes. The body of her father, the smiling face of Jack Butler, the bloody, broken remains of Damien Gould, the hunched figure of Ibn Fayoud in the back room of the Club Joey, the cool fingers of the woman in the Golf touching the back of her hand, and the photograph. Always that photograph.

The woman had not waited long before calling.

'Did you tell them about Ibn Fayoud?'

'Yes.'

'Just as I told you? He was the only person involved, no one else?'

'That's right.'

'You wouldn't be lying to me. I can check, you know. If you're jerking us off, those pics go straight to the press.'

'I'm not. How do I know you've destroyed the negatives?'

'You're going to have to trust me, aren't you? Just like I've trusted you.'

'Right.'

'We're watching you. Remember that.'

'I will.'

Of course, Kelly had said nothing to the police, or even to Nick about Ibn Fayoud. It would take time for the woman, or her people, to discover that the blame had not been placed fully on his fragile shoulders. The stories in the press had revealed that the police had been given a mere thirty minutes with him before he was bundled on to the jet bound for Qatar. Little would emerge of the investigations for days, maybe weeks.

But they would discover in the end and Kelly's career would reach its inevitable shameful conclusion; there appeared to be nothing she could do about that. It was for the sake of her father's memory that she had become involved in all this and to play along with criminals, simply because she was being blackmailed about something she'd never done, would be a betrayal of everything he had believed in.

Ride the horses, he would have said. Forget the world and ride the horses. And that is what she did.

Some time later she saw Nick at Windsor but he too seemed changed, distracted. At first, Kelly put it down to his own Jockey Club investigations into the case but, when Sheikh al Hassan made his announcement, she realized that drug-running was the least of his problems.

At the end of the season, the Sheikh would be withdrawing from English racing and setting up his international headquarters in France. Just like that. The vast network of breeders, trainers, jockeys, lads who were affected by the decision of the industry's biggest owner were treated to no more than a courteous expression of regret.

No wonder she had caught a distant, haunted look in Nick's face. Although he never spoke to her of his finances, she knew, as everyone in racing knew, that his bloodstock business was inextricably involved with the dealings of Sheikh al Hassan. If the cream of his mares and stallions were to be transferred to Chantilly and the rest sold off, he could be facing financial ruin. And the Jockey Club was not likely to retain the services of a bankrupt as a steward, particularly on the security side.

Typically, it was Annie who kept a sense of proportion.

'We never expected to get Ibn Fayoud's horses in the first place,' she said to Bill and Kelly at breakfast on the morning the news broke. 'From the racing point of view, it was a bonus.'

'If it wasn't for Ibn Fayoud, we wouldn't have gone to Tokyo,' Bill muttered drily. 'Some bonus.'

'And Shine On would have been sold outside the yard.'

'What will happen to him?' Kelly asked. 'Have you heard what the Sheikh plans to do with him at the end of the season?'

'Brompton-Smiley has said that, since he's been invited to run in the Washington Laurel

International, he should go. The Sheikh will decide after that.'

Kelly nodded. It was open knowledge in the Templeman yard that Shine On, who had recovered well from the Tokyo Cup, was likely to run in America. What was less clear was who would ride him. Cy was in no fit state to compete in one of the world's great races.

Now Annie looked at her husband across the table. He nodded, then went back to reading his newspaper.

'Kelly, we think you should ride him in America,' she said.

'What about Cy?' Kelly was surprised at her coolness at the news.

'It's not that the Sheikh's influenced by the court case.' Annie smiled. 'He's sensible enough to see that Bill and Cy are innocent victims. No, it's simply that he's your ride and you should never have been taken off him in the first place. You know as well as we do that if you'd ridden him in Tokyo he'd have won.'

Kelly remembered her reaction when the tables had been turned, when Cy was put up instead of her for the Tokyo race. He knew it; she knew it. That was racing.

'Great,' she said quietly. 'When is it? A fortnight's time?'

Annie nodded. 'Just over.'

'You'd better win it,' Bill murmured.

'I will.' If the horse runs, Kelly thought. If I'm still riding. If the photographs don't reach the press before then.

* * *

There were times when she managed to forget, sometimes for as long as a couple of hours, and that afternoon, riding Warwick, was one of them.

Kelly had only one ride and, on any other occasion,
she would have treated a two-hundred-mile trip to
ride a mediocre horse in a small, low-value handicap
as a routine chore but, since Gatwick, nothing was
routine any more. The horse she was down to ride was
Boardwalk, the one-paced gelding on whom she had
failed to win a seller last time out at Ascot.

Kelly remembered that evening vividly. It had been
her first ride since Pendero at Ascot, since her father's
death. Mrs Prentice, the owner, had been thrilled with
second place, but everybody else, including Bill and
Annie, knew that she should have won. Today she
would.

There were only four horses running, the race
having cut up badly with the hard ground, but on all
known form Boardwalk might as well have stayed at
home for all the chance he had.

Driving to the races with Billie and Annie, Kelly
had mentioned that Boardwalk lost his races by pulling his jockey's arms out over the first five or six
furlongs. Since none of the other runners were proven
stayers and were likely to be more bothered by the
rock-like ground than their horse, why not let him go
on? There was just a chance that he could give them
the slip. At worst, they would give Mrs Prentice a
good run for her money. After some discussion, they
agreed.

It worked, even better than Kelly had planned. As
the field raced down the straight, the favourite

Mighty Quinn was in a group of three horses, each of whose jockeys were biding their time, waiting for one of the other two to make its run. The fact that they were all looking at the bony hindquarters of Boardwalk as he rattled along happily in front of them seemed supremely irrelevant. He'd be stopping soon, right enough, then the race would start in earnest.

Boardwalk and Kelly Connor had other ideas. By the time they were halfway round the lefthand bend heading for home, the rest of the field woke up to the realization that the one horse they had discounted as a threat was galloping, ears pricked, as strongly as ever. Almost comically, the three jockeys galvanized their mounts into action and set off in pursuit.

Kelly knew that, when Boardwalk came off the bit, the others would be running on but she trusted in his gameness and her strength to get him to the line before they caught him. He faltered with two hundred yards to go and the most seasoned gambler would still have laid odds on any one of his three pursuers overhauling him.

As she heard the thunder of approaching hooves behind her, Kelly roared at Boardwalk, who was now rolling wearily like a ship in a gale. Using her hands and heels, she kept him together and all but lifted him over the line as Mighty Quinn surged up to him and past. Had the winning post been moved twenty yards back, there would have been hundreds of happy punters at Warwick. As it was, the result was greeted with a sullen silence, broken only by wild cheers from Mrs Prentice. Boardwalk had held on to win by a neck.

These days Kelly avoided the post-race celebrations

but on this occasion it was a pleasure to take a glass of champagne with Mrs Prentice who, even after the last race was finished, was still reliving her horse's victory and planning an impressive campaign for him next season. There would be a time when Annie or Bill would have to break it to her the way Boardwalk ran, his races hardly gave ground for optimism that he would make the transformation to a jumper, but now was not it. Smiling, they allowed their owner her moment of triumph and unbounded optimism. Reality could wait.

It was as Mrs Prentice recounted the race yet again that Kelly noticed Harry Short standing at the bar alone. Although he looked as red-faced and belligerent as ever, he seemed to be staring in her direction, occasionally jerking his large head in an unsubtle gesture of invitation.

'I think Harry Short wants a word with you,' Annie said softly.

'I was trying to ignore him.' Kelly stood up. Harry was not a person it was easy to ignore for long. 'This won't take a minute,' she said.

'Brilliant ride, Kelly.' Harry shook her hand with a smile that somehow deteriorated into a leer.

'Thank you, Mr Short,' Kelly said coolly. It was odd how the fat trainer unnerved her, even in a public place.

'Drink?' He turned towards the barman.

'No thanks, I'm with an owner.'

Harry frowned and looked around him conspiratorially like a joke villain. 'Wanted to give you a tip, darling,' he said. 'About your spot of bother.'

'Bother?' Kelly tried a smile but it lacked conviction. 'I've just ridden a 12–1 winner.'

'You know what I mean.' Harry was looking at her beadily, his little eyes sparkling unpleasantly above his fat red cheeks. It occurred to Kelly that he might be drunk. 'I've heard,' he continued, 'that your friend Jack Butler is in deep shit. Someone's after him, someone very big.'

'I don't see what—'

'If you want to know who was behind the Tokyo job, you better find Jack. He knows. But they're looking for him too. The word is they're not very pleased with him.'

'And who are they?'

'Can't help you there, darling.' Harry drained his glass. 'All I know is that a lot of money has been laundered through his shops. Naughty money. Drug money. And now Jack's lost his nerve. They say that it was Jack who tipped off the police about Tokyo.'

'Jack Butler? Why?'

'He wants out. And they're not happy about that.'

Kelly glanced back to the Templeman party. Bill was listening to Mrs Prentice, occasionally nodding with a polite smile. Annie was looking quizzically in her direction.

'I happen to know that it wasn't Jack who told the police about the Tokyo drugs run,' she said eventually. 'I think your sources may be stringing you along.'

'My sources are reliable. Take it or leave it.' Harry made as if to leave.

'Why tell me?'

The trainer hesitated, as if surprised by the question. 'Felt bad about the Pendero business,' he muttered eventually. 'Wanted to square it. Because, once they get Butler, they'll be after you. They don't like people who know as much you do.'

Annie was approaching the bar. 'Hi, Harry,' she said cheerfully. 'How you doing?'

'Good,' he said. 'Just sussing out whether this young jockey of yours was interested in riding for me now and then.' He winked at Kelly. 'Give us a bell once you've thought about it, eh darling?'

'Of course.'

The two women watched Harry push his way through the bar and out of the door. 'Thought you might need rescuing,' Annie smiled.

'Thanks,' said Kelly thoughtfully. 'What would you say if I told you that Harry had just done me a favour?'

Annie shrugged. 'I'd say you needed a double brandy to recover from the shock. Harry's favours tend to be to himself.'

Kelly started back to the table where Mrs Prentice was still talking about Boardwalk's victory.

'Maybe it's just a day for miracles,' she said.

That night Kelly put through a call to Ireland and asked Dermot Kinane about hot money being laundered through bookmakers.

'Sure, you're a little terrier, you are. Don't tell me you're still on the snoop.'

'I owe it to Dad.'

'Laundering, is it?' There was a pause and, in her

mind's eye, Kelly could see the Irishman sucking at his pipe before he continued. 'Well, it happens a bit.'

'What sort of people do it?'

'People with more money than they can account for. Thieves, drug pushers, anyone doing cash jobs that they don't want to declare to the Inland Revenue. Bookmakers, off-course as well as on the spot. It's a simple exercise with the right number of people working it for you.'

'So, do bank robbers use it?'

There was a sigh, as if Dermot were reluctant to reveal more. 'That's right. Irish bank robbers.'

For all his apparent vagueness, Dermot Kinane used words carefully but sometimes they needed to be decoded. The reference to Irish bank robbers was no pub joke. Before she could question him further, Kinane said, 'Kelly, we shouldn't be talking like this. Remember where I'm calling from. The lines aren't secure.'

'This is important, Dermot.'

'Hold on.' For a few seconds there was the sound of rustling paper. 'Call Mr Colm Hogan on this number. He lives near Royston. He can tell you something – in fact, he'll tell you a lot if you buy him a couple of drinks.'

Kelly took down the number and hung up. Irish bank robbers. We shouldn't be talking about this. It was unlike the old man to sound so rattled, so edgy. Lines weren't secure.

Then she understood.

Colm Hogan answered the phone with the quiet suspicion of a man used to receiving only bad news.

Kelly mentioned Dermot Kinane's name and suggested they meet. He showed little enthusiasm. Meet for a drink. Hogan laughed humourlessly and agreed.

They met that evening in a pub outside Cambridge. Hogan had been keen to meet at his local but, knowing that there was a stable yard in Royston and that some of the lads drinking at the pub might recognize her, Kelly had insisted he meet her where neither of them would be disturbed.

'Kelly Connor?' The man who approached her in the King's Head, Melbourn, was not at all what she had expected. Tall, pale and wearing a dark suit that had seen better days, he might have been an accountant, or a tax inspector fallen on hard times. Only the bloodshot, watery eyes behind the thick-lensed glasses and the high colour in his cheeks gave him away. 'Colm Hogan,' he said.

Kelly smiled and shook his cold, bony hand. Almost before she offered, he asked for a large vodka and tonic.

'Dermot sent his best,' she said as they found a table, outside in a beer garden. Hogan smiled wearily as if Dermot could send his worst for all it mattered to him. He drained his glass in one.

'What's it about then?'

'Just a spot of general information Dermot said you might be able to give me.'

'Is that what he said?' Hogan's voice was thin, correct with a fake gentility to it.

Kelly produced a fifty-pound note and put it on the table between them. 'Another drink, Colm?'

He looked at the money and for a moment Kelly

thought that the direct approach had been a mistake. But then he reached out and put the note in the top pocket of his jacket.

'That would be very nice,' he said with an insincere smile. 'Another large vodka for me and go easy on the tonic.'

She stood up and walked to the bar. She hoped Dermot had been right about this man.

On his third drink Hogan began to open up. He had known Kinane and Kelly's father at a time when they were riding and he was working for the Irish Jockey Club. He had trained as a laboratory technician and had been hired to test horses for dope after they had run.

'Interesting.' Kelly had decided that the best way to get information from this man was to take it slowly. On the other hand, she couldn't afford to wait so long that, by the time he reached the part of his story which concerned her, he was disappearing under the table.

Hogan shook his head. 'Worst decision I ever made. Should have been a scientist. Messing around with horse piss. Fucking horses.' The expletive sounded odd coming from him.

'What went wrong?' Kelly nodded in the direction of Hogan's glass. 'That?'

'No. I'd have the odd gargle, but nothing much. Not then.' He looked at her, challenging her to disbelieve him. 'Not until the boys got to me.'

'The boys.'

There was a long silence as Hogan looked around the garden. ' "Colm," they said. "You wouldn't be in the way of doing us a wee favour, would you?

263

Nothing much. Just now and then making sure that the sample for this or that race is, like, exchanged for another. We give you the clean sample on the day of the race. You lose the real one, all right? You're on your own when you make the test. What could be simpler?'' And I thought about it. These weren't just gamblers we're talking about. They were the boys.' A wheedling, pleading note had entered Hogan's voice, as if, right now, he was back in Ireland, trying to convince himself that he had no alternative. 'They had this sweet, sweet system of exchanging stolen money for nice, legitimate notes from across the counter. Plus a bit of interest. But,' Hogan sighed tragically, 'now and then it went wrong. Even when the boys had set up the race so carefully, when they had called up the trainers of the other horses and told them straight that, if they valued their kneecaps, their horse wouldn't win tomorrow – even then, there were mistakes. Fucking horses.' He pushed his glass towards Kelly.

When she returned from the bar, the Irishman needed no encouragement to continue with his story.

'It was easy,' he said, adding with a drunken smile, 'a piece of piss, you could say. Went on for two years. A truly sweet operation. Then,' Hogan's face clouded over angrily, 'then it got untidy. Somebody else started calling me. He knew everything. I thought I was finished. But all he wanted was to join in the game. Did the same thing. The gambles that man landed.'

'Did you have any idea who he was?'

Hogan ignored the interruption. 'But it was getting

silly now, silly. I couldn't understand how the stewards didn't see what was going on. I'd be getting calls from the boys, calls from this man – no wonder it got to me. I was telling the boys I was off the case. Said I'd work for them on the mainland if needs be. They didn't care. One day they'll call me. I'll get—' Hogan frowned with concentration '—activated. I'm a sleeper, you know,' he added proudly.

'What about the other man? What did he say?'

'Never heard from him again. Must have heard a whisper that I was off. Came here then. Started a new life.' Hogan stood up, swaying slightly. 'Must go,' he said.

'Who was he, Hogan?'

'I told you, didn't I? Just some fucking Englishman.'

Kelly watched through the window as Hogan weaved his way towards the bus stop. It would take a lot to activate him, to rouse this sleeper, but then the boys in the IRA were not without their powers of persuasion. She finished her drink and sighed. Colm Hogan, yet another loser.

Margaret Stanhope sat at Jack Butler's desk in Jack Butler's office and thumbed through his little red book. Conquests, contacts, conmen – it was all here. He must have been in one hell of a hurry to leave without it.

He wasn't holed up with a distant cousin, or a friend of the family, Margaret was sure of that. And with that little girl from accounts in tow, he was hardly likely to be hiding behind the skirts of one of

his many ex-girl friends. Which left villains. The old
con's network. It was a tough man's world, the criminal community, but Margaret Stanhope was at her
best in a tough man's world.

She was going to have to make some calls. It was
dodgy, of course, the chance of messy misunder-
standings occurring when you were dealing with thugs
and hitmen was high but Jack's behaviour left
Margaret with no choice. It was no good his doing a
runner just when she needed him most. She had to get
her hands on him one way or another.

At first, as she parked the car, Kelly didn't see the girl.
When she did, a blonde, waif-like figure standing in
the shadows, her instinct was not to get involved. The
girl looked like some sort of runaway, a schoolgirl
perhaps, and Kelly had troubles enough without that.

But then the girl walked slowly towards her as she
was locking the car. Kelly saw now that she was older
than she had thought, but her hair was lank and dirty,
and there was a bruise on the side of her face. She
was fumbling in her bag for something, talking to
herself.

'Can I help you?' Kelly said.

'Letter,' said the girl, at last producing a crumpled
envelope out of the bag. She put the envelope on the
bonnet of the car and started walking away, quickly,
unsteadily on her high heels.

Kelly picked up the letter which bore her name and
the word 'PRIVATE' on the front.

'Wait!' she called out. But the girl had turned the
corner. Kelly ran after her, but as she rounded the

street, the girl was getting into a car. The driver – he looked like a man – drove off before Kelly could even take the number.

She swore and walked slowly back to the car, opening the envelope as she went.

Inside was a note from Jack Butler.

Chapter 13

Dear Kelly,

I'm sure that by now somebody will have shown you pictures from the night of the Flaxton ball. It is the worst thing I've ever done in my life and I'm ashamed of myself. If you haven't seen them, I'll explain when I see you. I had no alternative, believe me. You're the reason why I've gone straight and why I'm being hunted.

I need to see you urgently. Please drive up and see me at the Coast House, Holkham, Norfolk (top bell) as soon as you possibly can. I want to tell you something important before I leave. You're the only person I can turn to who will understand. Please trust me. Tell absolutely no one about this note.

Yours,

Jack (Butler)

Kelly sat at the kitchen table and stared at the note. Neatly written in a careful, looping hand on cheap, lined paper, it might have come from a child. Jack (Butler). No longer the kingpin, but a fugitive, turning to her for help. It seemed absurd.

She felt weary, used. It was in this kitchen, at this very table, that she had read the letter from her father, his last message to her. What would he have done now? Believe a man who was corrupt, a bent bookmaker at the centre of an international dope-dealing ring? Trust him just this once? The shadow of a bitter smile crossed Kelly's face. Where had trusting people landed her, or indeed Frank Connor? Trust was a one-way street leading to compromise, danger.

And yet, she couldn't help thinking that Jack Butler was not the type to send fake SOS notes. He was on the run, Harry Short had already told her. Maybe, if she could reach him, he would provide the last piece of the jigsaw, allowing her to return to racing having laid her father to rest at last. She would drive to Holkham the following day, a Sunday, but she wouldn't just go without telling anyone.

She tried to get in touch with Annie, but she and Bill had gone to London for the weekend. Cy wouldn't be any use. She dialled Nick's number and cursed silently as she heard his answering machine. He was away at a bloodstock sale and wouldn't be back until Monday evening. After a moment's pause she said, 'I've heard from Jack Butler. He's in a place called the Coast House at Holkham. I'm going to see him tomorrow. I think it's got something to do with Tokyo.'

After she had hung up, Kelly found herself

reflecting on the strange life of Jack Butler. See him on the television or on the racecourse, even at a social function like the Flaxton dance, and you'd say that nothing could shake his confidence, his control over every aspect of his life. Yet now he seemed to be on the run.

Some fucking Englishman. She remembered Colm Hogan's words. Presumably Jack knew the IRA was laundering stolen money through his bookmaking system and played them at their own game. But how, why, did he become involved in the drugs trade? Kelly opened the fridge and poured herself an orange juice. She could see the temptation. Once there were large amounts of cash being lost over his counters, there was a certain logic in expanding his operation. But why did he need to? Was it Ibn Fayoud's influence? It seemed unlikely. Or maybe his father, Reg Butler. Nick had told her that he was an old monster; made Jack look like a babe in arms, he had said.

It was madness. She was a sane, rational person, and yet here she was looking for excuses for someone who had drugged and virtually raped her.

She turned off the lights in the kitchen and went to her bedroom, thinking about Nick Morley and how little she really knew about him – his past, or the way he made his living in bloodstock, what he really wanted, how he felt about her. Nick was one of those Englishmen who hoard the personal like a dangerous secret weapon that could fall into the hands of some unseen enemy. What would he do if she needed help?

She thought about his guardedness, the way he withdrew into himself. It was not so surprising – in one way or another he had been involved in under-cover work throughout his professional life. Racing, the army and, before that, if he was to be believed, childhood in a family deeply imbued with the English passion for privacy. As she undressed, she caught a glimpse of herself in the mirror. Thank God she was born Irish. Her father, Dermot, even Colm Hogan were possessed of an openness an Englishman of Nick's background would find alien. She wondered if Nick ever got drunk, ever spilt out his heart to an old friend, ever lost control, just for a moment. Somehow it seemed unlikely.

She put on her dressing gown, switching on the radio beside her bed. Although she had become used to living alone since her father's death, she didn't like the late-night silence of the empty flat. Maybe, when this was over, she would share a flat with someone – she needed company.

As she cleaned her teeth, the full absurdity of this idea occurred to her. Any day now, she could awake to find her name and her photograph splashed across the pages of some tabloid rag. The jockey who slept with a bookmaker. Kelly winced comically at her reflection in the mirror. It would be an inglorious end to her career. Perhaps, once she had heard Jack's side of the story, she would have the courage to tell Nick, even Bill and Annie, of the scandal that was about to break.

She wished Nick were here. They could talk, help each other. Although he was cagey about his army days, he would surely be able to shed some light on Hogan's story about the gambling activities of 'the boys'. Part of her longed to be able to pass over the responsibility of her knowledge to someone else but she knew that, until she talked to Jack, it would have to remain hers alone.

She turned off the radio and the bedside light, then slipped into her single bed. Staring into the darkness, she found herself thinking of Nick again. Perhaps it was companionship that she was missing, the sharing of a burden. Maybe, after tomorrow, it would be possible.

In the public bar of the Half Moon pub, Dagenham, a man sat nursing a pint of bitter. The look on his broad, ill-shaven face did not encourage small talk. At first glance, you might think he was a fat man caught up in some sort of daydream but look again and you'd see that the fat was muscle; you might even guess that nothing as innocent as a daydream would pass through the arid wasteland behind that low, furrowed brow.

Scag wasn't dreaming. He was remembering the job he had just done. What he'd be paid for in this very bar later tonight. Though, personally, he'd have been happy to do it for free. Because as jobs go, it was tasty – very, very tasty.

He shifted on his chair and belched happily. He was seeing something in his mind's eye – something that was better than the hottest, nastiest video. Because it had really happened to him that very afternoon.

The thing was, you didn't very often get the good stuff from Maggie. It was usually messy, cash-collection jobs. Flash gits who thought they could try it on with Jack Butler. Maybe Scag was going soft but brutalizing the older generation wasn't as much fun as it used to be. Once you'd seen one old geezer spitting his teeth out in a pool of blood on the floor, you'd seen them all.

But this was it. The good stuff. This made all the other crap he'd done for Maggie worthwhile. When he'd seen her, his girl, his blind date, walking down the street in that little dress, her face all puckered and worried, his heart just went boom-bloody-boom-bloody-boom. Was she a doll or what?

He followed her home, waited for a bit, then called from a phone box. Got a message from Jack, he said. Meet you at the pub. And she was out of the door, tip-tapping down the road, without so much as a second thought for her own safety. These young girls, no wonder they were getting into trouble all the time.

He wasn't rough. In fact, on the Scag scale of bad behaviour, what he did with Roseanne barely registered. He did slap her once, just after he had put her in the car but, after that, she was good as gold. Told him where Jack was when he'd told her to go home. Showed him the letter that he had sent to the Connor girl. And because she had been very good, he even drove her up to Newmarket to deliver the letter.

On the way, he'd tried to talk to her, but Roseanne just sat in the passenger seat and looked out of the window like it was the end of the world or something. Which was funny, because the way Scag had heard it was that they liked all that, girls. Bit of this, bit of that, bit of conversation, chatting up. But this Roseanne, she just would not be chatted up, moody cow.

Tell the truth, after they'd been to Newmarket, Scag had been well tempted to take her back to his gaff, maybe get a few mates round. But there was something about her little face, all smudged and defiant, that got to him. Basically she didn't look like a fun way of spending the evening. In fact, she might even have given him a spot of grief with the filth.

So he'd given her a friendly squeeze and pushed her out of the car round the corner from her house. She even sort of smiled at him and said thanks, like she knew that he was doing something rather beautiful, by his standards. It was one of the nicest dates Scag had ever had. And he was getting paid for it.

He pushed his way to the bar and ordered another drink. He had time to get another down him before Maggie's bagman arrived. It had been a very good day.

An autumn mist hung low over Newmarket as Kelly set off early that Sunday morning for the Norfolk coast. She had been there a couple of times with her father and associated the wide, wind-swept beaches, the acres of undulating dunes, with a peculiarly English form of holiday. The sea would be grey and distant, there would be the occasional families struggling with a picnic behind brightly-coloured canvas windbreaks. Even with the sun in the sky, it would never be quite warm enough. Beautiful but bracing, this stretch of coastland was ideal for the English at play. Of course, there would be fewer people than ever now that the summer holidays had ended.

The journey took longer than she had anticipated

and, by the time she saw the North Sea, the sun was high in the sky and Kelly was hungry. Jack could wait. She went to a pub, ordered crab sandwiches and thought of her father. He had loved it here, saying it reminded him of County Kerry. Not for the first time, she wished Nick was with her. He would appreciate the wild beauty of the place, the quiet of a coastal town left at last to locals.

The barman told her that Coast House was a mile from the village down a long drive leading to the beach.

'Popular with folk that like to be left alone,' he said, his grin revealing an uneven set of yellowing teeth. 'Honeymooners and the like. Park at the end of the drive and walk another half-mile and you'll see it.'

Sensing the man's curiosity as to why a young woman on her own would be looking for such an isolated guesthouse, Kelly thanked him and returned to her car.

The barman had been right. The Coast House was an ideal hideaway. The only passers-by would be the few hardy souls who were visiting the distant beach. There were two other cars parked at the end of the drive, and neither of them looked like Jack Butler's. She walked down the narrow sand track and, after a few minutes, came to a bleak Victorian building set back among the pine trees. An ancient sign announced 'The Coast House, Bed and Breakfast, VACAN-CIES'. It had almost been obscured by windswept sand. There was no sign of life.

She walked to the front door and rang the top bell once, then, after a minute or so, again, more persistently this time. Eventually a middle-aged woman in an apron appeared from the back of the house. Kelly told her that she was looking for Mr Butler.

The woman looked puzzled. 'No Butler here,' she said. 'No one staying at all except Mr Reginald.'

Kelly asked if he was staying on the top floor.

'Maybe.' The woman approached Kelly, her hands sunk deep in the pockets of her corduroy trousers. 'I thought you wanted Mr Butler. Mr Reginald said he wasn't at home to visitors.'

'I'm not just a visitor. I'm a friend. He's expecting me.'

The woman shrugged. She knew about friends. A lot of friends stayed at the guesthouse during the season, ordering up breakfast in bed, messing up the rooms, whispering in the television room. It was good money, double rooms going for a lot more than singles, but she didn't like it, all this friendship that seemed to be going around these days.

'He's out,' she said eventually. 'Went for one of his walks this morning. Not back yet.' She pointed in the direction of the sea. 'You'll find him down there.'

Kelly thanked her.

'Seems he's got lots of friends all of a sudden,' the woman called after her. 'Doesn't see a soul all week and then it's two people in a day.'

Kelly turned. 'Two?'

'Met up with some feller down by the beach.' She looked sheepish. 'Saw them through the window a couple of hours ago.'

Although it was barely three o'clock, some of the weekend visitors were making their way back up the path from the sea, having stayed long enough with the wind and the waves to justify a cream tea beside a fire. Some of them looked curiously at Kelly, a woman walking alone towards a beach that was virtually deserted.

After half a mile the path divided up. The right-hand fork led to an expanse of beach where one or two families could be seen attempting to play beach football or to read newspapers in the wind. Kelly hesitated and took the left-hand path through steppe sand-dunes towards another part of the beach.

At first when she heard it, she mistook the scream for the cry of a gull above the wind, but then she saw two people running with unusual urgency towards a distant dune. She left the path, finding higher ground from which she could see a family group gathered round something on the ground. Although they must have been more than two hundred yards from her, Kelly sensed an agitation among them. This was no holiday adventure.

She started running.

As she approached, a boy in his early teens ran past her, panting, his eyes wet with tears that had not been caused by the wind. She could now see that three other members of the family were standing by the body of a man who lay, face downwards, at the foot of a sand-dune. The mother was leading her daughter away. The father glanced at Kelly as she ran up.

'My son just found him,' the man said helplessly. 'I sent him to fetch the police.'

'Come away from him, Peter.' The well-bred tones of the man's wife cracked with panic. 'There's nothing you can do.'

There wasn't. The way the body was lying suggested that the man had been kneeling in the sand and had pitched forward when he had been shot. The sand around the head was darkened by congealed blood. A bullet hole the size of a small coin could be seen at the back of the neck.

Kelly crouched beside the body. Half-concealed by the sand, Jack Butler's face looked at peace, as if the manner of his death contained nothing that had surprised or even frightened him.

'He's dead.' The man was now beside his wife and had awkwardly put his arm round his ashen-faced daughter. 'I don't think you should touch him.'

Kelly reached out to touch Butler's pale cheek. It was cold.

'Shot,' he muttered. The man had a gift for stating the obvious.

Round the bullet hole, the skin was dark, burnt. Kelly stood up slowly.

'Close range,' she said. 'If you hadn't found him, he would have been swept out to sea with the tide.'

'Nothing we can do.'

'No,' said Kelly. 'Nothing anyone can do.' She took one last look at Jack Butler, lying tidily in the sand with a tidy hole through his neck. He had died more neatly than he had ever lived. 'I'll make sure the police have got the message.' She set off through the pine trees. With luck she'd be able to reach her car before the police arrived.

'Right,' she heard the father saying with a final, despairing attempt at authority. 'We'll just stay here then.'

John Francome

Sitting in her car, eyes closed as if to shut out thoughts of what she had seen, Kelly realized that it was pointless to run. She had been seen near Jack's body. It would take little – a photograph of her in the papers, a chance remark from Nick – to establish that she had been in Holkham on the day that Jack died. Running would only suggest guilt.

The body had been cold. If it was established that the murder had taken place during the late morning, Kelly's fears that she might be implicated in some way could be dispelled. She had been in the pub in Holkham. The barman with the bad teeth would remember her. She rubbed her eyes wearily. It had been lucky for her – and perhaps unlucky for Jack – that she hadn't driven straight to the Coast House.

She reached in her pocket for the note Jack had sent to her. *I want to tell you something important before I leave.*

Something important. Once, she had been certain that Jack held the answer to the most important question in her life, who had killed her father, but now it seemed that he too was a bit part player in the drama. He had used Ibn Fayoud as useful cover for his drug-running operation. He could even have been involved in the death of her father, of Gould, of Broom-Parker, but there was someone else giving him orders, someone higher up the chain of command.

Why was he running? Why did he have to die? Kelly remembered something Harry Short had told her: it was Jack who had blown the whistle on the Tokyo operation. She had dismissed the idea, knowing that

280

Nick had warned the police, but maybe there had been two tip-offs. Perhaps, for some reason – lack of nerves, whatever – Jack was trying to extricate himself from an operation that had grown too big, too dangerous. It would explain why he had tried to stop her going to Tokyo, if it was him. Kelly was now certain it was.

So the person, or the organization, behind the drugs operation had decided that he was a liability. They had somehow tracked him down and murdered him. Except it wasn't just a murder – Kelly remembered the dark skin round the bullet hole in Jack's head – it was more like an execution. Her stomach knotted at the thought that she knew too much as well. Was this how drug barons punished offenders? It somehow seemed too military. Or paramilitary. The boys.

Three police cars approached at speed up the coastal drive. They pulled to a halt yards from where she sat and six policemen, two in plain clothes, emerged, slamming the doors of their cars. They seemed relaxed, as if they knew that death was no emergency, a corpse could wait.

Kelly got out and walked quickly to where they stood. 'You'll find him straight up the path, three-quarters of a mile beyond the house.'

'Was it you who found the body, miss?' one of the men in plain clothes asked.

'No,' said Kelly. 'But I know who it is.'

She rang Annie that night, as soon as she had returned to Newmarket and poured herself a brandy to steady her nerves. The police constable who had taken her

statement had been irritatingly slow and sympathetic,
as if obeying some procedural handbook concerning
female witnesses of an ongoing murder situation.

She had told him everything directly relevant to the
case. How she knew Jack Butler, his connection with
Ibn Fayoud and the Tokyo run, the note she had
received from him. Occasionally, as she dictated her
statement, the constable would break off to greet
colleagues – a deputation from forensic, an inspector
from Norwich – before returning with a tolerant smile
to Kelly and her story. Used to being given the dull,
peripheral work, he seemed unable or unwilling to
accept the significance of what she was telling him.
Only when she haltingly told him about the photographs and how the woman calling herself Jill Turnbull
had tried to blackmail her did the man raise his eyebrows in surprise. Sex, drugs, blackmail – this one had
everything.

If, somewhere deep in his brain, the police constable
had grasped that the woman from whom he was taking
a statement had a motive for wanting to see Jack Butler
dead, he showed no sign of it. His brief was to take a
statement, not to rush about reaching conclusions.

No doubt the powers that be would want to talk to
her further but, once she had completed and signed her
statement, he let her go with a friendly, encouraging
wink. By this time Kelly was seething. The constable
was the wettest bastard she'd ever come across and she
hoped to God the rest of the Norfolk Police weren't
like him. If you phoned him in an emergency, you'd be
dead before he realized anyone was calling.

Back in Newmarket, it was Annie, to her relief, who

answered the telephone. As coolly as she was able, Kelly recounted the events in Norfolk, including details of the photographs.

Annie's reaction was to let forth a torrent of abuse about Jack. 'The creep got what he deserved,' she concluded. 'If I'd been here,' she went on, 'I would have come with you.'

'I left a message with Nick but he was out too.'

'Yes, he would be. There's a drinks party being held by Simon Brompton-Smiley at the Al Hassan stud tonight. He's meant to be explaining the implications of the Sheikh pulling out of English racing. Sounds like an exercise in window-dressing to me.' She laughed lightly. 'Bill volunteered to go.'

'Maybe I'll catch him there.'

'Except they won't let you in. This is an Arab function, remember. There will be tight security.'

Kelly thought for a moment. 'I suppose I'll just have to tell them I'm you.'

There was a pause from the other end of the telephone. 'You can tell them that if you like.'

'But you'd prefer me not to go.'

'Kelly, you're in enough trouble as it is at the moment. Why don't you just leave it all alone.'

'That's what I want to do,' Kelly said quietly. 'I think it's going to come out one way or another sooner rather than later. I want to hand my information over to someone with the power to do something about it.'

'Like Nick Morley.'

'Right. He knows the background, he's got the authority—'

'And you're in love with him.'

'No.' Kelly replied. 'I thought I may have been once, but not any more. No. We get on fine, but that's all.'

Annie sighed. 'We'll never win that bloody race in America.'

For a moment, after she had hung up, Kelly considered whether Annie was right. The Washington International could make her career. Although, on form, Shine On looked outclassed by an international field that included Badinage, the winner of that year's Arc de Triomphe, and Angel Dust, an American four-year-old that had been unbeaten in top-class company since he won the Laurel in the previous season, Kelly fancied his chances of running into a place. He had worked well since his return from Tokyo and, while other horses were losing their form after a long season, he showed no signs of going over the top. If he travelled well, if he got a good draw, if his jockey had her mind on the job, he could surprise them all. If.

She stood up and looked at her watch. It was almost seven thirty. She could get to the Al Hassan stud within the hour, speak to Nick and still get home early. In the morning, she was to ride Shine On for his last piece of work before he flew to America. This way she could wipe the slate clean, let Nick worry about the implications of Jack Butler's murder. It was time for her to be a jockey again.

It was eight fifteen when Kelly parked her mud-spattered Saab between a Porsche and a Mercedes outside the Fairfield Stud. She glanced at herself in the rearview mirror, and saw the face of a woman about to crash a party of Britain's racing elite, track down Britain's brightest Jockey Club administrator and tell him that Britain's best-known bookmaker had just been executed, possibly by Britain's most notorious terrorist group. And she hadn't even bothered to have a bath. Murder was a great motivator.

'Mrs Templeman,' she told the butler who opened the front door. 'I believe my husband's already here.'

The man directed her to a large room from where the hum of polite conversation could be heard. As she made her way across the panelled hall, she noticed him discreetly checking her name on a guest list on a table behind the front door.

For a moment, as she stood in the doorway of Fairfield Hall's reception room, Kelly thought her nerve might fail her. A glance around the room revealed several well-fed faces rarely seen outside the inner sanctums of the Jockey Club establishment: not only the racing managers of the rich and landed, the rich and landed themselves were here in force. In a corner, she could see her old friend Colonel Beamish giving Ian Gardem the benefit of his opinions, while on the far side Bill, looking as bored as ever, was in a group which included General Winstanley and the steward Lord Chester. Kelly took a bucks fizz offered by a waitress and turned away – she had to reach Nick before Bill spotted her and asked embarrassing questions.

'Kelly Connor.' The booming voice of Charles Caldecott made her wince. She might as well have got the doorman to announce her formally.

She managed a smile. 'Hello, Charles.'

Caldecott came to stand before her, beaming

aimiably. 'It's the mystery guest. Always turning up when least expected. What on earth are you doing here?'

'Feminine wiles.' Kelly sipped her drink. 'That, and the fact that I'm riding the Sheikh's horse in America on Saturday.'

Caldecott made a weak, whoops-silly-me face. 'Damn shame about the Sheikh pulling out like that,' he said, changing the subject quickly. 'A few people in this room will be sad to see him go, I'll tell you that.'

'Yes.' Kelly could see Nick across the room, deep in conversation with a man she recognized as Simon Brompton-Smiley. 'He paid quite a few salaries, one way or another.'

'Salaries? It's the unofficial trade that will be hit hardest, if you know what I mean.'

Nick had looked up and, Kelly sensed in an instant, had seen her. If she could just keep Caldecott talking, Nick would probably make his way unobtrusively to her. Once she had spoken to him, she would be out of here and on her way home before Brompton-Smiley became aware that he had an uninvited guest.

'Mmm?' She smiled warmly at Caldecott. 'I'm not sure I do know what you mean. What unofficial trade?'

'Come on, Kelly.' Charles Caldecott dropped his voice and spoke through his teeth like a bad comedian. 'When your employer has got so much money that your annual salary is what he'd pay one of his regular tarts in London or Paris, you have to look for the perks, the odd under-the-counter arrangement.'

In spite of herself, Kelly was intrigued by what

Caldecott was saying. He seemed slightly drunk and unguarded, like a man talking about his wife now that he knew the marriage was over. The Sheikh was going, so a few spilt secrets would hurt no one.

'You mean tax fiddles?'

Caldecott frowned, as if his listener was being extraordinarily slow. 'No need for that.' He dropped his voice to a murmur. 'You're in Kentucky for the sales, all right? You're representing our Arab friend who's interested in a yearling by Northern Dancer. It's going to go for two million dollars. What's to stop you tipping the seller the wink that the Sheikh's prepared to go to two and a half million and splitting the extra after the sale. Suits him, suits you and the Sheikh's not going to worry about the odd couple of hundred thousand, is he?'

'That really happens?' Kelly noticed that Nick was no longer talking to Brompton-Smiley and was casually making his way across the room in their direction.

'Every time a horse is bought or sold, the agents rip these Arabs off a treat.' Caldecott smiled as Nick approached. 'Talk of the devil.'

Kelly darted a surprised look in Caldecott's direction. 'Hi, Nick,' she smiled.

It was almost as if he had expected her. 'Delighted you could make it,' he said, watching her warily as if warning her not to speak out of turn.

For a moment the three of them stood silently. 'Charles,' Kelly said finally. 'I just need a quiet word with Nick for a moment. You wouldn't excuse us, would you?'

287

'Of course.' Caldecott grinned knowingly. 'I'll leave you two to it.'

Nick looked at Kelly. 'What the hell are you playing at?'

Kelly had to hand it to him, he knew how to keep up appearances. A stranger looking at them from a few yards away would have judged his manner to be that of just another guest. Politely interested in the conversation, even slightly bored.

'I'm not playing at anything, Nick, if you just listened.'

He smiled and nodded. 'I can't listen here. Ring me tomorrow.'

'It can't wait.'

'Jesus.' He sipped at his drink casually. 'First I get a message on my machine saying you're going after that bloody bookmaker, then you appear without warning or invitation at an extremely important drinks party. Have you gone quite mad?'

'Jack's dead. He's been shot.'

Nick raised his eyebrows and gave a convincing little laugh. She might have been telling him a joke for all the emotion he showed. 'Did you tell the police?'

'They know. Listen, Nick, I know now's not the time but I must ask you this. The gun to the back of the neck – it's an IRA execution technique, isn't it?'

A waitress appeared at Nick's elbow carrying a tray with food. 'Something to eat, Kelly?' he said. She shook her head. Presumably Nick's intelligence training helped him to behave like this but she found it unnerving. 'It's hardly the most unusual way of killing someone, if that's what you mean. Could be anyone.'

'I think the people who killed him were the ones behind the drug run and probably the death of my father.' Kelly added more urgently, 'For Christ's sake, stop smiling like that. Bill and Cy McCray are going to get slung into prison unless something happens.'

Nick turned slightly to acknowledge the presence of a plump middle-aged woman who had caught his eye. 'Triona,' he said warmly. 'Have you met Kelly Connor? The jockey?'

The woman gave a little squeal of pleasure. 'But I'm one of your greatest fans. You ride for Bill, don't you?'

'Yes,' said Kelly. Nick was backing away.

'Keep me posted about that,' he told her. 'Don't do anything until I ring tomorrow.'

The woman was talking about Boardwalk's win last time out when Kelly interrupted. 'Sorry,' she said. 'Would you excuse me? I'm not feeling well. Got to go.'

She pushed her way towards the door, walked quickly across the hall, nodding to the butler who said, 'Goodnight, Mrs Templeman.'

In fact, it was true. She was feeling ill. The contrast between the wild seascape of Norfolk and the comfortable interior of Fairfield Stud, between the desolate sighing of the wind and the sharp chatter of well-bred conversation, between the lifeless corpse of Jack Butler and the coldly smiling face of Nick Morley had suddenly made her feel faint. And now she couldn't remember exactly where she'd left her car.

Breathing deeply, she leant against Nick's Aston

Martin parked in the front row and squeezed her eyes
shut. It had been a mistake to drink a strong brandy
cocktail before she came here. In fact, it had probably
been a mistake to come at all. She had merely antago-
nized the one man who could help her.

'Stupid, stupid,' she said, straightening slowly. It
was getting dark now. She wiped her hands and made
her way slowly towards her own car which she had
spotted to her left.

Then she stopped. Something was wrong. She went
back to the Aston Martin and ran a hand along the
side of the bonnet. On the tips of her fingers were a
few grains of sand.

'You're chasing the wrong fox, darlin'.' Dermot
Kinane's voice was that of a man who had just
returned from an evening's hard drinking at the pub
and was unprepared for late-night calls about murdered bookmakers and suspect stewards. 'Nick
Morley is not your man, I'm sure of it.'

'But the sand, Dermot.' Kelly remembered the
wind and the way the sign outside the Coast House
had been partially obscured by blown sand.

'All-weather gallops. Paddocks. There's no short-
age of sand around Newmarket.'

Kelly wasn't convinced.

'I spoke to some people,' Dermot went on quietly.
'The Englishman who muscled in on Colm Hogan's
set-up can't have been Jack Butler. He lived in the
north – somewhere in Fermanagh, they say.'

'So there's no connection between—' Kelly felt
uneasy with the chummy euphemism used by Hogan

'—the boys and Jack Butler's little operation with Ibn Fayoud.'

'I didn't say that.'

'But—'

'Your man moved to the mainland but the word is that he still has Irish connections which are not strictly to do with racing.'

'You mean that the drugs operation had terrorist money behind it?'

'It's not just drugs. It's arms. I don't know how but they used to get hardware on to the mainland, using the trade in racehorses.'

'My God. So it was an execution. That was why Jack lost his nerve. He was playing out of his depth.'

'Kelly, listen.' Dermot sounded alert now, as if their conversation had cleared his mind. 'Nothing can stop these people. You're not dealing with some two-bit hoodlum with a grudge. These are Irishmen with a cause, working with Arabs. There's American business interests involved. For Christ's sake, you've found out enough about your dad's death to leave it there. Go to Washington and ride your race. Or you'll end up like Jack Butler.'

There was something in Dermot's tone which suggested that he knew more than he was letting on. Like many of his countrymen, he was torn between a belief in a united Ireland and a hatred of the viciousness and violence used to achieve it. Kelly knew that his contacts were a reliable source of information, that he wouldn't tell her so much over an open phone if he didn't know that the danger to her was real.

'You know who it is, don't you?' she said eventually. 'The Englishman.'

'I can hazard a guess. There was a man who lived in Fermanagh, a permit-holder who used to ride down in the south now and then. Suddenly, from being something of a loser, he starts doing very nicely. He goes back to England, gets on in the racing world. And now he's right at the centre of the Arab network. My hunch is that he's a puppet for the boys and they're working him, with or without his employer's blessing.'

'His employer?'

'Sheikh al Hassan.' Kinane paused. 'The man's name is Simon Brompton-Smiley.'

It was never beautiful, but it had never been this ugly. Snarling. Bitter. Nasty. And all with their clothes on. It was a shame it had to end this way.

Margaret Stanhope stood by the window of Room 501 in the Sheraton Park Hotel and stared down at the street below. She hadn't cried since she was a little girl until last night. Then she had cried a lifetime of tears for her one true love who had died, for the months and years of planning that had come to nothing, for the pain and disappointment of a wasted life.

It was her life she was thinking about. Trust that bastard Jack to get himself topped just when he was about to realize how much he needed her, just when it was all going to work out between them.

The flesh of Jack's flesh, Reg Butler, sat on the bed, thinking about his son. He looked old now – the idea of his even having a mistress seemed like a joke in poor taste. If it were not for the glitter of anger that shone in his eyes he might have been a pensioner reminiscing about the good old days.

Reg was bad at sorrow. When he was a young man, he used to be well known for striking out when he was down. It didn't matter who precisely he hit, it was just his way of expressing unhappiness. He liked to share grief, to pass it on to the next man.

Or woman. He had never hated anyone as much as he hated Margaret Stanhope right at this moment. Twenty-four hours ago, she had told him she had tracked Jack down. She had sent someone good, someone reliable to bring him home. Now the messenger had disappeared. Maybe some bastard had nobbled him, turned the messenger into a murderer. Maybe he'd got there too late, found the place stiff with filth, scarpered. It all boiled down to the same thing. His only son was gone. This bitch had screwed up.

'I need a name,' she said, like a sleep-talker.

'Fuck off.' Reg's voice was a cracked whisper. 'You're getting nothing.'

At first, when he had got the call from her, he hadn't believed she had the nerve to suggest a meeting. At a time like this. But then she'd asked whether he wanted to put her on to his wife right now or should she ring back later. She had dates of their meetings, notes about what they did, tapes even. Reg had just lost a son; the idea of losing a wife made him feel sick to the stomach. Reg Butler, ending his life alone – it was unthinkable. The woman on the bed beside him had no heart.

293

'Don't think I wouldn't do it either, you stupid old bastard.' Margaret still had her back to him, but he could sense the cold obsessiveness in her voice. 'I didn't put up with you all those times for nothing. Give me the name and you'll never see me again. Otherwise—' she sighed '—the missus is in for a nasty surprise.'

'The tapes, is it?' Butler reached for some prints. 'Like the photographs you took of my son with that little jockey – which you can't even sell now on account of dead bookmaker on the job being too tacky an item for even the scumbag press?' He tore the photographs into pieces and threw them on the floor. 'Some blackmailer you turned out to be.'

'Try me.' Margaret picked up the pieces and put them into her bag. There were some memories that should never be trodden underfoot.

Reg Butler sat for a moment on the bed, then stood up. 'Paper,' he said quietly.

Margaret watched him scrawling a name and a telephone number on a sheet of hotel writing paper. She wished he hadn't reminded her of Kelly Connor. If it weren't for that little bitch, Jack would have stood firm and would still be alive today. She had got to him that night even though she had been drugged out of her brain, she had infected him with something Margaret hated to the depths of her soul. Integrity. A sort of innocence. Love. And that had started the slide that ended with his death. Jack had been killed by love.

'He never fails,' said Reg, avoiding Margaret's eyes as he gave her the piece of paper.

She walked towards the door. 'Don't you want the tapes?'

The old man looked up. 'No.' He shook his head slowly, keeping his eyes fixed on her. 'The day you use them will be the day you stop living.'

Margaret paused. 'There weren't any anyway.' She opened the door. 'I hope he's good.'

She closed the door on Reg Butler, on part of her life.

Killed by love. Now it was Kelly Connor's turn.

Chapter 14

In the hot morning sun, Kelly was given a leg-up by Dennis, who managed a smile as Shine On arched his back in a skittish, good-natured apology for a buck.

'He's well enough,' he said, as horse, jockey and lad walked on to Washington racecourse. 'He may be one of the outsiders for tomorrow's race but, tell you what, I fancy him for a place.'

Kelly looked down at Dennis and smiled. It was odd but, since they had worked together in Tokyo, he had shown a new respect for her, as if he recognized that she wasn't just a jumped-up stable lass with nice legs and a pretty face but a fully-fledged jockey. 'A place?' she said patting Shine On's neck. 'What are you talking about, Den? We're going to win.'

Their optimism was not shared by the American press, who treated Shine On and his jockey as a novelty turn rather than as serious contenders for the Laurel International. The gossip papers were full of items referring to 'Britain's Knock-'em-Dead Racing

Sensation' and 'the Jock With a Hollywood Smile'. The *National Enquirer* ran a scurrilous piece revealing that Kooky Kelly had been dating shamed drugsbust American jockey Cy McCray, who had been helping prepare her for the big race. There was an invitation to appear on the *Johnny Carson Show* which Annie, who found herself acting as Kelly's minder, turned down. The last thing they needed was for Kelly to be transformed into a media star before she had even reached the start of the big race.

The experts in the more serious racing papers wrote with sober disapproval of the publicity, hinting that it had been encouraged by the race organizers and Shine On's connections. The Laurel International, they wrote, was too important a race to become a circus. The fact was that Shine On was among the outsiders, he had a bad draw and, for all her much-discussed good looks, his jockey was woefully lacking in experience. Those who took their racing seriously would be advised to ignore the fuss, which did little for the sport.

Kelly found it easy to dismiss the sillier stories – anyone who had survived the British press knew how to deal with gutter journalists – but she found the expert commentators' cool dismissal of her chances annoying. Annie helped to put their views into perspective.

'D'you know what these people said about Lester when he first rode here?' she said over breakfast at the Washington Park Hotel. 'The guy rides like a bum. He made them change their mind and so can you.'

She was due to work with Spritzer who had travelled over with Shine On from Ian Gardem's yard. As she made her way over to where Ian and Annie were waiting, Kelly noticed a knot of onlookers in the stands.

Journalists. A few would be there to sniff out stories about her but most of them wanted to see Spritzer who had won the St Leger last year. He had only been beaten once this season – last time out, in the Arc de Triomphe when, according to many who saw him, he was unlucky to lose by a short head to the French colt Badinage after being impeded by tiring horses in the straight.

There was no denying that Spritzer was impressive to look at, Kelly thought as Bill Ryan, his jockey, greeted her in front of the stands. A big bay horse with an intelligent, almost arrogant look to him, he had come into his own as a four-year-old. Of course, he had had a hard race last time out, but on the other hand Shine On had travelled halfway across the world and back. Never mind the home team, or the French Derby winner Kernac or a highly fancied horse from Germany called Millionaire's Row, Spritzer was going to take some beating.

Annie walked over to Shine On and checked his girths.

'All right?' she said.

Kelly nodded, thinking briefly how well Annie had adapted to her new role as trainer. 'Yes, he seems in great form.'

'Just a pipe-opener, remember,' Annie said quietly. 'If Bill Ryan wants to go on over the last furlong, let him. It's tomorrow that matters.'

Ryan was a quietly competent professional who had ridden against Kelly enough not to be taken in by her looks or the fact that she was a woman. He spoke little as they cantered down to the five-furlong marker but Kelly sensed, from the frequent glances in her direction, that he was assessing her horse. She smiled to herself – at least one expert was taking her chances seriously.

When they pulled up they let the two horses catch their breath and then turned in together and came up the straight, stride for stride. Shine On was a good mover but there was no denying that, beside Spritzer, he looked ordinary and Kelly felt he was taking two strides to Spritzer's one. At the furlong pole, Bill Ryan looked across at Kelly, said something she couldn't pick up and let his reins out a notch. As Spritzer lengthened his stride, Shine On responded but Kelly kept a tight hold of his head. By the time they passed the post, Ryan was three lengths clear.

Kelly smiled to herself as she let Shine On slow down to a walk. Doubtless the journalists in the stand had the copy they were looking for: 'Class Brit horse Spritzer sparkles in his gallop with disappointing Shine On.' None of them had felt what she felt. Her horse had been pulling her arms out at the finish and had worked as well as she had ever known him to.

'I think he'll go well tomorrow,' she said to Annie when she returned. Some twenty yards away, Ian Gardem was talking to his jockey, running a hand down Spritzer's front legs and patting him in a confident, satisfied way. It was doubtful if he or his jockey were dismissing Shine On's chances as easily as the journalists were, but their horse's wellbeing fully justified their confidence.

Annie walked with Kelly and Shine On back towards the stables. 'You've got quite a fan club here, you know,' she said. 'Apparently the owner is coming along tomorrow.'

'The Sheikh?' Kelly was surprised.

'He had to come to America for some business to do with Ibn Fayoud. Between you and me, I think he's less keen on moving his horses out of England than everyone thinks. I've had several calls from Brompton-Smiley asking about Shine On.'

The name brought Kelly up sharp. Preparation for the big race had proved to be the perfect distraction from the aftermath of Jack Butler's death. Shortly before she had left, two detectives had visited her and taken a further statement but, beyond that, she had managed to banish almost everything from her mind. This week was for racing; she would attend to the real world on her return.

'And your friend Nick Morley's here too. He's buying some mares and wants to look at American racecourse security.'

Her friend. Kelly winced as she remembered the last time they had seen one another. 'I know,' she told Annie. 'He's already been in touch. I said I'd meet him sometime today.' Maybe away from the pressures of home he would be different.

Back at the hotel, Kelly asked the desk clerk for her key. Apart from seeing Nick, she'd planned to do nothing except watch television, relax and read up the form of the following day's runners. The man behind the desk gave her the key to Room 1341 and invited her to have a good day. Kelly smiled and said she would.

In Room 1342, Margaret Stanhope sat reading yesterday's edition of the *National Enquirer*. She knew the story off by heart now – Kooky Kelly, indeed. She looked with loathing at the photograph of the Connor girl arriving at the airport earlier in the week. The jock with the Hollywood smile. Margaret narrowed her eyes. Tomorrow there would be an end to smiles.

There was a click from across the room. Donnell was at the desk, checking his gun yet again. Personally, Margaret could have done without the tedium of sharing a hotel room with a professional hitman with the conversational skills of the Statue of Liberty but it was simpler to get the room they wanted as a married couple. This was where they had spent their honeymoon night five years before. It was a romantic enough story to swing it, when backed up by a hundred dollar bill for the bookings clerk.

At least he didn't want sex; there was that. As soon as Donnell had been alone with her in the room, he had said, 'I sleep on the floor.' She had been polite, said they could both use the bed if he wanted but he had been like ice. 'I always sleep on the floor,' he said.

A gay hitman? Or was this some trick learnt in Vietnam where, Margaret imagined, Donnell had acquired his taste, his talent for killing? Don't talk, don't sleep on mattresses, don't touch women unless you happen to be murdering them at the time; the man was a crazy purist. Not that it made any difference, as long as he did what he was paid for. She watched the trim, balding figure of the assassin as he cleaned and assembled his short pug-like pistol, then fitted the silencer once more.

'All present and correct?' she said.

The man looked round at her, narrowing his eyes as if she were a stranger who had just come up and insulted the memory of his dear dead mother. For a moment, Margaret thought that he was going to kill her, just for the hell of it, even though she had only given him ten of the twenty thousand dollars he was to be paid.

He chewed thoughtfully on his gum, digging deep for precisely the right words.

'Shut the fuck up,' he said finally.

Margaret shrugged. She stood up and wandered out on to the balcony. A telephone was ringing from next door and, through an open window, she could just hear the voice answering it, laughing, carefree. Margaret smiled. Kooky Kelly. Soon to be the late Kooky Kelly.

As she listened to Nick's voice on the telephone, Kelly found herself wondering how she seriously could have suspected him of being involved in the death of Jack Butler. He sounded concerned, genuinely interested in the news about Shine On. He never said as much, but it was clear that he had timed his trip to Washington so that he could see her ride in the big race.

'Where are you staying?' she asked.

'Some people called Bruce,' he said vaguely. 'They've got a small palace in the north-west of Washington, where the diplomats and politicians hang out. I'm meant to be buying some mares from them.'

'When you're not dating jockeys.'

Nick laughed. 'Why don't you get a cab and come up here some time this afternoon? I've got to lunch here but afterwards I could show you the National Cathedral. It's spectacular.'

Kelly hesitated. She was hardly in the mood for sightseeing but the alternative of spending the afternoon in her hotel room or going over tomorrow's race yet again was even less appealing. 'Why the hell not?' she said.

They agreed to meet outside the main entrance.

Nick had been right. The National Cathedral was spectacular, a vast neo-Gothic celebration of American self-confidence. He greeted her by the main entrance, kissing her on both cheeks, holding her to him with an intensity which momentarily took Kelly by surprise.

'Shall we go in? Pray for your chances tomorrow?' There was something ironical and self-mocking in his smile, as if he were anxious not to reveal quite how pleased he was to see her.

'I'm a good Catholic girl,' she said. 'There's a time and a place for prayer.'

'Like down at the start.'

She laughed and they walked slowly into the great building. A boys' choir was practising in the crypt, and Nick and Kelly stood in the central aisle listening for a moment.

'Carols in October,' said Kelly. 'That must be a bad omen.'

'No.' Nick's voice was almost a whisper. 'They're boys from a local boarding school. It's famous for its singing. They'll be rehearsing every day from now on.'

Kelly looked at him. There was a strange glitter to his eye, as if he had been reminded of something distant and unpleasant. 'You're well informed,' she said.

He shrugged. 'I visit Washington quite a lot.'

He guided her to a pew where they sat, a congregation of two, listening to the carols. A young soloist had stepped forward. As he sang with all the confidence of youth, his voice echoed about the empty cathedral.

'Brahms,' said Kelly. 'It reminds me of my father. He loved carols.'

Nick was not listening to her but to the soaring voice of the chorister. 'The pure, unsullied voice of privilege,' he murmured, almost to himself.

'He's a good singer,' said Kelly, misunderstanding.

'And he'll be a good schoolboy, and good Ivy League graduate, and a good lawyer or businessman or politician until, in a few years' time, he'll be back here in the acceptable part of Washington. He'll take up the baton in national life, just as it was always intended he should. It's what Mom and Pop are paying for now.'

Kelly could hear that steeliness in his voice again.

'And some won't,' she said. 'Some will go their own way.'

'I was in the choir at Harrow.' In the darkness of the cathedral, Kelly could see that Nick was smiling now, an oddly cold smile.

'And you went your own way.'

'Yes.' It was as if he had suddenly awoken from a dream. 'That's what I did.'

The music had stopped now and the boys were collecting up their books, whispering and laughing in the crypt.

'I was going to be a lawyer,' Nick continued. 'That's what was planned for me. I had the brains, the education, the background. For some reason, maybe a fear of turning into a cold, loveless success like my father, I chose a career they would hate. They've never quite forgiven me.'

'They must be proud of you now.'

Nick looked at her as if she had understood nothing of what he had told her.

'Some go their own way,' he said and stood up.

Kelly felt a million miles from him. The music, the sound of the boys' voices had taken Nick into a cold, bleak land where she couldn't reach him and where she had no desire to go. He had business on his mind, and she had a race to win. She smiled to herself. Just ride the horses.

Blinking in the autumn sunlight, they emerged from the cathedral and turned left down the wide street.

'Now where are you taking me?' she asked.

He raised an eyebrow, once more his natural,

charming self. 'Back to my place?' he suggested. 'For a cup of tea.'

'I think I ought to get back.'

'Don't be silly. You'll only be bored and my hosts have a magnificent house.

Like most of their neighbours, the Bruces, with whom Nick was staying, lived in style; theirs was not so much a house as a residence. In the large sunlit room where Nick and Kelly were served tea by a Filipino maid, there was a grand piano in one corner and photographs on the wall, most of which showed a plump, distinguished-looking man with various political and showbusiness celebrities.

Over tea, Nick explained that Virgil Bruce III was at his office downtown and his family lived most of the time in South Carolina. 'He's an old friend,' he said. 'We do a lot of bloodstock business and I have an open invitation to stay here.'

For a while, they discussed the Laurel International which Nick, like Kelly, thought was a more open race than many of the American commentators assumed. Last year's winner Angel Dust was a worthy favourite, having remained unbeaten all year and with the advantage of not having had to travel far, but the European challenge could not be ignored. They'd already won a handful of American races that season. Nick seemed distracted when Kelly spoke of Shine On's chances. Then, quite suddenly, he changed the subject.

'Have you heard anything more about the Jack Butler business?' he asked. Kelly looked at him, surprised.

She shook her head. 'The police took a further statement.' She thought of Jack lying in the sand. 'Did you know that he was involved with the IRA?'

'Jack Butler?' Nick sipped his tea. 'It wouldn't surprise me. There have always been links between terrorists and the criminal community, and even if he didn't quite fit into that category, his father certainly did.'

'It's more than that. An Englishman was involved in a betting ring in Ireland during the seventies. I've been told that he's remained active for them, that it was this man who was working Jack Butler and the drugs run.'

'An Englishman?' From Nick's tone of voice, they might still have been talking about Shine On and tomorrow's race, but he was now deathly pale. 'The boys use a surprising number of Englishmen.'

'This one lived in the north and was involved with horses. Now he lives in England.'

Nick looked at her, coldly, almost as if he were daring her to go further.

Kelly smiled. 'For a moment, I thought it must have been you, but now I've got the name.'

'Don't say it,' he interrupted her. 'I know.' He poured them both another cup of tea, saying quietly as he did so, 'I suppose I had better tell you everything.'

For five minutes, maybe ten, he addressed her coldly, succinctly, as if he were in a military debriefing session, only his eyes, which were alive with excitement, betraying the enormity of what he was saying.

Although he had left the SAS several years ago, he was still retained in a part-time capacity by a counter-insurgency unit at the Ministry of Defence. They had been aware for some time that the IRA were big-time players in the drugs business, the substantial rewards of which helped pay for their terrorist activities. Jack Butler had become involved out of sheer greed and ambition. First he allowed his shops to be used to launder drugs money, then he, or possibly his father Reg, had been persuaded to step up the stakes by pulling Ibn Fayoud into the conspiracy.

The Butlers had made sure that the young Arab, who was already in serious financial difficulties, became hopelessly indebted to them; the Pendero race at Ascot was just one of several gambles which had intentionally backfired on the Arab. Once they had him well and truly hooked, they used his cover to smuggle heroin through the diplomatic bag system, and also through racehorses travelling the world.

For some reason, Jack Butler lost his nerve. By the time Kelly alerted Nick to the Tokyo run, they were already aware of what was happening. He had been unable to tell her, although it had been his influence which had helped free her at the airport.

Kelly interrupted to ask about Cy McCray and Bill Templeman.

'They'll stand trial.' Nick shrugged regretfully. 'We can't blow our cover to help them.'

'You mean the smuggling operation is still continuing?'

Nick nodded. 'They killed Jack Butler, but he was small-time. The show will go on without him.'

'But I don't understand how Brompton-Smiley's involved.'

'You were right. There was an Englishman involved with the IRA during the seventies. We knew it was going on when I was on the front line, but we couldn't place who it was. It was after he began working for Sheikh al Hassan that our intelligence boys got on to him. He was the one who suggested Ibn Fayoud as cover. He's not as stupid as he looks; the reason why the Sheikh's moving to France is that he knows we're watching him. Even with Interpol co-operation, he'll have a clearer run over there.'

'If he goes,' said Kelly.

Nick looked at her sharply. 'How do you mean?'

'The Sheikh watched Shine On work this morning. He told Annie that, if he won tomorrow, he'll reconsider his decision to move to France.'

'That will spoil a few plans,' Nick said incredulously.

'It seems that Sheikh al Hassan is a bit of a romantic. He said that watching a small stable pitching for one of the big races was more exciting than anything he had experienced with his bigger yards.'

'So,' Nick smiled palely, 'it could all go into reverse if the wrong horse wins tomorrow.'

Kelly looked at her watch. It was time to get back to the hotel. 'Not that I'll be worrying about that as I pass the post tomorrow.'

'Of course not,' he said quietly. 'I'll order you a cab.'

Nick's explanation appeared to have solved the mystery of her father's death and everything else that had happened. But while he was out of the room phoning for a cab, she couldn't help feeling nagging, inexplicable doubt.

She stood up, cursing herself for being unable to stop the questions in her mind, even when the answers appeared to have been supplied. There was something wrong. It was somehow all too neat. She looked at the photographs on the wall. Virgil Bruce III with Richard Nixon, with Jack Nicklaus, with Henry Kissinger, with Frank Sinatra, with Ronald Reagan, with – Kelly paused by a shot of Bruce with a man whose face was familiar to her, yet which seemed out of context here. Grey-haired, a man of power with laughing, watchful eyes. Who the hell was he?

Nick returned to say the cab was on its way. He stood before her in the middle of the great room and reached out to touch her cheek. His hand was cold.

'I wanted to talk about us,' he said.

Kelly moved half a pace backwards, thinking of an excuse. 'Nick, I've got too much to think about right now. I've got a race to win. Will I see you there?'

'OK.'

The doorbell rang.

It was only when she was in the cab, driving down the wide avenues of Washington on her way back to the hotel that she realized he had never wished her luck.

She was right about him. When she got back to England she'd find herself a man with a heart. Someone who really cared about her. Not Nick Morley.

*   *   *

'Busy day, lady?'

Kelly assumed that the black cab driver had seen her picture in one of the newspapers. Yet there was something oddly appraising about the way he looked at her in the rearview mirror which went beyond traditional American openness.

'Not too bad,' she said.

'You guys work even longer hours than a cab driver. Afternoon with old man Bruce then back to the hotel bars. Shit, you sure earn your corn.'

It was a moment before Kelly understood what he was talking about. She laughed; it was the second time she had been mistaken for a hooker. She was about to correct him in her most starchily British tones when it occurred to her that the driver might know something about the man with whom Nick was staying.

Misunderstanding her laughter, he went on, 'Jeez, the number of times I come to this district with young girls. I'm surprised the guys round here have time to run the country the way they behave.'

'Right,' said Kelly.

'And that Bruce guy, he's the worst, you know? Parties, girls.' The driver shook his head enviously. 'I don't know where he gets the energy from, that's the truth.'

'Maybe it's the southern air.'

'South?' The man sounded surprised. 'Old Virgil's been no further south than the Potomac. I read that he was born in the Bronx, changed his name when he moved from being an organizer with the Teamsters to setting up his own transport business. Irish family, he was. O'Brien or some such.'

Kelly heard Nick's voice in her head. An old friend. Old money. Certainly the house had old-world style. And yet there were no racing pictures on the wall, which seemed odd; just celebrity shots. It was then that she remembered where she had last seen the face of the grey-haired man in the photograph with Virgil Bruce III. It had been in a portrait in the house of Dermot Kinane.

Who did you believe? A security officer for the English Jockey Club who had saved you from arrest, or a Washington cab driver who read the gossip columns and thought you were on the game? Kelly looked out of the window. As if some evil genie had waved a wand, the wide sweep and lawns of the northern suburb had given way to dingy, inner-city squalor. Nothing was what it seemed.

Virgil Bruce III, old money, or O'Brien, an Irishman made good? She looked back at the driver's mirror and caught him darting another speculative look in her direction. Unlike Nick, he had nothing to gain from lying to her.

That picture. What would Virgil Bruce III be doing shaking the hand of the most famous President of Ireland in the Republic's history, a man celebrated not just as a politician but, in his youth, as a fierce fighter for the nationalist cause. Eamon de Valera.

Kelly smiled coolly at the cab driver and looked away. She wished that the Irish connection was a coincidence, but she knew that it wasn't.

'Dermot, the American business interests you mentioned. It involved Bruce, didn't it?'

It was difficult to tell whether Dermot's hesitation

was caused by sleepiness – it would have been one in the morning in Ireland – or his characteristic wariness.

'What are you talking about, Kelly?' he said eventually. 'For the Lord's sake, can you not concentrate on the big race you're riding tomorrow?' The words sounded familiar.'

'Tell me, Dermot. This is important.'

There was another pause. 'The name I heard was not Bruce, that's for sure.'

'He calls himself Bruce but he was born O'Brien. He's in transport. Very rich.'

Kinane sighed, as if he were tired of the subterfuge, of trying to protect someone too wilful to see that the less she knew the better.

'All I can tell you,' he said, 'is that there is an O'Brien who's known as one of the biggest sponsors of Noraid. He gives money to the IRA, maybe more than money but, heaven alive, it's a common enough name.'

'Where does he live?'

At first, Kelly thought Dermot had gone back to sleep. She repeated the question, raising her voice angrily.

'He comes from Washington.'

After she had bid Dermot goodnight, Kelly switched on the television without the sound and watched the flickering images of a game show as she pieced together what she knew.

Nick was staying with a man known to be involved with the IRA and possibly with drug-running. She thought of Brompton-Smiley's party in Newmarket,

Nick's lack of surprise at the news of Jack Butler's death, the sand on his car. She closed her eyes and for a moment saw once again the image of Jack's body in the north Norfolk sand. He had trusted her with his hide-out address, she had trusted Nick, leaving the address on his answering machine. Suddenly everything was making sense.

Trust no one. The words from her father's letter returned to her. So plausible, so attractive, so human despite his position of authority. But on the night of her return from Tokyo, there had been that strange moment in his flat when she had felt not so much an accomplice as a victim. There had been something dangerous, triumphant about him that night. Unthinkingly, she had remarked that there were always more where the Butlers and Ibn Fayouds came from and he had become distant and distracted, had compared catching dopers and villains with defeating the IRA. It was the same thing for him, he had said.

Kelly remembered his manner that very morning in the National Cathedral, staring at the boys' choir as if lost in his own, inhospitable world. His parents had wanted him to be a lawyer and he had become a soldier. He had been bright at school, but he had elected to use low cunning and courage for a career. Doubtless his family expected him at least to join a socially acceptable cavalry regiment; instead he went into the SAS. Perhaps, when others looked to him to pursue a successful career as a soldier, he had once again moved in the opposite direction. What more perfect rebellion than to go over to the other side, to become rich in the service of the ultimate outsiders, a force beyond any civilized society. Some go their own way.

The telephone rang. It was Annie, checking that she was all right.

'I'm fine,' Kelly laughed and reassured her that the night spots of Washington could wait.

After she had said goodnight to Annie, she reflected that she had caught Nick Morley off-balance during their meeting that day. He had seemed put out, unnerved by the idea that Sheikh al Hassan could reverse his decision to pull out of English racing. Yet it was Brompton-Smiley who, he claimed, needed to move his base of operations to evade the natural curiosity of the Drugs Squad. A change of heart by the Sheikh would put those plans in jeopardy.

In other words, it was in Nick's interests for Shine On to be beaten in the Laurel International. It was possible that his involvement was nothing more than a figment of her talent for paranoia, but Kelly didn't think so. Unwittingly, by revealing Sheikh al Hassan's uncertainty about the move to France, she had set a trap.

The call came at eleven, shortly after Kelly had turned out her light.

'It's Nick.' His tone was brisk, wakeful. 'Can I come and see you?'

'No, I'm almost asleep.'

'Listen, this is important. I told you too much today,' he said. 'I've been in touch with London. We're in deeper than we thought. They need Brompton-Smiley to go to France and to make certain that he does, they want you to lose tomorrow's race. Kelly, you've got to realize that this is very important. Human lives, government matters are at stake.' He hesitated. 'It's absolutely essential. I've never asked anyone to do this before and I hate doing it, especially to you, but these are my orders and there's nothing I can do. You do understand, don't you?' There was more emotion in his voice than Kelly had ever heard before.

'Yes,' she said. 'I understand.'

Chapter 15

'It's gonna be a helluva horse race.'

The voice of Sam Dimona, an ex-jockey who was now America's best-known racing commentator, echoed over the public address system in the ballroom of the Washington Park Hotel. His words were clearly some kind of catchphrase because the journalists and photographers gathered for the Laurel International Breakfast whooped and cheered as if they were at the Troubadour in Vegas and Frank Sinatra had just ambled on to the stage.

Kelly caught the eye of Bill Ryan who nodded briskly and looked away. If he was taken aback by the publicity hoopla surrounding the race, he was determined not to show it. Beside her at the long table reserved for the trainers and jockeys of runners in the big race, Annie had the fixed smile of someone who wished she was somewhere, anywhere, else. She had warned Kelly that the hype surrounding the International was unlike anything seen in

Europe, but nothing had prepared her for this.

They had reached the climax of proceedings, during which members of the press corps, who were restrained in an undignified rabble behind a silver rope, were invited to ask questions of the leading participants.

Kelly was relieved to see that most of the interest surrounded Eddie Marielita, the young Puerto Rican who had made his name as the jockey of Angel Dust and whose answers to the shouted questions belonged to the Lester Piggott school of economic communication. How was Angel? Fine. Was he going to win today? No problem. Who did Eddie see as his biggest rivals today? Anyone who started in the race was a rival. Was it true that his grandparents had flown up from San Juan to see him ride? Yes, it was. The track was riding softer than average today – would that worry Angel? No problem.

At one point, as the American journalists doggedly attempted to extract a quotable sentence from Marielita, Kelly thought she saw Nick at the back of the room but, looking more carefully, she realized that it was someone else. In spite of her determination to concentrate on the race, she had been unable to shake thoughts of yesterday from her mind. Maybe Nick was still working for the government. She remembered the feeling in his voice. Perhaps her own concerns, winning a race, even finding out who had killed her father, were insignificant beside the fight against terrorism. When all was said and done, today was just a question of one horse running faster than a few others.

The journalists were trying their luck on Paul Hiberdy, the pale, good-looking French champion jockey who was riding Badinage. Every question was translated by the horse's trainer and followed by a lengthy discussion in French between the connections before a brief answer was supplied by the trainer. Annie muttered that, at this rate, no one was going to get to the racecourse.

In the end, Kelly reflected, she had to follow her instinct. No one – not Annie, nor Dermot, nor, least of all Nick – could help her decide. As the journalists moved on to the American jockey who was riding the fancied five-year-old gelding Space Cadet, she thought of the person to whom she had always turned for advice, whose quiet wisdom had helped her so much in the past and, in the end, had helped him so little. What would her father have said?

Her reverie was broken by the sound of an American voice calling out her name. 'Kelly Connor, how do you rate your chances today?'

She smiled and said she rated them highly.

Another journalist asked whether she had any thoughts about being on a horse ridden last time out by American jockey Cy McCray. Before she could answer, Annie spoke up to point out that Shine On had been ridden in all his races this season by Kelly except for the last one. Kelly added that Cy McCray was a fine jockey and a friend and that, after she had won, her first call to England would be to him.

When another reporter asked whether it was true that she had been offered $100,000 to appear in *Playboy*, she'd had enough.

'Grow up,' she said to laughter from the other journalists.

As the questioning moved on to Bill Ryan, Kelly rubbed her eyes wearily. For some reason, the press here had taken against her and now she had given them ammunition to use against her. Arrogant, snooty, abrasive. The bimbo bites back. It had been a mistake, but then she had hardly slept during the night.

Along the table, Eddie Marielita was staring at her. Almost imperceptibly, he gave a practised, see-you-after-the-show wink. His vulpine smile was not that of rival and was more eloquent than any words he had uttered minutes before. No problems.

Margaret Stanhope was not used to taking orders unless they were from someone she loved and the only person she had ever loved wasn't giving orders to anyone these days. All the same, when Donnell told her to get her bags out of the hotel by seventeen hundred hours and to meet him in the bar of the Holiday Inn that night at nineteen thirty because by then the job would be over and he'd be on his way, she asked no questions. The man was a jerk but he had his area of expertise, and Margaret had learnt to trust experts.

That morning, as the day's racing celebrities were given their highly public breakfast downstairs, she had wandered about the hotel room in her under-clothes humming to herself. It wasn't that she wanted to do anything with Donnell – for her, social sex was only an occasional indulgence – more that she found his cold detachment something of a challenge. She still had a good body and liked to think she could influence the behaviour of most normal men by the promise of a share in her assets.

But Donnell was blind to her flat stomach, to her almost perfect breasts, to her long tanned thighs. She had sighed softly as she slipped on her nylon stockings, bitten her lower lip temptingly as she fastened her suspenders. But the bastard was as interested as if she were a slab of wet fish. She hated him – not as much as she would have hated him if he *had* tried to jump her, but she hated him all the same.

'So you'll do it when she comes back to the hotel?' Margaret looked at Donnell, who sat at the desk, staring out of the window. This was not a man, but a computer, a robot programmed to kill. Although he didn't seem to have stepped out of the light suit he wore, had slept in it as far as she could tell, he still looked as blandly immaculate as he had two days previously when she had first met him.

He gave the question serious thought and nodded.

'After five o'clock?' Margaret hesitated as Donnell narrowed his eyes. It annoyed her how those cold eyes made her flesh crawl – nobody, least of all a man, had frightened her like this for a long time. 'Or seventeen hundred hours, whatever you call it.'

'As soon as you get out of here.'

'So, by the time we meet in the Holiday Inn, she could have been found? The news might be out.'

Donnell stared at her. The publicity side of the job wasn't his problem.

'Fuck knows,' he said quietly.

* * *

If they had been in England, Kelly's big race build-up would have been simple – that is, the same as any other day, except for maybe arriving early to miss the extra traffic, then killing time chatting to the other jockeys outside the weighing room and studying the form. There was nothing strange or mysterious about it. Tennis players may hum their own special mantra, footballers may pray and cross themselves as they run on to the pitch, but jockeys just get on with it.

But they weren't in England. Here in Washington, on the day of the International, a jockey was news. Everything he said or she did was a potential quote or photo opportunity. Kelly was glad that she decided to walk the mile and a quarter course with Annie early that morning before the press were awake. The idea of going through the race before an audience of journalists more interested in her legs and face than in her ability as a jockey did not appeal.

It was a good galloping course and the going, which was on the soft side of good after some unseasonal rain, would suit Shine On. Since the race was run over a shorter distance than the horse had won over recently, Annie and Kelly decided it would be best to lie closer to the leaders than she normally did. They had been drawn one out from the inside track and the only way of ensuring a clear run would be to keep clear of the pack.

Force of habit had brought Kelly down to the race-track again later that morning, and now she wished she had stayed in her room at the hotel. As she arrived, she found herself surrounded by photographers. She pushed past them, ignoring their shouted questions, and walked to the area adjoining the course where the horses were stabled. There at least she would be free of the publicity circus.

She showed her pass at the entrance to a barn-like building where all the foreign horses were kept. Unlike Tokyo, Kelly reflected as she walked the length of the barn towards Shine On's box, the security here seemed impeccable. Only the immediate connections of each horse were allowed into the barn, which had cameras covering every loosebox.

Kelly quickened her steps. She remembered Nick's reason for attending the meeting: the Washington security force were going to show him round. No one had a better entrée to the stables than he had and, if she was right about him, no one was more determined that Shine On shouldn't win.

Seeing Annie and Dennis at the stable, she breathed more easily. After a restless night, her imagination was running away with her.

'Shaken off your journo friends?' Annie asked.

Kelly smiled. 'Just about. I don't seem to have made too big a hit with the gentlemen of the press.'

'I'm not surprised after yesterday. But don't worry. It's just that you're not playing their game. In Washington, turning down the chance to appear on *Johnny Carson* is one of the Seven Deadly Sins. Everything is showbiz here – politics, sport, life.'

'Crime,' Kelly added to herself, thinking of Virgil Bruce and his collection of celebrity photographs.

'You'll just have to prove your point by winning the race. An American trainer was saying there's a question mark over Badinage's ability to stay the trip on this ground. He reckoned that Stir Crazy's here to make it a true run race for Angel Dust, so he's certain to get tested.'

'Could be.' Kelly had also heard that, although the American colt Stir Crazy had some good form, his owner was being paid to run him as pacemaker for his more fancied compatriot.

The two of them discussed the race for a few minutes before Annie glanced at her watch. 'Gotta run,' she said. 'Simon Brompton-Smiley wants to see me before the races.' She slapped Kelly lightly on the arm. 'See you in the weighing room. Don't go talking to any strange journalists.'

'Are there any other kind?' Kelly turned to Dennis. 'Will you be staying with Shine On all the time this morning?'

Dennis looked at her in surprise. 'You bet,' he said. 'No one gets to see this horse without seeing me first.'

'Fine.'

With time to kill, Kelly left the stables and took the lift to the top of the stands where, apart from a few early racegoers, it was deserted. She was looking across the green swathe of the racecourse, planning her race and fixing the course in her mind when she spotted Nick walking from the racetrack towards the stands, deep in conversation with two men. She wondered briefly what they were discussing. Security? Heroin? How to stop villains? How to stop horses? They were too far away for her to see Nick's face but she could imagine his expression – concerned, frowning, a man at work.

She remembered his late-night call and the urgency

in his voice. Half the night she had tried to think of reasons why she should believe him, trust in the higher good which, according to his story, required her to throw today's race. We know best, he had been saying, trust us. It's more than a matter of racing, it's national security, life and death.

In the early hours of the morning, she had once more read her father's last letter to her – these days she always kept it with her. The men who had killed him had made it clear enough to him: 'friends in high places' was the way they put it. But it was her father's own words which finally convinced her. 'In this war, there is no neutral territory. You're either with the enemy or you're not.'

Kelly recalled a story that her father had once told her about Dermot when he'd been younger and very much involved with the Cause. It was at a time when the fighting between the two religions was at its bloodiest. Dermot was taking a lunch break with eight workmates in a hut on a building site. Suddenly a man burst open the door and stood there with a mask covering his face and a machine gun held nervously in his hands. Everyone in the hut jumped to their feet in terror, anticipating the certain burst of fire.

'Everyone who's Protestant lie on the floor,' screamed the gunman.

Dermot had said they'd had no idea which religion the gunman supported. There could be no knowing and no pretending.

Dermot and two others remained standing. One wet himself with fear waiting for the ultimate verdict.

As Dermot put up his hand to make the sign of the

cross, the man opened fire. Then he turned and ran out of the hut, leaving six men lying on the floor, their bodies torn apart by bullets. There were no half measures with these people.

The three men were approaching the stands. For a moment, Nick looked up and Kelly imagined briefly that he could see her, watching him. The enemy. It was difficult to see this man, who had once been her lover, as the enemy she was now convinced he was. She wondered how a mother could ever come to terms with a son who committed murder. She thought of her father, Damien Gould, of Jack Butler. Whatever devils drove Nick Morley – greed, ambition, or some deep-seated malaise of the personality that dated from his childhood – she'd been right: there was no place for humanity in his plans, no place for love.

Kelly turned to go back to the weighing room, taking a lift to the ground floor.

The doors opened and, as if her worst nightmares had become reality, the three men stood in front of her. The two men with Nick were broadly built and had brutally correct military haircuts. Villains, security chiefs – they all looked the same.

'Kelly.' Nick made no effort to stand aside. 'Ready to do your best for Queen and country?' Above the smile, the eyes were cold, professional.

Her mind was set. 'Of course,' she said, forcing herself to sound convincing. One of the men stood aside to let her through.

Although there were no other women riding in the Laurel International, Kelly was relieved to find that the women's dressing room was busier than it would be had they been in England. As she changed and prepared for the big race, several of the leading American women jockeys wished her luck. Maybe if the American press hadn't treated her like a joke contestant they might have put patriotism before sisterly solidarity but now they were right behind her.

It was a relief to ride out on to the racecourse for the pre-race parade. Now it was all over: the questions, the photographs, the speculation, the hype. Now it was a matter of horse and jockey. Away from the publicity circus, Kelly smiled and patted Shine On. She felt good, and so did he.

There were ten runners and, with the possible exception of Stir Crazy, they were all in with a chance. Angel Dust headed the parade and, from the reaction of the crowd, it was obvious that the tough, angular grey who had convincingly won the race last year was a big favourite. Behind him was Skillet, the American three-year-old who had broken the course record at Kentucky earlier in the season. The word in racing circles was that he was over the top, that he was half the horse he had been a month ago. As if to prove it, he was dripping with sweat. More impressive in the paddock had been Larkrise, a chestnut filly who had won her last two races, admittedly against moderate company, by six and ten lengths. Then there was Stir Crazy, pacemaker to Angel Dust.

The foreign challenge was the most formidable for years. Even if the chances of Shine On, last in the parade, were discounted, as they were by the majority of on-course experts, the claims of Badinage and

Spritzer, first and second in the Arc de Triomphe, Kernac, the Chantilly-trained three-year-old who had won the French Derby, and even the German horse Millionaire's Row were undeniable. Looking at the horses ahead of her as they filed past the stands Kelly remembered the words of the pinhead back at the hotel. Yes, it was going to be a helluva horse race.

Down at the start, there was less chat between the jockeys than Kelly was used to. Of the Americans, only Eddie Marielita seemed to be enjoying himself, patting Angel Dust, grinning occasionally at Kelly in a way he clearly thought was seductive. Bill Ryan's face was set in an impassive scowl and Paul Hiberdy, the Frenchman riding Badinage, looked pale and tense.

With the odd numbers going in before the even numbers, from left to right, Shine On was put in the starting-gate first. There then followed a delay while the handlers tried to get Kernac loaded. The delay helped no one, but Shine On, having been incarcerated longer than any other runner, was most likely to break slowly. Kelly touched his ears reassuringly as the American handlers cursed Kernac. Thank God he was a seasoned professional for whom a delay in the stalls was merely part of the business of racing. Beside her, Ryan was keeping Spritzer on his toes – another one looking for a good break.

'Good luck, Bill,' she said.

The Englishman looked over. 'You too.'

Then Kernac was in.

The crack of the starting gun, crash of metal, the yells of the jockeys, the grunt of racehorses lurching out of the stalls and into their stride, the distant roar from the grandstand – they all came together as the starter pulled the lever that sent the runners of the Laurel International on their way.

Kelly had heard that race-riding in America was much more of a bodily contact sport than it was in England. From the thud of bodies and curses behind her, the reports had been correct. Shine On, willing as ever, had been first of the field into his stride, allowing Kelly the luxury of a place on the rails without close company to her right and in front of her.

For one awkward moment, she thought she was going to have to make the running but, after two hundred yards, Stir Crazy surged ahead with Millionaire's Row and Spritzer sitting in his slipstream. At some deep, instinctive level, Kelly noted that the race was being run at too fast a pace for the ground they were racing on, and as more of the runners went past her on the outside she abandoned her plans and let Shine On settle in towards the rear. There were only a couple of horses behind her and for an instant her mind flashed to two people in the stands. Annie would think that she'd gone totally mad, and Nick – well, who knew what Nick was thinking.

As they passed the halfway marker, Kelly breathed a sigh of relief as the early pace began to tell on some of the runners. The pacemaker had started to lose his position, but the jockey on Millionaire's Row had begun to move. Bill Ryan looked as confident as ever. The French horse Badinage was dogging his footsteps on the inside. There was no sign of Angel Dust. Then Kelly felt and heard another horse clipping Shine On's heels. She took a quick peek over her shoulder. The American horse was right behind her.

Shine On was good round bends but he preferred a right-handed track. It was as he moved half the width of a racehorse away from the rails, taking the last bend, that Eddie Marielita saw his chance. As they turned into the straight, Kelly became aware of the local horse making its run on her inside. It was time to remind Eddie that all's fair in love, war and racing. Letting Shine On quicken slightly, she closed the door on Angel Dust to a torrent of abuse from the American.

Three furlongs from home. British-trained horses were in first and second places, but it was beginning to look as if Ryan's determination to avoid the trouble that had cost him the Arc had asked too big a question of Spritzer. Kelly saw him change legs and moved to his outside. She could take him any time but the last thing she wanted to do was to hit the front too early.

Paul Hiberdy on Badinage solved her problem by switching his challenge to the outside. Kelly had started riding. Stride for stride with Spritzer, she was half a length down on the French horse. As they entered the final furlong, the crowd's roar was deafening – and then Kelly, Ryan and Hiberdy became aware of what was causing it. A grey spectre in the form of Angel Dust, Eddie Marielita hunched up his neck, hit the front as if the rest of the field was walking.

On her inside, Kelly heard one of Bill Ryan's few utterances – a multi-decibel obscenity aimed at Spritzer who was losing ground with every stride.

Shine On had the edge on Badinage whose jockey was waving his whip like von Karajan going for the big finish in Beethoven's Ninth.

Shine On began to wander to his left and Kelly pulled her stick through to keep him straight. There was no need to hit him. He was running the race of his life. With less than a furlong to run Angel Dust seemed to have his race won, but Kelly could feel Shine On struggling to get back at him and she pushed harder than she ever had before to help him pull out a bit extra. He was like a tiger. Suddenly it was no longer a question of by how much the American hero would take his second Laurel, but whether he could hold on to win at all.

Limbs aching and lungs on fire, Kelly saw the post approaching as, stride by agonizing stride, Shine On pegged back Angel Dust's lead. Yards to go. There was a short head in it, if that. It was on the nod. As they passed the post, it seemed to Kelly that she had lifted the exhausted Shine On across the line. For seconds, as the two gallant horses pulled up, the roar from the crowd carried on. Kelly slumped forward as Shine On slowed to a canter, then a trot. Somewhere in the distance a photograph was announced, but she knew the result.

So did Eddie Marielita. As he turned back to the stands with her, the Puerto Rican pulled down his goggles and extended a hand. 'Eh, Playboy,' he said. 'I think you just won. You're a tough cookie.'

Slowly, as if from a dream, Kelly awoke to her immediate surrounding. Dennis was running towards her and, above the noise of the crowd, she heard him say – probably to Shine On – 'You did it!'

The generous American crowd, realizing that they had witnessed one of the greatest finishes to a Laurel International for years, applauded her and also Angel Dust as they made their way through the throng to the winners' enclosure. The American horse was still a favourite, but now they had another hero to cheer – the first woman to win the International.

There was a renewed round of applause as, some twenty yards ahead of her, Marielita took Angel Dust into the place reserved for the second horse. The cheer as she entered the enclosure was deafening. Kelly smiled at the flashing cameras, at the journalists already scribbling notes on their pads. So much for Kooky Kelly – tomorrow the headlines would not be of the girl who said 'No' to Carson, but of a new super-jockette. No one could change horses mid-stream more adeptly than a pressman.

She dismounted as Annie, momentarily forgetting that Sheikh al Hassan was standing behind her, hugged her with delight. 'You were brilliant!' The Sheikh laughed and shook Kelly's hand. Above the clamour, he told her that no winner had given him more pleasure. Brompton-Smiley stood by his shoulder, nodding like a toy dog. She went to weigh in.

'Congratulations.' A familiar English voice cut through the furore as she stood down from the scales. She turned to see Nick standing before her, pale, unsmiling. For an instant, she held his icy look before returning to the dressing room. No regrets. Whatever Nick and his friends had planned for her, there were no regrets.

She hardly had time to change amidst the congratulations of the American women jockeys before she was called out from the dressing room.

'Hey, your very own press conference,' said one of the women, laughing.

Kelly smiled. 'Just what I always wanted.'

The man at the door looked familiar, but it was only when he was taking her to the lift that she realized where she had seen him before. That morning. On the racecourse, with Nick.

The doors of the lift closed behind her.

'Where's the press conference?' she said, as calmly as she was able.

The man looked at her coldly. 'Ain't no conference for you,' he said as the lift descended. 'You goin' on a trip.'

Kelly reached for the alarm button, but the man grabbed her hand and pushed it away contemptuously. He opened his jacket, like a man showing off the designer label on his suit. There was no label, only a dark leather shoulder holster containing a neat, black pistol.

'This is crazy,' said Kelly quietly. 'You'll never get away with it.'

'Wanna bet?' the man said as the lift came to a stop. 'Looks to me like we're getting away with it.'

Now Kelly saw where they were heading. Below the stands, there was a car park used by the racecourse employees. It emerged by the main entrance on to the drive outside the course. The man in the suit pushed her out of the lift and, at that moment, a dark, anonymous Chevrolet swept round the corner and pulled to

a halt in front of her. The back door opened. Placing
a hand on the top of her head like a cop bundling a
criminal into his car, the man pushed her in and leapt
in the front passenger seat. The Chevvy set off for the
exit.

'Stupid.' Nick Morley, now in dark glasses, was in
the back seat. He shook his head uncomprehendingly.
'So stupid.'

As they approached the way out of the under-
ground car park and the Chevvy slowed down, Kelly
lunged for the door. As she did so the man in the suit
turned, brandishing a gun.

'Forget it,' he said calmly. Nick stared straight
ahead.

They emerged from the car park; the main road was
no more than fifty yards ahead but to reach it the car
would have to pass the principal gate out of the course
through which racegoers were leaving early to beat the
traffic. Kelly sat forward in her seat, turning her face
to the window.

Too late, Nick realized what she was doing. 'Sit
back!' he hissed.

A middle-aged woman attempting to cross the road
recognized her and shouted, 'Yo, Kelly, you did it!'
and tapped on the window. Now Kelly could see a
group of shabbily-dressed men, some of them with
cameras, standing by the entrance. They looked in her
direction – and started running for their cars.

'Shit.' The driver was trapped behind a stretch limo
that was dawdling its way past the entrance. Kelly
looked back and saw two, three, maybe four cars
pulling out behind them.

Journalists. Kelly realized that her image as a publicity-shy star, the Great Garbo of the racetrack, had offered her a lifeline. Some pressmen, sensing that she might try to leave the racecourse without subjecting herself to their questions, had staked out the main entrance and were now in pursuit.

One car Morley's wheelman might have lost in the Washington traffic, maybe even two, but there was no way that he could shake off the pack that was now following them.

'Act normal,' Nick told the driver. 'Go to the Washington Park, We'll lose the journalists and leave by a back entrance.'

Kelly looked across at him. 'Why?'

The man in the passenger seat whirled round angrily. 'Don't say a fucking word,' he snapped.

'No,' said Nick, like a man under deep hypnosis. 'Don't say a word.'

Until that moment Kelly had been more angry than truly afraid. Now she was terrified.

At the Washington Park, there were more journalists waiting in the lobby. Kelly was about to scream when Nick forced his hand over her mouth and bundled her to a door at the rear, while the two goons made it look as if they were all just playing a game. As Kelly was taken upstairs the back way, Nick reappeared to explain to the journalists that she was tired but would hold a press conference in thirty minutes' time at five fifteen. Before they could ask any questions, he had collected her key and was in the lift heading to her room on the fifth floor. With cool professionalism, members of the hotel staff prevented the press from advancing beyond the lobby.

'Here's what we're going to do.' Nick double-locked the door to her room after the two thugs had left, took off his dark glasses and sat easily in a chair. Kelly had no doubt that he was armed. 'We wait here for ten minutes. I take you down the way we came in and out the back to where the car and my friends will be waiting. You go with them. I'll catch up with you later.'

Kelly looked at him. The light curtains were drawn but the early evening sun shone in, giving his deathly pale complexion an odd luminosity.

'You're mad, Nick,' she said. 'You've been seen with me. If anything happens to me now, you're up to your neck in it.'

Nick shook his head. 'I brought you back here. You told me you wanted to be left alone for a few minutes. I came down to tell the press that you might be delayed. I went back up and you were gone.' He shrugged. 'Anyway, my credibility is perfect. I'm in charge of security at the Jockey Club, I'm a former army officer.' He smiled wanly. 'I'm an Englishman.'

'Just tell me why.' Kelly was close to tears but she sensed that the longer she could keep him talking, the greater the chance that Annie would arrive. She would know that something was wrong the moment she realized that Kelly had left the course without seeing her and without her gear.

'I told you.' There was no trace of regret in Nick's voice. 'If the Sheikh gets out of English racing, I have an escape route. If you hadn't won, I was all set up. If—'

'Maybe he'll go anyway.'

Nick shook his head. 'He's staying and anyway, you know too much.' He sounded weary rather than bitter. 'It would have been so easy. I'd make a killing from inside deals on the sale of his horses and set up in France.' He looked at Kelly almost tenderly. 'We could have been happy, you know.'

'We?'

'I thought you might come with me. We would have been good together.' He smiled. 'Kelly Morley, champion international jockey – it sounds good.'

Kelly realized now that he was insane. She laughed humourlessly. 'I may be ambitious but I'd rather die than marry a dealer in dope, a murderer.'

'I'm not really a murderer. Your father was never meant to die. It was a mistake. I told Jack Butler's boys only to frighten him but one of them hit him a bit hard. Of course, he was an old jockey and his skull must have been thin.' He ignored the look of cold hatred that Kelly directed at him. 'And it wasn't going to be drugs from now on. There's more money in weapons. Ibn Fayoud gave me some contacts in Libya. The boys had the money for it. Shipping high-class mares around the globe was going to be the ideal cover.'

'And now you're going to kill me.'

'I loved you.' He moved close to Kelly as she sat on the bed and for a moment she thought he was going to kiss her. 'I would have done anything for you.'

Then something behind her seemed to attract his attention. He looked up, then back at her, as if torn by a moment of indecision. 'Don't move,' he said quietly.

At first, Kelly thought that it was a journalist who had somehow penetrated the hotel's security cordon, but then she realized that Nick was looking over her shoulder towards the balcony, out of the window.

It seemed to happen in a fraction of a second. Nick dived for the window, through the curtains, turning as he went so that his back shattered the glass. Against the evening sun, she saw the silhouette of Nick and a balding man in a light suit struggling. One of them was pushed back against the edge of the balcony and, at the moment when he began to topple backwards into the void, there was a muffled shot. Suddenly there was only one man left on the balcony. Slowly Nick turned towards her.

He stepped carefully through the shattered window and, as he smiled at her, she saw the small circle of red on his white shirt slightly to the left of his regimental tie.

'I loved you,' he said softly, before crumpling to the ground.

It was two hours before the police had finished with her, and now she sat in Annie's hotel room, pale and shocked.

'We must ring Bill, Cy,' she said quietly. 'They'll be free soon.'

'Later,' said Annie.

And Kelly sat, as Annie placed an arm round her shoulder and spoke soothingly about a future of horses and races and winners and no death. Free – now Kelly was free too.

'I can't understand,' she said yet again.

'Don't try. It's all over.'

Kelly thought of all the threats, the murders which had happened because of one man's restless unhappiness with what the world had to offer him. Maybe it had all been worth it. A trade in drugs, in weapons, in human misery had been terminated. Maybe she had been wrong, all those weeks ago, when she had said to Nick Morley – the late Nick Morley – that there was no end to evil, that wrongdoing would be there as long as there was greed in the world. Maybe it had all been worth it. Maybe.

At ten past eight, Margaret Stanhope, sitting alone in the bar at the Holiday Inn, sensed that it had all gone wrong.

She looked at her watch. She had given Donnell an extra forty minutes which, for a man of his precision, was more than enough.

She stretched her legs, carefully watching a group of three men who were deep in conversation at a corner table. Villains. Washington or the Wirral – she could tell a villain anywhere. Her hand smoothed down her skirt; she crossed her legs. The older fat one was calling the shots, the bald one was neither here nor there, but the younger guy, the one with the long dark hair – he was where tomorrow's power would reside.

Margaret stood up, draining her tequila. It was good to be a survivor. So the little Connor girl would live to ride her racehorses while she, sauntering now across the barroom of the Holiday Inn, would go back to riding her luck. Horses or luck. When it came to true future success – a Tudor mansion in the suburbs, a holiday home in Florida, servants, money like it didn't matter – Margaret knew where hers would be. The man with the dark hair looked up at her. She gave him her smile. Her best, winning smile.

'Hi,' she said.

BLOOD STOCK

JOHN FRANCOME & JAMES MACGREGOR

'Dick Francis's nearest rival in the pen and quill stakes'
Daily Mail

As a racehorse, Moondancer had been a champion; but as a
stallion he was a total failure. So when he is found dead in
his box at the Drumgarrick stud one morning, his owners
feel more relieved than sorry, and promptly make a
massive five million pound insurance claim.

But then Drumgarrick's owner disappears and his son
Fergus is left facing financial ruin . . . and a corpse. A
brilliant amateur jockey, Fergus has a vested interest in
seeing the claim is met in full. But Jack Hendred, the
insurance investigator, is sure that it is fraudulent,
and determined to prove it . . .

The lush countryside of Ireland forms the background to
this gripping tale of intrigue and greed in the bloodstock
business. An attempted betting coup at Leopardstown,
hair-raising National Hunt racing scenes, two grisly
murders and a dramatic Dublin trial are the ingredients
of this new high-voltage thriller from the winning
team of Francome and MacGregor.

'The racing feel is authentic and it's a pacy,
entertaining read' *The Times*

'Rattling good storytellers' *Horse and Hound*

'Gets off to a galloping start . . . with a surprise twist in
the final straight' *Evening Standard*

'The local characters are well drawn, the suspects
gratifyingly violent, equally motivated and suspicious'
Books Magazine

'A captivating read . . . goes at a cracking pace all the way'
Woman and Home

Don't miss *Declared Dead* by Francome &
MacGregor, also from Headline

FICTION/CRIME   0 7472 3416 7   £3.99

K I M O N O

f o r a

C O R P S E

'The Japanese answer to Maigret . . . sheer delight'
OBSERVER

JAMES MELVILLE

The world of designer fashion is unfamiliar
territory to Superintendent Otani. However,
the worldly Inspector Kimura has enjoyed
more than a passing acquaintance with several
models in his time, and is considerably more
knowledgeable about such things. But neither
has ever before had to deal with such a varied
assemblage of creative temperament as that
currently gathered in Kobe for a hugely
prestigious international fashion show.

Tempers are always frayed at such times, so
Otani tends to take hasty accusations and
hysterical threats with a pinch of salt. But when
a colossal chandelier crashes among visiting
dignitaries at the opening ceremony, it's clear
that more than professional jealousy is at work.
As the ornate fabrics are peeled away, the
discarded silks reveal another face of high
fashion – an ugly mask of greed, envy,
blackmail and – in hideously apt garb –
murder . . .

FICTION/CRIME   0 7472 3115 X   £2.50

A selection of bestsellers from Headline

FICTION

A RARE BENEDICTINE	Ellis Peters	£2.99 □
APRIL	Christine Thomas	£4.50 □
FUNLAND	Richard Laymon	£4.50 □
GENERATION	Andrew MacAllan	£4.99 □
THE HARESFOOT LEGACY	Frances Brown	£4.50 □
BROKEN THREADS	Tessa Barclay	£4.50 □

NON-FICTION

GOOD HOUSEKEEPING EATING FOR A HEALTHY BABY	Birthright	£4.99 □

SCIENCE FICTION AND FANTASY

RAVENS' GATHERING Bard IV	Keith Taylor	£3.50 □
ICED ON ARAN	Brian Lumley	£3.50 □
CARRION COMFORT	Dan Simmons	£4.99 □

All Headline books are available at your local bookshop or newsagent, or can be ordered direct from the publisher. Just tick the titles you want and fill in the form below. Prices and availability subject to change without notice.

Headline Book Publishing PLC, Cash Sales Department, PO Box 11, Falmouth, Cornwall, TR10 9EN, England.

Please enclose a cheque or postal order to the value of the cover price and allow the following for postage and packing:
UK: 80p for the first book and 20p for each additional book ordered up to a maximum charge of £2.00
BFPO: 80p for the first book and 20p for each additional book
OVERSEAS & EIRE: £1.50 for the first book, £1.00 for the second book and 30p for each subsequent book.

Name ....

Address ....

....

....